JONATHAN ESCOFFERY is the recipient of the 2020 Plimpton Prize for Fiction, a 2020 National Endowment for the Arts Literature Fellowship and the 2020 ASME Award for Fiction. His fiction has appeared in *The Paris Review*, *American Short Fiction*, *Electric Literature* and elsewhere. He is a PhD fellow at the University of Southern California and in 2021 was awarded a Wallace Stegner Fellowship in the Creative Writing Program at Stanford University. *If I Survive You* is his first book and was longlisted for the National Book Award for Fiction in 2022.

Praise for *If I Survive You*:

'A stylish debut ... Escoffery's interracial sensitivity, coupled with the courage to move beyond the politeness that silences meaningful conversations on race, creates moments where I wanted to snap my fingers, like at a poetry slam'   *Guardian*

'[An] astonishing, compassionate entrance to the literary scene'
i Newspaper

'Brilliantly energetic ... This is Escoffery's debut, but his talent feels fully formed and raring to go; highly recommended'
Financial Times

'Humour and a flair for second-person narration illuminate the experiences of a Jamaican family living in Miami in this invigorating series of linked stories ... A commanding debut from a talent to watch'   *Observer*

'Smart, savvy and snappy ... A superb debut'   *Daily Mail*

'Unmissable ... *If I Survive You* is rare in that it has the heft and heart of a novel, with the refined finesse of the short story ... The only thing to do is eagerly press it into the hands of others'
Irish Times

'Sings with authenticity and heart'   *An Other Magazine*

'Novels crafted from a series of interlinked stories are a tricky proposition ... Get it right, however, and they add up to vastly more than the sum of their parts. Escoffery gets it right'
Marie Claire

'A gifted, sure-footed storyteller, with a command of evocative language and perfectly chosen details ... Makes me eager to read him for a long time to come'   *New York Times Book Review*

'A ravishing debut ... The book feels thrillingly free ... [Escoffery's] stories also stress the ebullience, the possibility, that can emerge from in-betweenness' KATY WALDMAN, *New Yorker*

'It's rare for a story collection to break out of the gate with as much buzz as Escoffery's debut, but his linked tales justify the unusual attention ... Fine details, wit and dazzling verbal versatility'   *LA Times*

'With disarming humour and sympathy, Escoffery devises an intimate exploration of intergenerational conflict'
New York Times

'This is a compelling hurricane of a book that sweeps the past, present and future together into one inextricable knot. This is where Jonathan Escoffery's career begins. There are no limits to where he will go' ANN PATCHETT, author of *The Dutch House*

'An electrifying, enthralling debut about identity and belonging. Jonathan Escoffery illuminates both beauty and trauma and the ways in which so many of us Jamaicans are still looking for home within ourselves ... this spectacular collection introduces us to an amazing new voice'

NICOLE DENNIS-BENN, author of *Here Comes the Sun*

'There is a beautiful economy in the telling that never sacrifices the depth, complexity and richness of the worlds these characters inhabit. Jonathan Escoffery's is a strong, much needed new voice in our literature' PERCIVAL EVERETT, author of *The Trees*

'I am also reading Jonathan Escoffery's *If I Survive You*, a family mosaic, about a Jamaican family in Miami living in a world filled with hope and contradiction'

A. M. HOMES, author of *The Unfolding*, on Twitter

'An astonishing book of stories, one that roves between darkness and humour as quietly and unsettlingly as a millipede over a doorstep' MICHAEL MAGEE, author of *Close to Home*

'A collection of brilliant wit, real heart and electric humour'

NANA KWAME ADJEI-BRENYAH, author of *Friday Black*

'It's truly a feat that a book of short stories tackling such big stuff – family, love, violence, race – could be so damn funny. Escoffery is a writer only just getting started, and his first book is a welcome reminder of what fiction can do'

RUMAAN ALAM, author of *Leave the World Behind*

'Joyously funny and intelligent'

JO LLOYD, author of *The Earth, Thy Great Exchequer, Ready Lies*

'Funny, angry, sad, vulnerable and sly ... A towering masterpiece'

NIKKI MAY, author of *Wahala*

'A tender and wise debut with a fat, pulsing heart. I'm here for whatever Escoffery writes next'

SABA SAMS, author of *Send Nudes*

'Marvellously inventive ... Redefines what we mean by a novel and a collection of short stories'

KIT FAN, author of *Diamond Hill*

'Jonathan Escoffery has achieved what all great literature manages to do: he invites the widest of audiences to revel in the unfamiliar' MOSES McKENZIE, author of *An Olive Grove in Ends*

'A magnificent debut ... Escoffery is a writer to watch'

MAURICE CARLOS RUFFIN, author of *We Cast a Shadow*

'A keen and witty observer with range and style. An exciting new voice' GABRIELA GARCIA, author of *Of Women and Salt*

IF I SURVIVE YOU

JONATHAN ESCOFFERY

4th ESTATE • London

4th Estate
An imprint of HarperCollins*Publishers*
1 London Bridge Street
London SE1 9GF

www.4thestate.co.uk

HarperCollins*Publishers*
Macken House, 39/40 Mayor Street Upper
Dublin 1, D01 C9W8, Ireland

Hardback edition first published in Great Britain in 2023 by 4th Estate
First published in the United States by MCD,
an imprint of Farrar, Straus and Giroux in 2022

10

A catalogue record for this book is
available from the British Library

ISBN 978-0-00-850121-1 (hardback)
ISBN 978-0-00-850122-8 (trade paperback)

These stories previously appeared, in slightly different form, in the following publications: *Passages North* ('In Flux'), *The Paris Review* and *The Best American Magazine Writing 2020* ('Under the Ackee Tree'), *Zyzzyva* ('Odd Jobs'), *Electric Literature* ('Pestilence'), *Prairie Schooner* ('Independent Living', published as 'Chasing Carlos'), *American Short Fiction* ('If He Suspected He'd Get Someone Killed This Morning, Delano Would Never Leave His Couch'), and *AGNI* ('If I Survive You').

Title page and chapter-opening art by Lubov Chipurko/Shutterstock
Designed by Gretchen Achilles

Set in Fournier MT Std
Printed and bound in the UK using 100%
renewable electricity at CPI Group (UK) Ltd

MIX
Paper | Supporting
responsible forestry
FSC™ C007454

This book is produced from independently certified FSC™ paper
to ensure responsible forest management.

For more information visit: www.harpercollins.co.uk/green

To Mom, Dad, and Jason

CONTENTS

IF I SURVIVE YOU

IN FLUX

t begins with *What are you?* hollered from the perimeter of your front yard when you're nine—younger, probably. You'll be asked again throughout junior high and high school, then out in the world, in strip clubs, in food courts, over the phone, and at various menial jobs. The askers are expectant. They demand immediate gratification. Their question lifts you slightly off your preadolescent toes, tilting you, not just because you don't understand it, but because even if you did understand this question, you wouldn't yet have an answer.

Perhaps it starts with *What language is your mother speaking?* This might be the genesis, not because it comes first, but because at least on this occasion you have some context for the question when it arrives.

You immediately resent this question.

"Why's your mother talk so funny?" your neighbor insists.

Your mother calls to you from the front porch, has called from this perch overlooking the sloping yard since you were allowed to join the neighborhood kids in play. Always, this signals that playtime is over, only now shame has latched itself to the ritual.

Perhaps you'd hoped no one would ever notice. Perhaps you'd never noticed it yourself. Perhaps you ask in shallow protest, "What do you mean, 'What language'?" Maybe you only think it. Ultimately, you mutter, "English. She's speaking English," before going inside, head tucked in embarrassment.

In this moment, for the first time, you are ashamed of your mother, and you are ashamed of yourself for not defending her. More than to be cowardly and disloyal, though, it's shameful to be foreign. If you've learned anything during your short residence on earth, you've learned this.

It's America and it's the eighties, and at school, in class, you pledge to one and one flag only, the Stars and Stripes. *Greatest country on earth* is the morning anthem. It's the lesson plan, a mantra, drilled into you day in, day out—a fact as inarguable as two plus two equaling four—and what you start to hear, as you repeat this to yourself, is the implication that all other nations, though other nations are seldom mentioned in school, are inferior.

You believe this.

It's an easy lesson to internalize, except that your brother, Delano; your parents; nearly all your living relatives are Jamaican. When your play cousin moves from Kingston to Miami, to your Cutler Ridge neighborhood, winding up in your third-grade class, refusing to pledge allegiance to your flag, you know to distance yourself from her. You say a quiet thanks that your last names are different.

If you'd had any context for the question of what you "are" when it first came, you might have answered, *American*.

You were born in the United States and you've got the paperwork to prove it. You feel pride in this fact, this inalienable status. You belt Lee Greenwood's "God Bless the U.S.A." on the Fourth of July, and even more emphatically after visiting your parents' island nation for two weeks in your ninth summer. You disagree with every aspect of the island life, down to the general lack of central air-conditioning. You prefer burgers and hot dogs to jerked or curried anything.

Back at home your parents accuse you of speaking, and even acting, *like a real Yankee*. But if by *Yankee* they mean *American*, you embrace it. "I speak English," you respond.

Your parents' patois and what many deem an indecipherable accent still play as normal, almost unnoticeable against your ears, except that it is increasingly paired with the punitive. For instance, when your mother says, "Unoo can spill di t'ing on di tile, but unoo can' clean it?"

And your brother says, "No me, Mummy."

And you say, "I didn't do it, Mom."

She'll say, "Den who did? Mus' be a duppy."

The duppy becomes the scapegoat for all the inexplicable activity that takes place in and outside your house. The duppy broke your mother's vase, then tried to glue it back together. The duppy hid your brother's report card underneath his mattress. The duppy possessed your father, dragged his body out for drinks after work, and didn't bring him home until morning.

A duppy, or ghost, or even a grown man, can be difficult to discipline, so you and your brother alone share the punishments.

In school, when your world geography project is announced and you're made to choose from a list of countries to present on, you choose Mongolia. It's not till another student chooses Jamaica that you consider the tiny island a worthy option.

Part of your project requires preparing a dish native to the country you've chosen. This is fourth grade. Your mothers do the cooking. When they meet one another on presentation day, eyes ringed dark from having wrestled with foreign recipes late into the night, they nod imperceptibly, too exhausted for pleasantries.

As your classmate begins her presentation on Jamaica, your mother sucks her teeth—a sound akin to industrial-strength Velcro ripping apart—drawing glances from several of the other parents. "Me could've brought in leftovers," she whispers, leaning in, "if only you chose home."

———

On career day, your father stands in front of your class and identifies himself as a general contractor. The block letter alphabet strung along the edge of the blackboard arcs over his wavy black hair. Below the arch, he unspools a foot of measuring tape with the tip of his thumb, then releases it, causing the tape to zip back into its case. The sharp whiz emitted by the swift violence of the retracted tape gains your classmates' undivided awe. Your father repeats this action several times before deigning to speak. Your classmates hold their breath in anticipation.

As he explains that "when man need dem bat'room fix, is me get all di plaster an' PVC an' t'ing, an' is me make di worker man come nice up di place," a string of snickers breaks out from the classroom's back row.

Your teacher shushes the students, but as your father continues his speech, her face crinkles, head bobbling to the beat of his patois. You concentrate on the pink surfacing over her cheeks, the color spectrum helping you determine the magnitude of this disaster. If she remains light pink—a shallow blush, a rose petal, a ballet slipper—you'll know this is a faint debasement, to be forgotten in the weeks ahead. But as her skin brightens, flashing past punch, nearing violet, you recognize this as catastrophic.

You question why you didn't insist your mother come in your father's stead. She knows better how to iron out her words for American ears, as she must for work every day.

Earlier in the week, you asked her about the details of her secretarial position. From the edge of your bed, your mother explained that she works in the office of a company that ships jet engines internationally. The hem of her nightie shimmied as she skipped across the room to pull down the globe from atop your bookcase. "You see here. And here. And this here." She kneeled at your bedside, pointing to Germany, then Brazil, then to the chain of Hawaiian Islands, singing, "We go all-around-the-world," dancing her slender index and middle fingers across oceans and lush green continents before lifting them to tap your nose.

"We?" you asked her. "You don't get to go to these places, do you?"

Your mother blinked twice, then walked the globe back to its shelf. "Someday," she said. "Someday maybe when you're all grown up." She added, "Better you ask your father to visit school. Him they'll find exciting."

In your fifth-grade history section, you learn more about the founding of America. You learn about the subject referred to simply as "slavery." It's an abbreviated, watered-down lesson, much like its subject heading. It's: *Mostly good people made a big mistake.* It's: *That was a long, long time ago.* It's: *Honest Abe and Harriet Tubman and M.L.K. fixed all that nasty business.* It's: *Now we don't see race.*

An air of shared discomfort infiltrates the classroom during this lesson; the students agree this was a terrible event. You're mildly aware that some of your classmates are supposed to have descended from the perpetrators of this atrocity and that some descended from the victims. You're not quite aware that many descended from both. Should *you* feel slighted by this country you love so dearly?

This is not the first time you've heard of the transatlantic slave trade, as your father never misses an opportunity to denigrate your country of birth. In his boisterous version of the lesson, you learn "that's why these Black people act so, the ignorant monkeys. Them come out o' bondage not two seconds ago, now them must act civilized? Boy, I tell you, White people wicked, you see." At the height of his lecture, he'll add that slavery ended in Jamaica *hundreds of years* before slavery ended in America, a claim you'll later learn is off by hundreds of years.

He has a word, a Jamaican word, for the Blacks of either nation he deems disreputable: *butu.* If ever you do something that might cause him shame, he'll say, "You can act like real butu sometimes."

=====

"What am I?" you've repeated to your mother by now. You've been asked enough times by strangers to begin seeking answers.

Her response seems prepared, but not as clearly defined as the question demands. Your mother tells you that you are made up of *all sorts of things*. She lists countries, several countries, and assigns *great-grand this* and *great-grand that* to these many nations. Your mother rarely attaches names to these forebears, so you easily confuse them. "Our last name comes from Italy," she says, "by way of England." Most of the countries she lists are European, and though she's sure to add Africa as though it were a country or an afterthought, she never mentions race.

You want a one-word answer.

"Am I Black?" you ask her. That, after all, is what you want to know. Race has descended upon your world, sudden and grating, and what you fear most is that others recognize in you something that you've yet to grasp.

When only the kids asked, you assumed that their limited experience in the world left them similarly ignorant. But now adults are beginning to fish for answers. Some of your teachers simply gawk at you, while others ask how it is you *speak so well*.

At first, you'll reply, "I'm American," certain they are distinguishing between your accent and your parents'. This answer only further confuses your teachers. Later, especially when asked by teachers whom your parents have never met, you realize they mean something else entirely.

"Are we Black?" you ask your mother.

Agitation grips her. A shudder takes her bright, freckled flesh and wiggles it over her bones as she quickly finishes the family genealogy, down to the last shaky details. "Your father's father's mother was Jewish. Your grandmother's mother was Irish," she says. "Your grandmother's father," and she lowers her voice to a whisper when she says this part, "may have been an Arab."

You stare at her blankly, noting, "You haven't answered the question."

Her agitation inflates to ire. "Chuh. I was never asked such stupidness before coming to this country. If someone asks you," she says, "tell them you're a little of this and a little of that."

You see that her response is final. Again she's avoided the one-word answer, what you'd hoped was a simple yes or no.

The few decidedly Black kids in school find you befuddling. They are among the first to insist that you state your allegiance. "Are you Black?" they demand.

You're a rather pale shade of brown, if skin color has anything to do with race. Your parents share your hue. As do their parents. *Their* parents, your great-grands, occupy your family's photo albums in black-and-white and sepia tones that conceal the color of their skin. Some look like they might guest-appear on *The Jeffersons*, while others look like they'd sooner be cast on *All in the Family*. Your best school friends, José and Luis, are the two whose skin tones most match yours outside of your home. But when they flip back and forth between English and Spanish, you feel excluded. And when they flip their hair back and forth in mock head-banging motions when singing your favorite rock songs, it becomes painfully apparent that yours isn't long or loose enough to bang along.

Additionally, your neighbor Julie informs you that—after half a decade of friendship—you are no longer allowed to play together. "Because your family doesn't believe in God."

"Of course we believe in God," you know enough to say.

But she just shrugs and says, "My dad says Jamaicans don't."

Your mother tells you and your brother one day, "Unoo better no bring no nappy-headed girls home." In your mother's defense, or perhaps to further disparage your mother, her list of girls not to bring home will stretch to the point where you'll wonder if she ever wants you to bring home girls. "Don' bring home no coolie," she'll start to warn in middle school. Upon seeing your uncut-coffee-colored Panamanian prom date, she'll lock herself in her bedroom. For her, your mother will have no words at all. And after you graduate, she'll say, "Please, just not a White girl. Promise me that."

But this is fifth grade still, and you're confused about this first warning. What constitutes "nappy" hair to your mother? You study hers—as fine as José's and Luis's guitar-string fibers— then study the cotton candy curls on your head. You wonder about your own hair's nappiness. You wonder who can't bring *you* home.

=====

The duppy returns, more mischievous than ever. It hides your father in a bar, in a bacchanal, in a dimension where your mother can't reach him. Before he rematerializes, plastered in J'ouvert paint, your mother reports him missing. As she talks to the police over the telephone, you and your brother huddle near enough to hear the man on the line say, "Ma'am, I can't make out a word you're telling me. Is there someone there who speaks English?"

She passes you the handset before breaking into sobs. The man asks you to describe your father. "He's six foot one," you tell him. "Skinny."

"Black or White?" the man asks.

You look to your brother. "Not White," you say.

"Black, then."

"Brown," your brother says.

"Your father go missing often?"

"How often is often?"

The disembodied voice tells you, "Ever."

"Oh," you say. "Then too often."

———

On the day you are scheduled to begin the sixth grade, a hurricane named Andrew pops your house's roof open, peeling it back like the lid of a Campbell's soup can, pouring a fraction of the Atlantic into your bedroom, living room—everywhere—bloating carpet, drywall, and fiberboard with sopping sea salt corrosion. It disinters the kidney-colored fiberglass from the walls and ceiling, splaying the house's entrails on the lawn. The storm chops your neighbor's house to rubble, parks a tugboat at the far end of your street.

In Andrew's wake, your family flees Miami-Dade to Broward County, where your mother's company has temporarily relocated.

At your new school, you again fall in with the brown boys. These boys, you come to learn, are the Puerto Ricans. One, Osvaldo, takes you under his wing. You sit with his crew in the lunchroom, and every once in a while, when they break into Spanish, you stare into your lunch tray's partitioned green peas and orange carrot cubes. If you are still enough, no one will notice you in these moments—you'll become invisible. If no one can see you, no one can realize tú no entiendes, that you don't quite fit. Osvaldo seems aware that you don't speak the language, but he's forgiving of this fault and steers the conversation back to English.

Perhaps it's that you've taken to shaving your head, removing the thick curls that might otherwise peg you as different; or perhaps you look enough like these boys, despite having a touch more Africa running through you; or perhaps they assumed you understood that at this school and at this age people stick to "their own kind." Either way, it dawns on you just a beat late that these boys believe you, too, are Puerto Rican.

They make cracks about White people: "White people smell like cocker spaniels. But only when they're wet."

They take cracks at Blacks: "Why do Black people stink so bad? It's so blind people can hate them, too."

Finally, one day at lunch, a member of the group asks you, not without a level of disgust, why your parents never bothered teaching you Spanish. You expect Osvaldo to intervene, but he awaits your answer with equal anticipation.

"Because they don't speak Spanish," you say.

The boys share confused glances. "Your grandparents didn't teach them Spanish?"

"My very Jamaican parents speak only English," you clarify.

"Wait," Osvaldo says. "You're Black?"

The trouble is not just that you've outed yourself, but that there is another set of boys with whom this group happens to be at war. The factions claim turf around the schoolyard, occasionally brawling under a nearby overpass. Your newness left you ignorant of the beef, but you're told these rivals hail from an island just two over from Puerto Rico: Jamaica. Osvaldo supplies this information as a parting gift. You are no longer welcome at his table.

The Jamaicans, some of whom are in your classes, look nothing like your family or the family friends who fly up for visits. And from the skepticism you find in their faces, you're certain that you scarcely resemble anyone they hold warm feelings toward. You wonder if there are two Jamaicas.

The difference can be noted in the names they and their American counterparts assign you: *light bright, red naygah, White boy*. At times, they simply call you *Spanish*. Now that you've been booted from the brown enclave, your vulnerability becomes your fragile, frantic, solitary friend.

Your brother, Delano, having four years of experience on you, and picking up on your ever-deepening entrenchment in this liminal space, finally clarifies things: "You're Black, Trelawny. In Jamaica we weren't, but here we are. There's a 'one-drop' rule."

With a smirk, he adds, "Sorry to break it to you."

=====

You attempt to befriend your Jamaican classmates. These attempts involve enduring humiliations, including quizzes about what Jamaican cities you can name (*Everyone knows Kingston. That doesn't count*), and what patois you can speak (*You know what's a batty boy, batty boy?*), and what Jamaican dances you can perform (*You can Bogle? Show us!*), till it becomes obvious they will never accept you among their ranks, especially not after you spent time with the browns. Members of both groups go out of their way to trip you in the halls or knock over your lunch tray.

You disappear to the library's Science Fiction and Conspiracies section during lunchtime. It's the one place you feel safe. This double exclusion will solidify one thing for you: you are the black sheep, if nothing else.

=====

Your brother starts traveling south, back to Miami with your father on weekends, his chafed leather tool pouch shoulder-slung, like a heavyweight championship belt. His biceps grow round and taut overnight, as though tennis balls had been implanted beneath the skin overlaying his arms, forced in with a shoehorn at the crooks. Softballs bloom inside his shoulders. The skin darkens, terra-cotta–colored under the facial hair that's sprouted on his cheeks, his cheekbones burned ashen.

"Roof work," he explains. "Di sun wicked, you see." He says this grinning, thumb-brushing his chin hair, modeling skinned knuckles.

With your father's guidance, he is rebuilding: rebuilding the house, the life Andrew washed into oblivion. He is constructing manhood.

They disappear Friday nights and reappear Sundays. You're told they sleep in a tent pitched in the wreckage of the living room or kitchen, depending on which they worked over that day.

You beg your father to bring you on these trips, to allow you to join in rebuilding.

"This no pickney business, boy," he says. His decision is final, rendered before you even ask.

Weekends, you sit with your Sega and kill things: vampires and aliens and time.

One Sunday night, your brother returns to your bedroom, reeking. You could scrape the salt, sweat then left to crust, off his arms. You could pat his clothes and disappear into the plaster cloud emitted. On his breath you taste beer, warm and stew-like. He climbs to collapse on the top bunk, his tan boot dangling over the mattress's edge. You wonder if he'll make it to class the next morning, but you don't say this.

You say, "How much longer?" You say this every Sunday night. Always, the answer is vague, placating: "Soon come."

You translate, then repeat this to your teachers, any who will listen. "Not long now," you say. "Here's my homework. You can grade it if you want, but don't expect me back Monday. I'll be gone any day."

Every Monday you return, they say, "With us another week, Miami?"

You gaze into the chalkboard, forcing your vision to double over, working to deaden the expression in your eyes, in your voice. "It won't be long," you say evenly.

This time, "How much longer?" is met with your brother's yawned "It almost done. It going to be nice, bredren. Better than before. Stronger."

"I hope soon. I don't belong here."

"Thing is," Delano says, stifling a burp in his fist, "you won't go back. Not there."

"What do you mean I won't go back there?"

He pauses, perhaps sobering a little, realizing he's said something he shouldn't have, then commits. "Dad told me this weekend. You and Mom aren't coming with us."

———

On move-out day, your father shakes your hand firmly and tells you, "Soon, yeah?" He wears an expression that suggests there should be more to say on such an occasion, but he can't bring to mind what that thing might be.

Your mom can hardly tear herself from Delano, and when she releases him from her embrace, she bounds back into the apartment without a glance at your father. Your brother offers you a bunks, folding his fingers into his fist, knocking his knuckles against yours. "Likkle more, rude boy," he says, smiling for your benefit. It's a gesture. *It's not that bad*, this gesture says, though you all recognize that it is exactly that bad.

=====

A week before the start of seventh grade, your mother moves you back down to Miami-Dade County, to Kendall, where no one is American. You might be a *gringo*, you might even be *Black* American, but solidarity under the Stars and Stripes has ended for you.

In school, Black girls still scream *red* at you when you walk through the halls. The boys still make fun of the way you speak, calling it *White*. You, of course, deny any connection to Whiteness. You swear allegiance to Blackness. It's the music you listen to now, the baggy clothes you wear.

The most popular kids in your predominantly Hispanic middle school are Black. They're viewed as the most charismatic, the most athletic, the least likely to give a fuck. You want in on this Blackness, on its enigmatic pull. You mimic these boys. You ape the way they walk and talk. Specifically, you begin to drag your feet and limp, then bop, and limp, then bop, then limp when you walk home from school. Your new walk has less the effect of helping you blend and instead makes you stand out as having special needs, but no one gains cred beating on a disabled kid, so you keep it bopping. You begin to drag your words and cut consonants, cut entire syllables, 'cause fuck 'em if they' keeping you out the circle o' Blackness.

The member perks are simple: No one will fuck with you once you're a card carrier. The neighborhood gangs, comprising mostly middle-class, suburban Latinos, are wary of the Blacks, whom they vastly outnumber, but who have brothers and cousins and uncles in Overtown and Liberty City and in prison who are famous for having murdered people. Being Black, you realize, might save your life.

But somehow you keep falling short.

When you do stupid shit, it's embarrassing. When they do stupid shit, it's contagious.

They call each other *nigga* and *dog*. Then the Latinos say *my nigga* and *dog*. Then the Whites say *my nigga dog*, even if quietly, even if looking over their shoulders first. Even if ironically, but that's how it infects you.

First you say, *My bad*, and giggle. Pretty soon it feels more right in your mouth than *sorry*. Years later, you'll see it on *Friends* and hear it on the nightly news.

Now when people ask, "What are you?" the answer is simple: "Black." And soon enough, people start to believe you.

———

Weekdays, your mom leaves her office at 5:00 p.m. and reaches home around 7:00. Her company's post-Andrew relocation to Fort Lauderdale has become permanent, inescapable. Your mother's commute threatens to steal hours from her life, so she fills these hours with *Speak Italian Now!* on cassette. Somehow it's her American accent that grows stronger. She collapses in front of the television at night with barely the energy to ask, "Are things okay with you?"

"Things are okay with me," you say, no matter how things are.

"How are your grades?"

"My grades are okay."

"And your friends? You making friends yet?"

"My friends are okay."

The house your mother purchased is larger than the one you grew up in, and much emptier. She spends her weekends furnishing the common areas with armchairs and artwork and rugs, but the rooms never seem to fill. A third bedroom, the one she keeps for your brother—the whole reason you moved back to Miami-Dade—goes largely unused.

Although the household earnings have been halved by your father's departure, she can afford this home through the magic of an adjustable rate mortgage. "It's an investment," she tells you. "It's a good time to buy."

"I'm confused," you say. "Did you buy the house, or does the bank own it?"

"I bought it," she says. "And the bank owns it."

━━━

Your father visits infrequently and takes you exactly once to his and your brother's house. On the drive down, he listens to talk radio. It's a spectacle of active listening. The show's segment is titled "Race Wars."

The host is saying:

"My money is on the Hispanics, you know, because these people have shown a remarkable ability, ladies and gentlemen, to get anywhere they want to go. To cross borders, boundaries—they get anywhere. They can go without water for a long time and they will do things other people won't. Dishes, gardening . . ."

Your father slaps his knee and cackles. "Ignorant monkey," he says, before leaning in and turning the radio two or three notches louder. He smooths his mustache with two fingers, kneading the smile from his face when he notices you watching.

"The Blacks—now, I know you're going to say this is racist—but the Blacks have no chance. None. And I'll tell you why. They can't swim. It says it right here. Almost half of all re-corded drowning deaths among people aged five to twenty-four are among Blacks, according to this study in *The American Journal of Public Opinion*."

"But what kind of . . . chuh . . . rubbish." Your father lowers the volume. After ten seconds or so he chuckles and says to himself, "The man have a point, though."

Upon entering your father's house, you see that the living room's gray-blue carpet has been replaced with bright white tile. The juice stains and stiff patches of fiber that mapped your childhood have vanished with the carpet. Most notably absent is the wall that once separated your bedroom from the kitchen. They've converted your room into a kind of dining area. A green-and-white lawn chair and a burgundy office chair sit on either side of the unvarnished dining table. The house is pristine, except for the coffee mugs and newspapers that litter the table's rough surface.

Your brother, a junior in high school now, reclines shirt-less against the lawn chair's vinyl straps, flipping through the classifieds. He's lean and ripped and looks ever more like your father's son.

As you survey the interior, your father looks over your clothes disapprovingly; his ears perk up at words you do or don't use. You're unsure which, though you've used few in his presence. "Boy, you gallivanting with these Black pickney?" he says.

You look to your brother, who lifts his muscular shoulders, then sets them back in place before returning to circling job postings.

"More and more you're turning into some kind of Yankee butu," your father says.

"Don't blame me 'cause you used me for a green card," you respond. "I didn't choose to be born here." You are grasping more about your position in the world, even if you understand little about what you might do to alter it.

———

In high school, teachers stop asking how you *learned to speak so well*. They stop asking much of you in general, until you're accused of plagiarism when your research paper sounds "too sophisticated." You might talk and dress Black, but you still write *White*, and there's a discrepancy to account for.

Your blaccent, you realize, might get you kicked out of school.

Your science teacher, Mr. Garcia, forces you to rewrite the essay to "make it sound like someone like you wrote it." You rewrite your thesis: *Niggas be like, Why for when bullets fly, niggas die? Newton says it's 'cause objects in motion be staying in motion. That was one scientific nigga, my nigga.*

Your revised paper earns an emphatic checkmark and a D minus.

In February, when teachers speak of the atrocities perpetrated against Blacks in America, you nod, then dissociate, thinking, *It's not my history. My family wasn't even here back then.* Simultaneously, you cultivate disdain for America, though America does most of the legwork. You suspect, on some level, that this disdain functions because you believe this history is your history.

Still, you hope that looking outside the United States will offer a kinder alternative to the oppression-centric narrative for people of the African Diaspora. At best, what you discover are loopholes in the designation of Blackness, terms like *half-caste* and *mulatto*, semantic parachutes that might allow an escape from Blackness. You reject these terms, come up with your own: *Half-rican* and *Negro-light*.

When you meet boys your color and darker, boys with kinkier hair, fuller lips, and broader noses, who cling to their Puerto Rican or Cuban or Dominican heritage in an exclusionary way, as in, *I'm not Black; I'm Dominican*, you join your friends in calling them sellouts. Uncle Tom—ass, self-hating-ass Negroes. You want Black people strong and unified, after all.

But one day, after one in a never-ending string of racial injustices gets concentrated media coverage, a band of Black American boys walks past, screaming *chico* and *oye*, and at first you stand idly, searching out their target, thinking, *Someone's about to get it*, not realizing it is you who will receive the sharp edge of their vengeance. A dozen dark hands ram you against a chain-link fence, shoving your body, as though pushing to strain the Blackness from your flesh before the White that remains can be justly smote.

Before a punch lands, though, Shells, your mutual, unquestionably Black friend, ambles by and gives you a pass. "Nah, he's cool," Shells says noncommittally. And this is enough.

How can your Blackness be so tenuous?

How would speaking Spanish make you not Black? you want to know. How does being from an island in the Caribbean make you not Black?

No, seriously, you'll want to know this, because some of the Jamaicans in your circumference start to openly make similar claims. *We're very different* culturally, they say. You've heard this from your own family. This becomes popular enough that even your Black American friends repeat it back to you.

At the warehouse where you work, a White coworker asks you to help him "nigger-rig a pallet."

"Is that really the kind of thing you want to say to me?" you ask him.

"What do you care? You're not Black. You're Jamaican," he says. "I have a Jamaican friend who explained the difference to me." You wish his friend could come explain the difference to you.

Suddenly, Black Americans are the only Blacks. Blacker than Africans. Black in the (lowered voice) *bad way*.

———

As you learn more and more about what it means to be Black in America, you finally make strides to understand your Jamaican heritage.

You start simple.

Suddenly, you like jerked and curried everything. Your flag switches from red, white, and blue to gold, green, and black. You fill your drawers with Jamaican flag bandannas and wristbands. Your one-word answer switches to "Jamaican," which you find more inclusive, all-encompassing.

Plus, the times "Black" failed to satisfy and you followed with "American," the askers shook their heads and said, "No, stupid. Where are your parents from? You know what I'm asking."

"Jamaica" is the solution. "Jamaican" is as specific as it gets.

But half the time, when you answer "What are you?" with "Jamaican," you're told, "You don't sound Jamaican. If you're Jamaican, where's your accent?"

———

You go deep. Not Shaggy, *Mr. Lover Lover*, radio-friendly deep. I talking Capleton, *More fire*, Mixx 96 underground-radio deep. Panyard warehouse dancehall deep. Me say, me can' rate rap music, 'less unoo say Kool Herc, a Yardie, invented hip-hop deep. Or Biggie's moms is Jamaican deep. And he's the best to ever do it deep.

You no turn Ras, but you chat 'bout I and I principles deep. You no praise Selassie, but you big up Marcus Garvey deep. You'll chant, *Fire 'pon Bush*, but still rate Colin Powell deep.

Bully beef deep. Build a Saturday soup with chocho deep. You nyam Marie Patties and Sango's deep, like unoo live 'pon Colonial, like you live 'pon ackee and saltfish diet deep. Fish and festival deep. Johnnycake and fritters deep.

You can chat 'bout Seaga versus Manley deep, JLP versus PNP policy deep, deep like Red Stripe versus Heineken. I talking Bayside Hut, heel an' toe on di Bookshelf riddim deep.

Deep like, *Why'd the Wayans have to do us like that?* deep. Deep like you root for Screwface in *Marked for Death* deep.

———

When you're out in Miami, let's say at Dolphin Mall, and the cashier addresses you in Spanish, and you say, "Sorry, I don't speak Spanish," then answer the requisite survey on why you don't, you'll be offended when the cashier tells you, "But you don't look Jamaican."

"What do Jamaicans look like?"

She'll rub her forefinger against the skin of her wrist, as if trying to remove a smudge, and say, "Black."

She promises you that you must be Dominican.

———

When you finally move away for college, what shocks you most is how no one in the Midwest assumes you are Puerto Rican or Dominican. Here you are simply, unquestionably Black. No one asks, "What are you?"

Instead, your classmates ask what it is like to have just survived Katrina. You explain that thirteen years earlier you lived through Hurricane Andrew—that Andrew was Miami's Katrina. At this, they blink and lose interest.

In seminars, people want to know the Black perspective on things. Their eyes flash disappointment when you say, "I'm probably not the one to ask." You suspect this is always the right answer, no matter who is asked. You wonder if denying to yourself and others that you've had the typical "Black experience" is integral to the Black experience.

You wonder what would've happened if a real Black man had gained admittance. You envision your classmates running for their lives. You picture your classmates throwing their pale, naked bodies at his very dark feet. You wonder if another Black person will ever be admitted. You watch as the years go by and none are.

In the Midwest, you are unquestionably Black; still, you'll marvel at just how white your skin gets in the winter. You'll stare for hours in the mirror at your hair, the loosened curls, newly freed from the weight of Miami's humidity. Some of it shoots straight out in singular strands, while other parts cling in wavy, feathery tufts, and still others spiral in tight coils. Not even your hair agrees on what it should be.

In the halls of your university's English department, your Korean friend accuses you of perming your hair. Your White classmates yank at it in seminars, then apologize, then yank at it in bars and don't. You thought this was just a stereotype, that the myth was grossly overblown. You are embarrassed for humanity.

You stumble drunkenly out of a dive bar and into a cab one night. You tell the Somali driver, "Take me to Black people." He nods and takes you downtown, to a hip-hop club. When you enter, you nearly tear up with joy, feeling the thumping bass vibrating through you. But when you peer into the crowd, the duo-chromatic pattern, the repetition of very dark men grinding against very pale women, will startle you.

———

In the Midwest, what comes into question is not whether you are Black but whether others around you are really White. Your Chinese American friend, Caitlyn, confides in you that she *feels* White.

"What does Whiteness feel like?" you ask her. "I imagine it's like walking barefoot on a shag rug."

"Oh, I forgot," Caitlyn says. "You must hate White people."

"Why should I hate White people? I moved all the way to the Midwest to discover White people."

"I just mean that people expect me to have some kind of minority perspective on things. Like I'm supposed to be the ambassador for Chineseness. My mom and dad are the only Chinese people I know. Plus we're so well-off. I guess I feel too privileged not to be White."

"That must be difficult."

"I know how this must sound, especially to you, but that doesn't change the way I feel. You wouldn't understand. How could you?"

"It sounds like you'd prefer if people treated you less like a generalization and more like a human being. Like how White people treat White people."

She bites her lip cautiously, then says, "Right."

"And your outward appearance is the only thing preventing this from becoming a reality."

"Exactly!" she says.

"I know what you're feeling," you say. "And I don't think it's Whiteness."

━━━

You attend what the students at your university refer to as a party. You've been to parties, of course, but here there is a distinction made between *parties* and *dance parties*. At dance parties, people have permission to dance. At parties, people have permission to stand awkwardly, discussing their studies, shielding their stomachs and chests with red plastic cups, or else bob dizzily around these cups, holding on for dear life.

In Miami, as far as you are aware, all parties are dance parties. You are way behind on the learning curve for small talk.

You meander through your host's crowded living room toward a partially formed circle of women whom you recognize from class. They are taking turns speaking passionately about something or other. You hope it's a topic you can contribute to. You're all English majors and transplants to the Midwest—you should have shared interests and experiences.

They make room for you to complete their circle but continue speaking rapidly, looking only into one another's eyes. One of them is saying, "It's like with me, people here find out that I'm from Mexico and they think of Mayans. My family's bloodline goes directly back to Spain. I'm no *Indio*. I mean, not that anything's wrong with that, but there's a clear difference."

"I know," the other black-haired woman in the conversation says. "I'm from Argentina. We're more similar to Europeans than South Americans."

"It's so true," the third, a brown-haired woman, says. "Just because my mother is Jewish, all of a sudden I'm treated like I'm not White here."

"Oh, *you're* White." The Mexican places a sympathetic hand on the brown-haired woman's arm. "Don't worry."

"Aw, you're White, too," she says, returning the arm pat.

"*I'm* White," the Argentine says, shakily. She blinks back tears.

"Oh, of course you are!" the other two say. "We're all White."
"*We're* White."
"We're *White*."
"We're White," they say.

———

You start to date two White American women casually, simultaneously. They both happen to be called Katie. Nearly every woman in the Middle West is called Katie. Or Caitlin. Or Kathryn. Or Kathleen. But these two are Katie. They're both in their mid-thirties and seem to be going through the same crisis that led them to date you in the first place.

They worry aloud about their fast-closing window of opportunity to have children. They speak carelessly about the fact that they come from wealthier families than you (they never actually ask). You're insulted, considering how much of your scholarship and student loan money you spend on your clothing, and how much time you put into your general appearance, but ultimately you come to understand they're both right. Although they haven't outright said so, the Katies believe they are smarter than you, but that you are better looking than they are, and they're willing to trade their money and brains for your youthful attractiveness.

What you don't tell them, what you keep closely guarded, is that you dicked around after high school, performing unskilled labor for years before bothering to apply to college, that you're a handful of years older than they assume. Brown guys don't get frown lines, so you're never asked what you're doing in undergraduate classes. Besides, the Katies already have your narrative written out in their heads, and who are you to disappoint them?

And what you like about them is that they're so taken by your . . . your what, exactly?

They try to play it cool in the beginning. But soon they let slip comparisons between you and other men they've dated. Or imagined dating. These comparisons are meant to sound complimentary.

Katie says, "Your skin's so much smoother than guys I've been with. I didn't think it could be so smooth. Be grateful you're not all ashy."

"Who knew your lips would be so soft?" Katie says. "Like plush little pink pillows. Thank god they're not all chapped and burnt-looking."

Katie even says, "There's pink in your nipples! Brownish-pink, but pink. I didn't think that was possible." Sooner or later they each begin obsessively to insist, over and again, "But you look mixed."

"I am mixed," you say.

"No, I mean biracial."

"Well, when you add it all up——"

"No," they say, "I mean like one of your parents is White."

———

In a diner at one in the morning, a woman tries to sell you the Koran. When you refuse, she curses you for betraying your Arab heritage. You promise her you have no Arab heritage and that you are not Muslim. At this, she passes a hand over your face and says, "Of course you are. Look at you."

———

Your two Black friends in the Midwest incessantly ask what you've done to your hair to make it look so. Actually, they point to it and say, "You don't wake up like this, do you?"

"No. You don't," the other says.

"I wash it from time to time," you answer.

They stay mad at you for *dating only White girls*, then for *dating only Asians*. They get mad at you for dating their Haitian friend. They're mad when you break up. "Like anybody cares where you put your raggedy dick," Sheila says when you point this out to her. "I told Gabriella not to mess with you," she adds. "You're on some taste-the-rainbow shit."

"Stick another fork in Black Love," says Neya, whipping her head this way and that.

You wonder if your and Gabriella's love could have qualified as Black Love. Your complexion is further from hers than from the Katies'. You're careful not to wonder this aloud.

When Sheila and Neya notice a family photo on your bookcase, the one that includes your dad, they go apeshit. "Oh, he has good hair," they say. And "Oh, no wonder. I thought your father was Black. I thought you were just light-skinned."

You want to point out their use of such a denigrating phrase as *good hair*, and to ask where this tribe of *just light-skinned* people is supposed to originate. You want to know if your father isn't Black, and if his hair alone disqualifies him. Instead, you blurt, "My mom's is straighter. What makes his so 'good'?"

They lean in close to inspect the photograph, then pull away, laughing. "Your mom's hair isn't straight," Sheila says, a string of giggles chasing her words.

You look to your mother's image—at the bangs, the hair cascading over her shoulders—then to Neya, whose laughter has stiffened into a smirk. "Her hair isn't really straight," she agrees. "That's nothing but a perm."

———

At the formal events you attend in the Midwest, you still manage to be surprised that the only Black people present are there to serve. Somehow you're still surprised when Black staffers stop you to say, *You look just like a guy who works here.*

Black bartenders refuse your order until you acknowledge this statement. They rush to wait on your friends and colleagues, but for you they stand idly by, smiling crookedly, as though you've told a joke, or as if they've remembered something amusing and you've said nothing to them at all. They might produce a damp rag and wipe down the bar before making eye contact. They might shuffle the ice scoop through the cubes in the freezer or stack cocktail napkins atop the dispenser, though the white paper squares are already beginning to lean.

When they finally acknowledge you, they make a production of sizing you up. Their heads wag especially slowly if you're accompanied by a date. "You look like a guy who works here," they say. And if you repeat yourself, if you ask, "Could we have two whiskey gingers, *please*?" they'll bare their teeth, look deep into your eyes, and say in the slowest possible cadence, "You look just like a guy who works here."

And you'll nod. You'll nod or go thirsty.

"That was really weird," your date might say on the walk back to your table. She might go so far as to explain microaggressions to you.

You'll take your seats, move on from this indignity, until the waitress comes around, quietly and briskly placing plates before the other guests at your white-linen-clothed table. She'll save your plate for last, as seems to be the protocol. If you're not paying attention, if you're engaged in conversation, she'll tap your shoulder, interrupt you mid-speech, and say: "You look just like a guy who works here."

You'll understand that she means, *You look like a guy who should just work here*, of course, especially because ever since you left Miami you've felt consumed by the idea that no one in this entire state looks anything like you. You wish some Dominicans would move into town.

Still, on buses and on downtown street corners, drunk Black men stop and point at you, saying, "We're brothers. Don't you forget."

———

In Jamaica you're brown. Your peers look overwhelmingly like you, some varied combination of African and European, with splashes of Indian or Chinese. They look like your family and sound like your family, and this makes you feel at home, even among strangers. Your peers here recognize mixed features as common within the middle class, and for once, on this grant-funded excursion to your parents' country, the eyes on you don't question or judge, but accept.

Until you open your mouth.

"Oh, a Yankee this," they say when they hear you. "But your parents them must be Yardies. Me can see it 'pon you." Some assure you that, no matter where you were born, you have "Jamaican blood." Others, the younger ones especially, find it preposterous that you would even utter the words *Jamaican* or *Jamaican American* to describe your ethnicity or as any other kind of self-identifier. "But what you know 'bout Jamaica?" they ask.

You've been taken in by this particularly skeptical mix of men and women in their early to mid-twenties, perhaps because they feel sad that you lost out on a proper Jamaican upbringing, or perhaps because they all seem to be home from the medical schools and law schools and universities they attend abroad, and having been away from Jamaica themselves, they need a foreigner present to remind them that they belong here.

Whatever the case, they succeed in convincing you that your parents ruined your life the moment they abandoned the island. Your new companions take you for fish and festival at Hellshire Beach, where onyx- and camel-colored bodies glisten in the turquoise water. They take you to National Stadium to see the fastest women and men alive qualify for their Olympic runs. They order their helpers to cook you jerked pork and stew peas and roasted breadfruit. They take you on boat trips and to nightclubs with names like Fiction and Envy. You count all this as research, postponing indefinitely your visit to the library at the University of the West Indies.

Your companions' parents insist you meet their friends' or siblings' daughters. For the first time in your life, someone's mother—several mothers—thinks you're an appropriate match for her daughter, and you agree. You want to propose to them all, to add posthaste to the caramel-beige population. These are the girls your mother wanted you to bring home, you realize: these walking multiculti mosaics, these brides of racial ambiguity.

Where else are people like me mass-produced? you ask yourself. And *How can I ever go back?*

On drunken nights you try your best Jamaican accent, which might pass under the thumping subwoofers' bass, or when everyone in your proximity is wasted, but having spent the last few years sequestered in the Midwest, away from the music and food and people so easily located in Miami, you've already lost a large percentage of your parents' tongue. At hearing your attempts, your companions crack smiles, then look away, pretend not to be embarrassed for you.

Eventually, you'll admit to yourself that you are tired. Tired of trying to convince anyone of anything, especially yourself.

When you're brought to the house your grandparents owned before they died, the one you visited as a child, you realize how small it is when held up next to your memories. You realize everything is relative.

═══

One afternoon, reclining in a lounger on your hosts' veranda, you set aside the bottle of Wray & Nephew long enough to ask two of your companions the question that brought you back to Jamaica to begin with, the one you've come to write about.

"Among your friends," you begin, "do people tend to think about or talk about their ancestral roots? Pre-Jamaican, I mean." You've been thinking about your mother's list of European grands and how your parents still speak so highly of the British school system that educated them, pre-Independence, and you think of the Rastafarians who extol Ethiopia and Mama Africa. But what you want to know about is contemporary middle-class twentysomethings. You want to know how you might feel had your family never left. "Do any of you look to England or West Africa as, you know, the motherland?"

"But what kind of foo-foo thing you asking?" Zoë, the light-eyed browning, says. You've fallen in love with Zoë alarmingly fast. You've spent the last several nights fantasizing about penning a letter to your father, begging that he send a dowry of sorts, any financial support that might allow you to remain in Kingston and court Zoë. Should you marry her and return your line to the island, perhaps in ten, twenty years America would be a blip in your family history, a bad dream to be forgotten. Back in Miami, Delano and his new wife have already begun making full-blooded Jamerican babies who may or may not grow to embrace their heritage.

For her part, Zoë returns your flirtations but guffaws at how slowly you speak, the grating way you bend your vowels, and how hard you land on consonants. "Is Afer-i-kuh your motherland?" she says in a voice that's supposed to sound like yours. "Only Yankees think 'bout these things 'cause them have no culture. Them lost."

"So typically," you say, "Jamaicans just feel . . . Jamaican?"

Zoë's cousin Steven turns to her. "Boy gone, you know. The whites lick off him head and him gone-gone." And to you, "Ease up, man. The rum there going mash up that t'ing between your ears." Steven's the son of a friend of a friend of your mother's who was supposed to show you around Kingston but who immediately pawned you off on Zoë and her girlfriends. You could kiss Steven for this.

"You think French people don't feel French?" Zoë asks. "You think the Irish them don't feel Irish?"

"That's different. You're not the original inhabitants of this island."

"So what? How long we must go back? You think generations never migrated throughout Europe?"

"I'm talking about colonialism, mass enslavement."

"Chuh. Only you Yankees hold on to that," she says. "That's what separates us from all of unoo."

You wonder about the relationship between ahistorical thinking and contentment.

You've been surprised at how forgiving you can be of Zoë's political views. Perhaps she has a point. Or perhaps this is love: blinding. When you told her you'd like to travel up to Accompong to pay homage to the Maroons who successfully fought off the British slavers, she said, "You mean dem likkle mud hut people?"

You say now, "But the poor people we pass on the street, the ones living in shacks and busing for miles to come clean your house, they can't see you all in nice cars and nice clothes and houses and think there's one Jamaica. They're still suffering the results of colonialism, no?"

"Well, you see, some people don't wan' work hard," Zoë says. "Me know it sound wretched to say, but——"

"Must be you want brown people in houses and Blacks in tin huts."

"Class issues, bredren," Steven says. "There's no racism here. We're all Black, man."

You decide to press the issue no further, fearful you'll offend your hosts. But later, when you ask about the private security forces whose billboards litter Kingston's skies—the ones who are said to arrive during home invasions and shoot thieves on sight—and how it is they distinguish between the robber and the homeowner, Steven points out, "They wouldn't shoot people who look like us. Them only shoot you if you're black-Black."

———

Your reentry into the Midwest is startling, much more jarring than when you first left Miami. You begin to feel pangs of loneliness, discontent. You realize—with bemusement at first, then with despair that reaches like an icicle from your diaphragm to the base of your gut—that you disagree with every aspect of life in your Upper Midwestern town, from the meat raffles and tornado warnings to the tater tot hotdish and the passive aggression, right down to the general lack of central air-conditioning.

You miss Jamaica and its people. You write to Zoë for several weeks, but the messages taper off as the fall semester gets underway.

One night, you get into it with Neya and Sheila about your feelings of isolation.

"What do light-skinned tears taste like?" Sheila asks. "Are they hydrating?"

"Maybe if he'd date Black American women . . . ," Neya says.

"Where are these women?" You make a show of surveying the room. "There's not another in this bar. There isn't one in my whole department."

"See, that's your first problem," Sheila says. "What kind of Black man studies literature, anyway? We can't afford to have college-educated artists. We need to be building wealth in our communities."

"Because the world needs another MBA," you say, referring to

Sheila's grad school ambitions. "Or, worse," you add, turning to Neya, "another lawyer."

You're three deep in tequila shots and the surface of your high top is littered with beer mugs, all of which have been emptied. You look to your left, toward the bar, hoping to spot the server to order another round.

Instead, you see what, for a split second, you believe to be your mirror image. There's a very light-brown young man sitting on a stool at the bar, and as you turn toward him, he turns toward you. His hair is shorter than yours, though, and his eyes are lighter. His lips are rosy in his golden face.

You would normally look away, but you keep your eyes planted on him for the moment. Your intense interest in studying mixed people's features, in parsing what makes them like yourself, has only intensified since moving to this city that has next to none. It's like belonging to a club you're not allowed to talk about.

The man at the bar smiles and approaches your table. He says his name is Justin. Justin appears to be alone. Perhaps he suffers from a similar affliction.

"Grab a seat, Justin," you say. "We were just discussing Black responsibility in the twenty-first century."

Justin looks to your companions as though to ask, *Is he serious?* You wonder if he'll engage, if he even identifies.

"What we were discussing," Sheila says, "is whether we need another artist in the Black community. How does that advance us?"

"Well," Justin says. There's a hint of thoughtfulness in the way he speaks, or maybe in the pause just before. "The artists are the heralds. They're our mirrors, our light. They reflect our reality, past, present, and future. Without them, we wouldn't have much gauge of whether we've progressed or not. We'd be like children, groping for each other in the dark."

Neya laughs.

"Just great," Sheila says.

"A poet," you say.

"No, not really," Justin says. "I'm a musical theater major, though."

"Tell me, Mr. Musical Theater," Sheila says, "what can your musicals reveal that a census or a Pew report can't?"

"Well," Justin begins again. He squints, and his jaw looks marginally stressed for a moment. He exhales slowly, as though he were releasing cigarette smoke. His jaw relaxes. His beauty marks dance around his face as he speaks. "A census tells us the what but not the why. But even if we have the why—let's say wealth disparities result from discriminatory housing practices—we still wouldn't have the humanity that's essential to conveying the real message, that human lives are at stake."

"Plus, factor in representation in a larger sense," you say. "If I don't create characters who look like me, who will? Visibility is important. Otherwise, it's as if we don't exist."

"Right," Justin says.

"Well, aren't you fric and frac?" Neya says.

"You're a writer?" Justin asks. "I wonder if you wouldn't mind looking at a piece I've been working on. It could use another set of eyes."

———

You meet Justin at a coffeehouse. You're meeting him so he can give you a copy of the story or play or script he's been working on. You're not too clear on those details. He's got it in hand when he greets you.

"This is the piece you wanted me to look at?"

He says yes but keeps the manuscript on the table beneath his folded arms. "Thanks for agreeing to." He looks around the café. "I've never been here. It's a nice choice." His fingertips flick the corners of the manuscript, giving it bunny ears. "Sorry. I'm just a bit nervous, I suppose."

"How come?"

He shrugs and looks down at his hands. "I've actually never done this kind of thing before."

"Listen, don't be nervous," you say. "It can be awkward at first, putting yourself out there. Putting so much trust in someone else. Exposing yourself. I mean, we all worry about what people will think. It's only natural. But after the first time, it gets easier. You'll get used to it, and pretty soon you'll start to love it."

"I hope so," he says. He twists a silver ring around his pinky.

"Can I ask you something? I don't mean to be intrusive, but I'm curious."

"You might as well, at this point." Justin smiles.

"What's your background?"

He sits a bit straighter. "Like, educationally?"

"I mean where are your parents from?"

"That's an odd question," Justin says. "They're from here. As were their parents before them."

"Yeah, but I mean racially," you say.

He stares at you in silence, looks around, faces you again. "Do you have some kind of fetish or something?"

"Fetish?"

"I get it if you have a type, but—"

"Type?"

"I'm not into the whole exotification thing."

"Type? What do you think this is?"

You stare at each other, each waiting for the other to clarify things.

"I just came to read your story, dude."

"And help me expose myself?"

"I meant creatively."

"I'm actually going to go now."

"Wait," you say.

He hesitates a moment, hands poised to push himself up from the table.

"Can't we be friends?"

He laughs. "I already have friends," he says. "Besides, I think you have some issues you need to work through."

———

In the final fall semester of your undergraduate career, you force yourself to stare into the fire red bursting in the leaves, to take in the breeze, crisp and invigorating along the skin poking out from your sweater, to tell yourself, *This is magic. This doesn't happen where I'm from—I've come so far.*

In the blistering, skin-biting nights that follow, though, you wish only that you were back in Miami, saturated by swampy warmth, engulfed in the sticky-hot. But you are not in Miami. So you puff hot breaths into your scarf to melt feeling back into your face. Tuck your head and lift your boots, trudge silently through the snow.

In the midst of the first snowstorm of your final semester—before your kitchen's lights flicker to black and your cell loses its signal—you make a decision. You call your mother to tell her. "I have news," you say over the wind ripping at your living room window, the one missing the glass storm window. You press the meat of your palm into your left ear cavity and shout into the receiver, "I'm moving home this summer. Right after graduation."

"I have news," your mother responds, her voice irritatingly soft. "I'm moving home this summer, right after graduation."

The window frame shudders and you wince away the idea that your mother is parroting you, that you've been away long enough for her to have grown senile. "You are home," you say.

"No," she says. "Kingston. Me get a job offer."

"You haven't lived there in thirty years, almost."

"It's time," she says. "This place too hard for a Black woman."

"Which Black woman?"

"This Black woman. You feeling all right?"

You hang up and call your brother. "Mom says she's Black and that she's moving to Jamaica. Those might be signs of dementia."

Your brother chuckles quietly, a sound affirming that he's never been particularly bothered by happenings in the lives of others. "We all have to be what we have to be sometimes."

You want to tell him where he can shove his platitude—to say, *I didn't imagine this. This hasn't all been in my head.* You nearly say, *It must be nice to be welcome in the country you were born in, to have a homeland to escape to.* You say, "The connection's bad. I'll call you back."

You dial your father. "I'm coming home," you tell him.

He pauses a long while, so long that you check the phone's display to confirm that he's still on the line. "Trelawny . . . you think that's a good idea?"

"You don't?"

"Well, what you can do down here? There's no jobs." He reels off a list of keywords, seemingly excerpted from the evening news: *mortgage crisis*, *foreclosures*, *recession*, *economic downturn*. "Better you just stay there," he says.

"I'll have my degree. That should help me find something."

"Degree in what? English? Them don't speak English here. How that can help you get job?"

"Maybe I'll work with you."

"There's no work," he says. "The people can' keep the houses them have, much less build new house. Even your mother's house them foreclose on."

"They did?" You think about her adjustable rate mortgage, about the bank doing the adjusting.

"Where you will live if you move back?" your father asks.

You fumble over the words: "I'll figure it out." You say, "Listen, I'd better go," before you can succumb to the realization that his invitation to move in with him, the one that is more than a decade late, is not coming.

———

A couple of months before you graduate, before you load up your Dodge Raider and drive the 1,811 miles back to Miami to figure things out, you decide to take a DNA test. You spit into a tube, mail it, and await the findings. Six weeks later an email notifies you that your results are ready. You log in to your account and a box pops up stating that you are 38 percent West African. This is your highest percentage from any single region (as large and varied as this region may be). This feels right, or at least it doesn't strike you as particularly wrong, given your Jamaican parentage and the history behind the populating of the island.

But when you click to pull up your complete ancestral breakdown, the top of the page shows 59.9 percent European ancestry (British, mostly, with the smaller, broken-down percentages spanning the continent). The bottom of the page shows 1 percent Middle Eastern ancestry. The remainder is inconclusive.

"Holy shit," Katie says from beside you on the couch. She backs away so she can take you in anew. "I'm dating a White boy."

You, Negro, are mostly European.

"You're still Black," Katie says, turning serious.

This is the first concrete data you've been provided about your race, though it's actually closer to your ancestral ethnic makeup. Race, you know, is a social construct. It can't be measured, because it doesn't exist—biologically. If the results had shown 99 percent European and 1 percent African, as long as your skin held some degree of brown and your hair still coiled, you'd still be Black and only Black by American standards.

You think of the times you're asked to check a box—on the census or an intake form at a doctor's office or a teaching evaluation at the end of the semester. It's one of the few times when you're asked to self-identify by an entity incapable of correcting or denying you, at least in that moment. You may now scrawl, *A little of this and a little of that* beside the "Other" box, but this new information doesn't mean you should check Black *and* White.

First, the entire project of Whiteness means "to the exclusion of *and*." Second, you are not the progeny of a Black person and a White person. You are the offspring of two Others.

You're brown, but not that kind, and not that kind, and not that kind.

Black means expansive enough, inclusive enough, to contain the whole of your European ancestry, to bear the whole of the continent: your French, your Italian, your Irish, your English, and Black, your Black, you're Black, then why do they keep asking?

You'd hoped that receiving scientific evidence would make easier the process of claiming one thing or embracing being multitudinous. Would empower you to say, *Regardless of what you see me as, I'm this*. To say, *I'm this, regardless of what city or country or company I'm in*. But nothing's changed. Not even the testing of your DNA can help you answer, in one irrefutable word, "What are you?"

UNDER THE ACKEE TREE

f you are the only son of uptown Kingston parents, then you will have options. You can take Daddy's Datsun or Mummy's new '68 VW and fly past street urchins who sell bag juice and ackee at red lights down Hope Road to pick up Reyha or Sanya or Cherie.

If a Reyha you pick, you will carry she to drive-in, where you can stroke she hair while unoo watch Bond 'pon big screen. Reyha's family own the bread shop on Barbican Road, where she work most afternoons, and you like sniff she hair since it always smell of coco bread or spice bun.

Is Cherie you like slow wine plenty nights down a New Kingston, whether Epiphany or Dizzy. She tease you, you see? Push up hard 'pon you in corners and grind she pelvis into yours before she laugh and push away.

A Sanya you like chat bad word with, so she you take a Hellshire to sit seaside and nyam escovitch snapper and chat bare fuckery till them tell unoo, You no see the sun gone and is time fi move you batty?

If you no careful, life go so carefree, till you daddy say, Time to get serious, boy, and stop all the play-play. Time to get job. Time to be a man.

If him say so, tell him say you wan' go a foreign fi art school and learn fashion design, and don' him see how your sketchbook full up with concepts and him can' see you stylee?

But if you say that, him will answer, Fashion? A my son a si' down an' sew panty an' frock? Wha' kind of little-gal fantasy that?

But, Daddy, man in Europe study fashion from time, you will tell him.

Me know, him will say. Batty man.

You'll ask him, How you can be so small mind? You'll puff up your chest and pace the veranda and wan' fling him furniture, because him can' beat you like him did beat you when you were a pickney.

Even he know him can' discipline you like before, so him say it calm: No bother with no foo-foo art school. If you can' be serious, you go work for me. And if you can' do that, you can leff me house.

And it don' feel then like you have too many options at all.

So you start oversee him construction jobs, though is little you know 'bout how man build house. Mostly, is make sure man show up on time and don' leave early. Mostly, is hunt worker down at bar after them disappear for lunch. When you run them down, the worker man malice you and call you rich man' boy, though your daddy' business not so big that him wealthy.

You don' like the job, but your father say, Since when man supposed to like job?

But him pay you and let you use him work vehicle and soon

after you can afford apartment in Mandeville, and after that you feel large.

If you carry on like before with Reyha and Sanya and Cherie, is Sanya who will come beat down your door and cuss you while Cherie sneak out back. You'll make promise and beg you a beg for she hand in marriage one time. Is Sanya you love, like you love bread pudding and stew, which is more than you have loved before. You love that when she walk with she brass hand in yours, you can' tell where yours ends and hers begins. You love that where you see practical solution to the world' problem, Sanya sees only the way things should be; where you see a beggar boy in Coronation Market, Sanya sees infinite potential.

Most of all, is she smile you fall for. Sanya' teeth and dimples flawless and you hope she'll pass this to your pickney, and that them will inherit your light eyes, which your father passed down to you.

Sanya' tall. You tall to rass.

She quick-tongued, and you passed six A levels. So your children will be bright.

You only hope them get she teeth.

If you marry she, you will have garden wedding, and you will design your suit and pay tailor to stitch it nice. You will send out invitation, and it will seem like the whole of Kingston will come celebrate unoo and see how you and Sanya styling. All nine Panton sisters line up as Sanya' bridesmaids, and it' good you keep plenty friend from school who can balance your side. Mrs. Panton give Sanya away, since she daddy dead and gone. Later, in Mandeville, if you breed she, you'll make a boy, and it seem your every want must come to pass. You will thank Sanya for the boy, though you know it man give Y chromosome—you no ignorant gully boy. But you thank her still. And though it too early to know whether baby will have she teeth, him have your eyes, so blue them nearly violet, so you quietly grateful she no interfere with that. You will make the boy' middle name Christopher, after you, even when most people know you as Topper. You will make him first name Delano.

You'll drive Delano up and down mountainside when him bawl and can' sleep. And you don't speed like you did speed when it only your life JA' potholes threaten so, you drive the car slow-slow. Sanya will sing Irish hymns to Delano, the ones she grandmother sang she when she was a pickney. And when neither she nor you can hold open your eyes, you will ask Jodie, your helper, to push him stroller 'round the block until him drop asleep.

If the night sounds shift from croaking lizard to machine gun ra-ta-ta-ta, you'll ask Jodie not to walk with Delano at night.

Your father will blame Independence for the way things go, but you'll say, No, man, is the prime minister and all him socialist fuckery that cause the trouble.

Don' *you* voted Manley into office? him will ask you, like is you alone had the one vote.

Fool me once, you'll admit to him. But me never vote for him in seventy-six.

Is rumor say Manley buddy up with Castro, and what him thought, the Yankee them was going let a next island in them backyard turn communist? Rumor say it CIA flood the garrisons with cocaine and make JLP rude boy war PNP badman with automatic rifle, when just yesterday them could've murder each other only with stone and rust blade.

If it just themselves the idiot boys slaughter, won't nobody care 'bout them butu war. Soon shots grow close, though, and is uptown woman them kill in crossfire and police say them can' chase the boy back in them slums because ghetto youth now out-gun policeman. Then the military must get involved.

You daddy call, and you know from how him voice shake the war come show up at him doorstep. Gunman lick down them door and tie up you mummy and daddy, and thief off them money and jewelry and everything. Daddy them pistol-whip and you mummy . . . God knows how them feel her up so, even when she old to rass. But him tell you say it could have gone worse.

How it can go worse? you ask him. But not a month pass before them rape your neighbor and kill her husband in front of she.

The fucker them is all one man in your eyes. No, two man: Seaga' man and Manley' man. Though Uncle Sam' man also tryin' swing JA' elections.

From then you send off for U.S. visa and ask your daddy' brother fi sponsor unoo, since him been in the States for time. Things move fast: your visa come through and you ask your mummy and daddy whether them think you should really go, and them say, Boy, wha' wrong wi' you? You can' see the whole of we island turn into war zone? And, This what we gained indepen-dence for? Them say, Better g'wan save yourselves.

Jodie ask can you bring she to the States, but you can't afford to keep helper now. You tell she you mummy and daddy will take her, since them helper old and soon need help.

You think 'bout a New York, but is Miami you settle, be-cause you visit your uncle Michael in Brooklyn one November, and if the fall can lick off your batty with cold tongue so, you no wan' know what winter go do. Plus the sister Sanya' closest with, Daphne, take up with a man from Miami and is there she start spend half she time.

Is Miami you have your second son. At hospital, when them hand you the boy' birth record to sign, under him birth year, 1980, in a section marked "Race of Father" them type "Negroid." You tell the nurse, Me learn 'bout Negro, but what is *oid*? But she don' bother with you.

You name your second son Trelawny to remind yourself of home. It long enough after you reach that you miss JA bad-bad. You miss walk down a road and pick Julie mango off street-side. When you try pick Miami street-side mango, lady come out she house with rifle and shoot your belly and backside with BB. In the back of your Cutler Ridge town house, you start try grow mango tree and ackee tree with any seeds you come by, but no amount of water or fertilizer will get them to sprout.

In spite of him name, Trelawny grow up strange. Foreign. You blame the nursery school teachers where you and Sanya leave him when you go work each morning, where you bring him from him turn six months old. You blame yourself since you can' afford to let Sanya stay home like when Delano did born. Still, when the boy start talk, you can' believe it: is a Yankee voice come out. You read and talk to him as much as you can, but the boy no wan' pick up nothing you say, not like him brother.

Him no say *mummy* for him first words; him say *mom*. Him have Sanya' dark eyes and none of she teeth or dimple. Him grow and soon it pain your ears to hear the boy say *water*, which him pronounce "wah-der."

You can' spend all day talking to the boy. You work twelve-hour shifts on used-car lot, sometimes selling car, most times selling nothing, until the day you take a man out for test drive and him stick him pistol in your gut and drive out all a Everglades and tell you say, Get out and walk, and if you turn around you're dead.

You walk and walk and wait to die, and when you hear him pull off, you walk some more. You no bother go back a work. Work fi wha'? So them can shot you? If you wanted bullet in your back you could've stayed a Kingston.

It four weeks before you admit to Sanya what happened and that you leave the job. In that time, when the house empty, you start sketch landscape from home off memory. You sketch Dunn's River Falls and Cockpit Country and Fern Gully, and it shaky at first, but then your steady hand return to you. You take a dozen sketches to the weekend flea market down the road and stand up all morning, but don' nobody wan' buy no colorless landscape. Them want garish flamingo watercolors like the lady at the next table selling. But you can't afford paint or canvas, or the time it take to put the two together. And when Sanya start ask where you find time to draw, and how it is your car sales drop from little to zero, you have to tell she the truth.

Sanya look at you cross and say, You think me wouldn't rather stay home and doodle?

You know she right, but she didn't have to put it so.

You call your daddy and say you wan' expand him business into the States. But him say, The business barely holding on since Manley piss off the IMF and make price of everything skyrocket. You say, But, Daddy, don't Seaga is prime minister now? But all him can say is, Chuh. Still him send you small loan through money wire.

You start basic. You go 'round and gather up man all a flee JA crime wave and see what all them can do. Is roof you can repair?

Unoo know plumbing system? You can fix AC? You use you father' loan to put out advertisement and soon you start broker deals, send man out on job and collect small fee off it. It don' pick up straightaway, and Sanya make more from she secretary job than you. She bright, so soon she them make office manager, even when no man wan' woman manage them. Still, your combined income less than what you alone made in Jamaica and it seem you never can catch up back. But if you scrimp and scrounge and keep in luck' favor, you family can just keep afloat.

———

If years slip by, Delano will grow athletic and is he the neighborhood boys will wan' quarterback when them play American football in the street, and him afi quarterback for both teams, or else the boys cry, It no fair. Him start smile with him mummy' mouth, and you can see how the young girls already crush after him. It seem him can do most anything. Him ask for guitar and lesson, and him pick it up fast-fast. The boy sing out in him bedroom, "Where Did You Sleep Last Night?" and "Purple Rain," and play along as he sing. Then him play "Pass the Dutchie" and you know him never learn that from him teacher.

Trelawny no wan' bother with sports or music. Him take book and you find him hiding in closet with flashlight. When you ask him a question, him twist up him mouth and stare on you blank with him big black eyes. If you say, Answer me nuh, boy, him look 'pon him brother, and if Delano repeat your question, Trelawny finally answer, like him need him brother to translate.

Every day is a next thing. Him start draw on him bedroom walls, and no matter how you threaten him with belt, him can' stop. Him get As in class but can' figure out how to tie him shoe, so him sneakers must have Velcro. You tell Sanya, Something wrong with the boy, but she tell you, Be patient. At him school open house, Trelawny' teacher say she wan' put him in t'ing called Gifted. You say, Wha' that, special ed? She say is for advanced children so him don't get bored, but you tell her, Teach him to tie him shoe, then we can talk.

Then him start shit him pants, even when he long past potty training.

If you take him for doctor visit, the pediatrician will come out the examination and say Trelawny have anxiety. What him have to be anxious about? Him no pay bills. Doctor say, Just give him time.

Then Hurricane Gilbert come mash up Jamaica, and you can think 'bout nothing but how the people back home devastated. You can' get through to your parents, and the news say hundreds dead across the Caribbean. You call you friend them and Sanya' sisters and everyone you can think of in Jamaica to see whether them can check on your mummy and daddy, but don' nobody phone work. The feeling you get is that everybody' dead. And you never should have left them behind.

You sit Delano and Trelawny down for breakfast the next morning and try teach them them culture to make sure it survive. The tropical market on Colonial start carry canned ackee and green banana and salt cod, so you cook the boys ackee and saltfish and try explain why it Jamaica' national dish. You see this here, you say. The ackee grow in a pod and it must open on it own or else the ackee poison you. You point to the picture on the can, so them can see how it grow, and it remind you that you never eat ackee out of no can before. You tell them, Enslaved Jamaicans used it to kill off slave driver and free themselves to the mountains. But you don't know if them legends true.

Delano say, I remember Jodie used to cook it for us.

Trelawny say, It looks like scrambled eggs.

You think me would stand up a two hour and cook the thing if it only taste like eggs?

It better than eggs, Delano say, but when Trelawny taste it, him spit it out and say, Eew. How him can say *eew*?

Then your father call and say everything okay. Mostly it man who live in zinc house and homeless who live in the gullies that dead. Man and them children. Him say it just as well, since the people in the garrisons so ignorant, them don' bother get prenatal care, then wonder why them baby come out malnourished or deformed. You say, Daddy, when you ever set foot in a tenement yard to know poor people' business? And him kiss him teeth like him done with you.

Him say, Send what you can, so you go buy canned food and baby formula and get the boys to help gather up them old clothes to send. You can' help hoping it only bad-mind people the storm kill off—the ones who wrecked the island with them violence—so JA can return to how it was in your youth. But you know it never go so. It always innocent randomness choose to kill.

Work pick up, because now it seem you know everybody that gone and flee Jamaica. If not gunman, is Gilbert send them here. South Dade start fill up with Yardies, and if you hang out where them hang out, you get job, since them no wan' bother with the Spanish man who them can' understand or the White man who can' understand them, even when all three speak a English.

But Sanya no wan' see you hang out. She wan' see you home.

She start malice you and say, If a work you go work, is how you smell of overproof? Is how you come home two in the morning? She don' understand it through socialize you get job. Each time you come through the door, she there 'pon the phone with Daphne a tell out your business. And Daphne the worst ear she could bend, since she man left her with pickney and never look back. You wan' say, *Tell her. Me no have nothing fi hide.* But when Sanya tell it, the truth make you sound villainous. It seem like one long fight you're locked in.

Then Jodie call one day and you say, Jodie, if you go call long-distance me know someone de go dead. But you never guess she would've say is both. You know is gunman finally kill off you mummy and daddy, and you never should have left them there, but Jodie say it car accident kill them.

You call Uncle Michael in New York and tell him say is time fi go home. You both fly back straightaway to arrange funeral and when you go to collect them body, the policeman on duty have your daddy lay out on the gravel, baking in the rhatid heat.

Your uncle say to the copper, How you can have him on the ground like dog? And him say, Please, please treat him with dignity. All from him breasts to him belly a tremble with rage.

The copper say, Morgue full up. There's no place else me can put the t'ing.

Uncle Michael cry, T'ing? T'ing? And him start bawl. Is then you know the man turn soft in a New York.

You tell the copper, Hear me nuh, boy. Take out a next corpse and bring my father inside until the undertaker reach. You can cuss and talk 'bout what him muma fi do and say duppy de go haunt him for disrespect the dead so, but you know it the twenty dollars U.S. that make the man do what you say.

Him and him partner lift your father inside and dump out a next corpse on the roadside with the others.

Only a Kingston have more dead than morgue, you tell your uncle. You tell him, You forget how things work down here? You say, That no Daddy, you know? Daddy gone.

But all him can do is cry.

The day before funeral, you pick up Sanya and the boys from Norman Manley and carry them to you mummy and daddy' house, where you and Uncle Michael and Jodie staying. And the car ride somber like you never seen your pickney and wife. But in the afternoon, after sun shower pass, Delano and Trelawny go out in the backyard and pick up sticks and fight and scream and laugh, like them little bodies can only hold so much grief.

At funeral, crowds come from so far as Negril, which take longer to reach from than Miami and maybe even New York. Mrs. Panton attend, now walking with cane, along with eight of Sanya' sisters, all but Daphne. Each say, Me sorry, Topper, and each look enough like Sanya that it remind you she no look 'pon you with such kindness for time. Even Reyha come to the repast and squeeze your hand when she think Sanya no look, and you resist sniff she hair to see whether she still smell of spice bun because Sanya always a look.

Is not till after funeral—after Sanya carry the boys back a Miami and Uncle Michael fly back a New York and after weeks sorting your parents' affairs and after schoolboy show up at your daddy' door and hand you him grade sheet and say your daddy promised to pay him tuition if him do well, and you tell him your daddy dead, and the boy start cry, like is he fate dealt the harshest lick, so you write out check to the academy, and after you slip under the white rum one mournful evening and let Jodie crawl 'pon your lap and start ride your cocky while unoo bawl 'bout how your mummy and daddy gone, and after you return home—that Sanya say, Things must change now.

How you can say so, you ask her, when me parents dead a three week?

She say, Me no wan' dead before you decide to come home at night.

But you no ready fi hear that. You rather sleep 'pon sofa. You rather things were the way they were in Mandeville, when you could take care of she and Delano, and she no worry so much 'bout where man supposed to be. You wish for some way to go back, but if a Kingston you stayed, your parents still would've dead. If a Kingston you stayed, you could've dead long time.

And you don' wan' admit you start get used to American convenience, too much to go back. But you know Sanya' right, something must change.

Then Hurricane Andrew hit and everything change.

House roof tear off and you all must cram up in apartment in Fort Lauderdale. And for a month or so, it seems you and Sanya must come together and make up. But with everyone house blow down, and FEMA start hand out check, is more work than all the years you've been here combined. You start recruit man from Miramar, where must have more Yardman than all South Dade' neighborhood. And you're on the road from dawn till deep night getting man working. Sanya stop complain because she know people need them house fix. And she know is like gold rush how the jobs come in. And even she get a next promotion at work, so in all the destruction unoo find your silver lining.

It nearly a year before your house can fix because you're so busy a make money, you only can fix your house part-time. One day you're back down a Miami and it late and you decide to stop by the Fence, where all the Yardies start reconvene, even when the house next door still have blue tarp for roof. You sip 'pon your white rum when you feel tug from behind and you turn and see Cherie, still look the same like she travel through time. She hug you up and say how she sorry to learn 'bout your mummy and daddy. She tell you how she move up here when she house get destroy in Gilbert. You say, Boy, seem like storm knock we back into each other' arms. But you no mean nothing by it.

If she hear song she say is she favorite, she'll take your hand and pull you to the dance floor. She start grind she pelvis into yours and you feel you're a young man again. But after three or four dance your legs start ache and you know it time to put an end to the reunion. You know there's no returning to youth. You kiss Cherie' cheek and when you think she going beg you fi stay, she give small wave and start dance with a next man.

The drive back long, and when you reach, Sanya is up, waiting on the couch, like she have a sixth sense for Cherie alone. Wha' you a go do? she start yell. Wha' you go do? And is phone she have in she lap. Is just dance, you start say, when you're sure is a *suss suss* business get back to she, but she say, Jodie call. She say, She call and the boy have your eyes.

If Sanya throw the phone you won't bother block it. The handset clip your forehead and leave gash that later scar because you never get stitch. You deserve the scar and much worse. Especially since the vexation mark Sanya with white streak through she hair that show up overnight.

You sleep with she the whole time? Sanya want to know. And you knew she would think that, if she ever find out, even when you never look 'pon the girl Jodie before the funeral. And you can see it in Sanya' eyes that suspicion start flood all she memories. Now everything sour, down to the root.

And you beg her. You tell her is Jodie take advantage of you in your weakened state. And of course you never touch the girl when Sanya was pregnant with Delano, even in the time you and Sanya stop having sex.

Sanya smile when she say, I believe you. And you go in to hold her and she box your face, even as blood leak from your forehead into your eyes. I believe you will regret this for the rest of your life, she say. And you know she mean it with that demented smile. And you hate yourself for taking away part of she and replacing it with disfiguration. And more than that, you hate that she is right.

———

If you go see the boy, it will be late summer. Jodie' family called and called to tell you say you must come see your baby, but them never let you talk to Jodie and so you wan' ask if there's a baby fi true or if this a kidnap scheme. But you no wan' put that idea in them head.

Still, you fly down a Kingston alone, since your shame won't let you bring witness. You hire car and drive to a shantytown buried in the mountains, halfway to Spanish Town. She cousin call the last time to say the baby sick, and is him give you directions, since where she live now don't have phone, and when you pull off highway and start drive down dirt path and see shacks made of lean-to zinc, you can see don' nobody here have phone. The shantytown walled in, like this a housing scheme, and you wonder whether it have name like Tel Aviv or Jungle or anything that signal man like you should not be here. Man who maybe should be here guarding the entrance and him tell you, You better park and walk in.

You made sure to leave home everything valuable, because you hear stories that things so bad now in JA that man hand get chop off with cutlass because thief want him wristwatch and don't bother asking. The cash you brought over you hide in your sock.

You approach the guard and him say, White man, you 'ave business 'ere?

You almost laugh, but say, Is me you think is White man? And him say, You the whitest man me ever see, and him no say it with humor.

You say you're there to see Jodie and the man wrap him arm around you and show big teeth and say, Cousin! You know him not the same man you spoke with on the phone, because this man say a whole heap of words now, and you can' understand half of it, because you never hear a bush patwah like that. You wonder whether everyone in this shantytown is Jodie' cousin.

Him start walking you inside and telling you how beautiful the baby you make is, but all you can think 'bout is how it good your mummy and daddy never lived to see this. More than that, you think 'bout how you break Sanya' heart. And about how she make you choose between Delano and Trelawny to take back to the house you finally rebuild and how she say she will never set foot inside that house again. You told her you don' wan' take either son from she and she say, You think I go let you walk away from your responsibilities? Like that your plan the whole time. She say, You will take Delano, because me don' trust you with Trelawny. And you can' deny you felt small bit of relief.

Jodie cousin walk you past a group of barefoot pickney kick soda bottle back and forth between them and woman who all a carry bucket of water on them head, and when you peek in the gaps in them lean-up tin walls and see is all one room and no plumbing or bathroom, you wan' shout, *But how people can live so?*

You know then that you must take Jodie and the baby back with you, because no boy of yours can grow up in such circumstance—if the baby truly yours.

The man who say him Jodie' cousin walk you into a rusted hovel and there you find Jodie sit down on a blanket on the dirt and hold a baby in she arms, and when she see you, she look up and smile. But the smile demented, like how Sanya smile the night she find out, and you never realize till now is a second woman you mutilate.

You kneel down next to she and when she hand you the baby, is two things you see: Him have your eyes, fi true, so him must be yours. And that the baby dead from time. Jodie' cousin stand up at the entryway and menace you with him big teeth and say, You just miss him. You hand the baby to Jodie and untuck the bundle of cash you hiding in your sock and leave it in Jodie' lap. Then you go back to the car and drive straight to the airport, certain them could no drag you back to this godforsaken island again.

———

If you're a man who utterly failed his child, you can either lie down to join him in death, or you can do more for those remaining. If the latter you choose, the first thing you can do is call your wife and beg she to take you back. You can leave message on she answering machine and explain there's no more reason you must be apart, and if it embarrass she feel, no one up a stateside has to know. At least, no one has to talk about it.

But if you do this, man will show up at your door early one morning, and when you answer him, Yes, I'm Topper, him will smile and hand you a manila envelope and say, You've been served.

It Trelawny you start worry after, because even when Delano don't do too well in school, him is a boy who will make something out of nothing. The day him graduate, Delano start him own landscape business with money you loan him and have man your age working under him. But when you pick up Trelawny from Sanya' new house in West Miami, the boy can' hold nobody eye when him talk. And him barely talk, like him 'fraid of his own voice. Him dress up in baggy clothes and hoodie, like him hiding, even when it summer.

You stop bring him down to your house, because the first time you see how it pain him to watch him brother and you living where him once had a proper family. It loss him feel, but you wonder whether it also envy of him brother. You take Trelawny out to eat instead every few weeks.

And every few weeks him seem to change who him trying to be. First, is only tegareg rap music beat out his headphones. Then it booguyaga dancehall. When you ask how it only ghetto music him listen to, him say him wan' connect with him people. You say, Boy, them butu singer not your people. You think your grandfather would let them type of man on him veranda?

But Trelawny say him don' remember him grandfather too well.

If you buy two acres of land in Palmetto Bay and start make

plans to build new house, you'll try involving the boy. You sketch design of what the house could be, and it good to feel your hand drawing over paper after so long. You try show Trelawny your mock-up and where him room might be when he visit, but him no bother pay much attention and stare out restaurant window instead. You know him resent you for the divorce, and you wonder what ideas him mother put in him head. You almost tell him it Sanya split up your family and make you choose Delano over him, but you no wan' have to explain the reasons why.

All now when the cancer start to take Daphne, Sanya no wan' hear nothing 'bout how you keep she in your prayers.

When the construction soon start, you ask Trelawny if him wan' help, the way Delano helped rebuild the Cutler Ridge town house, but him say, How much does that pay?

You tell him you're trying to teach him something, but him say, I already learned Lincoln freed the slaves. Him add, Maybe Delano should have paid attention in school.

The boy think him smart, you see?

Back home, you ask Delano why him brother must be so cantankerous.

Delano say, We all have to be what we have to be.

You ask, Who told you that? And when him shrug you say, Unoo go soon learn: if you wan' make it in this world, you best be better than that.

━━

One day, while you and Trelawny out at lunch, Delano page you and say him have surprise, and you're to meet him at the construction site in Palmetto Bay. When the two of you reach, you see is full-grown ackee tree Delano have him crew transplant in the backyard. Him say man in Coconut Grove paid them to chop it down, but him save it and bring it here instead. Them had to get tractor and trailer and permit to transport the thing, and if you have any luck at all, the tree should survive and start bear fruit in a year or so. Your eye start water and you see how it not everything lost after all; you see your legacy can grow, even in a foreign soil.

You thank Delano with handshake, and out the corner of your eye, you see Trelawny look bewildered, like him don't get the point, like him don' understand why him brother would bother.

———

When he finally take himself away to college, you hope Trelawny will meet people like him, people who find them worth in books. Sensitive people. Him swear say him hard, since him put off college to work warehouse job where him drive forklift and perform manual labor. But when you suggest that him throw out him wardrobe and buy proper clothes when he arrives in the North, suggest that him is old enough to stop wear clown clothes, Trelawny look like him wan' cry. How him can upset so easy? Miami too rough, too much like home for the boy. You don't see how him can survive here, where man always try test you, and always try get over. So you're glad when him leave for someplace he can find his true self.

But when him graduate, Trelawny move back.

You ask him, What you go do now? But him only shrug and stick him hands in him pockets and say him go figure it out. But you no see him figure nothing. Only him hide in the room you give him in your new house. Only him sit down 'pon him computer and do God knows. Seem like college only make the boy less fit for work.

This is how it's done now, Trelawny tell you. You apply online. No one wants me showing up in their lobby, reeking of desperation, him say. No one will hire me if they suspect I need a job.

But what kind of backward thinking that? You tell Trelawny to check his brother for work, but him say, You think I got my BA so I could start mowing lawns?

It just as well because Delano' tree service struggling through this Great Recession. And now Delano have wife and pickney of his own, so him can' carry his brother. And your business grind to a halt, so it better you just retire from now.

Anyway, you can' tell Trelawny nothing. Him think them teach him everything up north and the whole of Miami is ignorant. When him reach back, you tell him that with all the job loss him better stay away from certain neighborhood, and the boy say, There's no such thing as a bad neighborhood, and it's systemic racism and white-collar greed cause the crime—like him knowing the source can stop bullet; like him will sit down with robber and explain to him 'bout subprime mortgage and school-to-prison pipeline.

Even if things tight, you'll decide to hold retirement party, since you reach the age where all your friends start die off, and you wan' show people the house while there's still people left to show. Plus you start feel you no have too many ifs ahead, only bleak certainties.

Your house finally finish the way you want, with in-ground pool and bar, and more fruit trees flanking your ackee tree, lining the back garden. It the house you always dream 'bout design and a part of you sad Sanya will never see it, since she still hate your guts after all these years.

She called before Trelawny graduate and told you how she was moving back to Kingston. You said, Sanya, you crazy?

But she say, Just look after the boy nuh.

And the boy Trelawny back not a two week and him say him going invite up him friend from JA—girl he meet when him spend him summer break in Kingston.

You think, Careful she not after you for green card, but it not nice to say those things. Instead, you ask the boy where him did apply today, and him admit him no apply for job today at all. Instead, him say him worked on application for a grant to go live in Jamaica for a year and do research.

You must wan' study how to get your brains blown out, you tell him.

Him say next him go apply for Jamaican passport.

You say, Boy, is a death wish you and your mother share?

But the boy just turn back to him laptop like you not there speaking.

The night of the party, you make Trelawny help set up tiki torch poolside and get the yard trim up nice, and you get caterer to set up buffet in the backyard and have them serve a jerk pork and 'bout three sets of curry. You put out old table, so man don't bruk up your good dining table with them dominoes. You drape lights from the roof of the pool deck and turn pool light on, so everything glow, even when you know none of your friends wan' take off them shirt and frock to get in no pool at night.

The ackee tree bearing fruit now and some of the ackee pods start open, so you buy salt cod to pair with it for breakfast the next morning. The invite list long and even Uncle Michael fly down from New York and you can' believe how him get mawga and him tell you him can't believe how you get old.

Delano come with Shelly-Anne and them two boys, and when Shelly ask whether you wan' hold the baby, you say no, because both him boys get your father' eyes and you think 'bout Jodie' baby and the thought sick you.

Delano get him band to set up on the patio and play roots music and them bring all the young people, and all your old crowd from the Fence come through. Even Cherie show up eventually, but she don't want nothing to do with you, besides be friends.

Trelawny' girlfriend, Zoë, show up, too, and you can' believe how the girl gorgeous, like girl you would've date in your day. And Trelawny stand up straight and tall like you never see him stand up. And him finally wearing clothes that fit properly. Still, you don' want to admit you wonder what she can see in him. But maybe she see something you can't.

The party go on late and man start in on the white rum and maybe you take down too much, because Trelawny start look 'pon you sideways. But the boy always look at you sideways, so you don' know. In the kitchen, you start talk politics back home with Zoë, but Trelawny keep interrupt. Trelawny say Manley had the right idea, wanting to spread wealth to the poor people.

You tell him, Boy, is Manley mash up the country. Equal parts he and your CIA.

Then we should have stayed to defend it, the boy tell you, like he was there.

If we stayed, you wouldn't be alive. Me can promise you that.

Then how come Zoë is here? he asks you. And him laugh. Her family stayed. They turned out fine. More than fine.

Zoë nod, but you can tell she' uncomfortable.

You don' wan' say it, but ask her, Is how much bar your windows have? How much guard dog in your yard? You can walk down your street and feel safe?

She say, Me have car, me no need to walk nowhere, and she laugh, too.

You tell Trelawny, Pickney who grow up in a hellhole can't know the difference.

Zoë start say, It have its problems, but—

Trelawny cut she off and say, I was just there and it's better than this.

Better than what? you wan' know.

This . . . second-class citizenship, him say. And you don't know what rubbish the boy talking now.

What them teach you at school? you ask. Only self-pity?

Him say, You and Mom never should have left.

And that really make you vexed, so you say, Look here. Don' tell me 'bout my business when you never lived through it. Talk 'bout Yankee business. No bother talk to me 'bout Jamaica. Don't care what them showed you on vacation. You spend three week in JA and you think that make you more than tourist?

Him shrug and look 'round with him eyes low, like him embarrass, but you go on: Boy soft like you never could have make it. Boy who can' take get him hands dirty. Your brother maybe, but you wouldn't last a day. Soft boy like you would've dead long time. So just be grateful we left. Even if our leaving what make you turn out so . . . And you know you must stop talk, but you add the word you been thinking ever since him reach back a Miami, and long before him left . . . defective.

And you know from everyone face you take it too far. Trelawny won't even look at you, but him head nod slow-slow.

Uncle Michael looking at you disappointed and Shelly start carry she pickney away. You think him might need air, so you say, Trelawny, do me a favor, go take down some ackee for me nuh, so I can make it for breakfast. And him nod still and you can' be sure he even hear, but then him stand up and walk out back. Make sure it the open ackee only, you yell after him, because you can' tell if the boy remember anything you taught him from him was a child.

You try smile with Zoë, but she look to the front door like she wondering how she can reach home. You start get up and Uncle Michael say, You don't have to give the boy such a hard time, you know. But him them already turn soft, so you no bother with the old man.

You go out to the patio and wonder why everyone is turned around in them chairs, peering off into the dark, but then you hear it: loud grunt and dull thud. And you see Trelawny' silhouette under the ackee tree, all with ax in him hands. And him talking to himself now. And him swinging the ax.

And you start after him, but Delano grab your wrist and shake him head and hold you back. And is then you know it serious. And you think how Sanya' right, you regret everything. And you wonder if it's you must be defective since you ruin everyone.

And you know the boy ruin, because is same words him repeating like warped 45:

I'll chop down your tree.

I'll chop down your tree.

I'll chop down your fucking tree.

ODD JOBS

The exotic-animals dealer made me kneel on a caiman's tail. The reggaeton video producer paid in medianoches. The caterer forced me to serve poolside in glitter and a Speedo. But the gig that saved me after my father kicked me out was Chastity's. Her Craigslist ad read:

I'VE NEVER HAD A BLACK EYE . . .

. . . and i want one. i need bruises for a photo project but i also want to see what it feels like. i dont need any roiders here or knockouts just a solid sock to the face. thanks.

compensation: idk $35–40? i wasnt really gonna pay a lot for this, but we can discuss.

must not have ebola or a problem hitting a girl.

sorry, no black guys.

But I responded to her post anyway. I'd reached the point in my starvation where personal ethics and phenotypic traits couldn't deter me.

She'd wanted to meet at a coffeehouse, but I wrote back, *How am I going to punch you in the face at Starbucks?* The money wasn't much, but after a flurry of email exchanges, I discovered that, of all Greater Miami's sprawling suburban neighborhoods, she lived in Saga Bay, five minutes from where I'd parked my SUV for the last couple of days.

I was anxious to move on from the shopping center, as one of the security officers had begun circling in his golf cart, despite my alternating parking spaces every two hours or so. But in my bright red '87 Dodge Raider, who was I fooling? I'd backed the Raider into a space in front of the bagel shop, damn near on the sidewalk, so I could catch their Wi-Fi on my otherwise-useless phone. When the guard finally tapped his fleshy knuckles against the tinted glass, I wriggled from the Raider's bed into the driver's seat, turned the key in the ignition, and cracked the window.

"My man," he said. "You living out your car, my man?" His head swooped, glimpsing the Raider's contents through the narrow opening. I'd abandoned most of my books and photo albums in my father's garage, along with my diploma, still enclosed in the cardboard envelope it had arrived in. There in the car remained the dead giveaways: my kitchenware and the duvet I'd needed up at college. Clothes piles were lumped in the Raider's cargo area, doubling as my mattress.

"My lady ran into Publix," I told the guard, maneuvering my head into his line of sight. "She'll be out in a few."

He made the face I'd been receiving more and more lately. The *I don't care that you're lying, just don't infect me with your poverty* face. The *If your family let this happen to you, then you probably deserve it* face. The *I don't trust you around my kids* face I'd received from my sister-in-law, Shelly-Anne, the week before, when my brother invited me for dinner but not to spend the night.

"Hold up." A chuckle bubbled out of the guard's throat. "Trelawny?"

Through the dust-beaten windshield: cars zipped along Old Cutler Road. I could take it north, connect with U.S. 1, then get up to Hollywood Beach or Fort Lauderdale, where next to no one knew my name. South would take me to Florida City, then the Keys. If only I had gas money.

"We went to school together, man."

"Yeah, I remember." But he could tell I didn't. Something like defeat eclipsed his vision; to find himself unremembered wrecked his Tuesday. "Last name Johnson, yeah?"

"St. Pierre," he said. A familiar scar cut through his eyebrow, making me think we had met, had maybe called each other friend, but I remembered high school like I remembered dreams, in waves, with little recall for faces or what they should have meant to me. We watched each other through the crack, neither asking what had landed the other here. "Listen," he said. "I'll give you another hour, then you have to bounce. My supervisor's a dick and I can't lose my job over you."

The sixty-minute reprieve St. Pierre offered was as much kindness as I'd received in the two and a half months I'd been living out of the Raider. I glanced down at my gas gauge, at the glowering orange light, and did the math. I could probably get the Raider a couple of miles up the road. Wherever it died, the cops would have it ticketed and towed within days, then I would never get it back.

St. Pierre lingered outside my door for some reason, I guess to ask, "Ain't you go away to some bigwig school? Marquette or Notre Dame or someplace? What happened?"

"Graduation."

He laughed, stretching his arms over the Raider's roof before flinching from the heat, drawing them to his sides. His nose brushed the glass, eyes filling the space above. "Them degrees don't do much for people like us, huh? They're going to hold us down either way. 'S'why I didn't bother."

"Smart," I said, wondering what the hell he meant by *people like us*. I *had* bothered, had faithfully followed the upward mobility playbook in order to wind up an *extraordinary* failure. And this asshole wanted us in the same category. I'd experienced similarly artificial camaraderie with fellow second-generation immigrants I met at college, who thought themselves transgressive in electing to take literature courses when their parents expected them to go to medical school. "I'm supposed to be a doctor," they'd say with ease, as though they'd already earned their future prestige and wealth, as if it were there to be plucked from the garden of their parents' devotion and preparation—imagine moving through the world with such confidence! When invited to share the expectations my Jamaican parents held for me, I recalled the last recommendation I'd received from my contractor father and explained, "I'm supposed to work at Home Depot."

St. Pierre was saying, "You'll cook yourself like this, with the windows up." He said it like I hadn't noticed I'd been broiling for the last eight hours. "Some lady fricasseed her toddler just last week. Saw it on the news." An ache in his voice made me know he was a father.

"You're trying to son me?" I asked him.

"Say again?" Sweat threatened to spill over the lower rims of his eyes.

"Do I look like a baby, you yappy fassyhole?"

St. Pierre appeared more aggrieved than I might have intended, and as I could not stomach his expression—an expression that connoted, *I own a mattress and have Tupperwared food refrigerating*—I kicked the engine on and peeled out.

It occurred to me halfway to Chastity's that I might have asked St. Pierre if his dick supervisor was hiring. When my father put me out, back in May, I'd phoned the warehouse where I'd risen from pallet jack jockey to certified forklift driver before leaving Miami for college, but the manager, citing my degree, deemed me overqualified—he didn't believe I would find job satisfaction loading and unloading shrink-wrapped boxes of imported bananas. I wasn't worth the cost to HR.

But what else was out there for the class of 2009? The forty-thousand-dollars-a-year entry-level positions I'd been promised all my life no longer existed post-recession, and even the lowliest jobs wanted five-plus years of experience. I graduated with a 4.0 and couldn't get an interview for an unpaid internship.

Thankfully, Chastity hadn't expressed any interest in seeing my résumé. Hers was a two-story town house with a vaulted ceiling and a fenced-in yard. She looked surprised when she opened the door, and I thought I might have the wrong house before recalling that I wasn't to have shown up Black. But enough people in Miami claimed they couldn't tell what I was, so I'd learned not to short myself before they did. If she asked, *Aren't you . . . ?* I'd answer, *Nope*, and leave her the burden of providing evidence to the contrary. But she didn't ask. Instead, she spread her bare arms the width of the doorway, blocking my entry.

In her white maxi and gold belt, tousled hair falling down her front and back, she looked as though she'd recently escaped from a Grecian urn. Then again, my ability to fixate on faulty associations had grown powerful under the August sun.

There weren't any cars in her driveway, no signs of life beyond her threshold. "Who else is home?" I asked.

"Why?" Chastity said. "You planning to rape me?" On the floor behind her, I spotted no blue tarps or black plastic or anything that suggested I wasn't meant to make it out alive. Still, she might take this opportunity to stand her ground—arguing later that I had reduced her comfort level, or property value, or whatever it is my skinfolk are authorized to be slaughtered for these days.

Chastity didn't appear to be experiencing any particular discomfort, so I asked, "Is this really for a photo project?"

"Does it matter?" She unclenched the doorjamb and leaned her shoulder against it.

"I printed our emails," I lied, "and forwarded them to my brother. Just in case." The latter statement should have been true. But Delano wouldn't have been happy to hear from me, not after the previous week's dinner, not if his wife had told him what I'd confessed to her. Plus I didn't need him knowing the depths to which his kid brother had sunk.

Chastity held her elbow in her palm and pinched her nose, deciding. I'd caught my reflection in the Raider's darkened windows; I looked more than slightly stepped on. There was no way she was letting me through her door. "You're taller than I might have wanted," she said. "I think it's best if it's straight on. I don't want to be punched from a downward angle. Take your shoes off first."

"You've given this some thought," I said, entering. I kicked off my flip-flops in the foyer and followed her past a heavily air-conditioned dining area. I hadn't felt seventy degrees in what might have been weeks, and the cool air made my damp flesh tingle. I wondered about the odds of her letting me use her shower after.

It's important to build rapport with your employers, so I asked what she'd been up to today, to which she responded, "Besides this? Eating shit." That's Miami for *little else of consequence*.

In the living room, a mammoth flat-screen paralleled a teal sofa. Above the TV, a rash of quinceañera portraits distended the wall. She wore braces in the photographs and looked younger, though not much. "This is your parents' house?" A purple backpack slumped on the floor beside the couch, its unzipped mouth gaping stupidly. I dug my arm in and pulled from its depths Millett's *Sexual Politics*. On the inside cover a stamp declared the book the property of the library at Florida International University. "You're in college, then. Class of?"

"Let's skip the chitchat," Chastity said. "Right here in front of the couch is fine. Are you ready?"

But I was shook. Reality began attaching itself to the moment in the form of family photos on the walls and side tables. Young Chastity and her little brother at Epcot Center—at the beach, even younger, clutching a yellow plastic bucket and shovel. Or maybe reality was what I'd been living those months on the streets, this being its opposite: a middle-class facade, with its attendant codes of conduct. I dumped the book on the floor and turned toward the entrance. "This was a mistake."

Chastity snatched my wrist. "Wait." Her eyes flickered, and I felt she was trying to communicate something profound. "Do you understand the kind of psychotic responses I had to sift through to get you here? The dick pics? The run-on sentences? I can't start over."

"I'm sorry that happened to you." I placed my free hand over hers and removed it from my wrist. "Why don't you revisit your short list?"

"I don't understand the problem." Her eyelids wrinkled. "I'm paying you to do it."

"All the same," I said. "I'd recommend seeking a different kind of help."

Chastity yelled, "Shove that paternalistic crap up your ass," which only hastened me down the hall.

"I'd love to avail you," I said over my shoulder. "Theoretically."

That didn't have the soothing effect I'd hoped it would.

Chastity screamed, "Coward," the word shrinking me in the foyer.

I toed my sandal, terrified of what would happen if I reached for the doorknob. All I needed was to get caught fleeing this screaming White woman's house for some neighbor to decide to play hero.

Chastity must have mistaken my hesitancy for a negotiation tactic, because she said, "Fine. I'll give you eighty. And you don't even have to use closed fists. Just slap me a little."

I'd been back in Miami three months, and the forty she'd originally offered was as much cash as I'd seen in a single day. Eighty dollars was a gold mine. "What time do your parents get home, exactly?"

"We've got a solid forty minutes," she assured me.

With the promise of four Jacksons searing into my medulla, I sat Chastity at the edge of the couch. I slipped my forefinger beneath her chin, nudging it upward, and she looked me in the face with these enormous brown eyes, the kind that—by some evolutionary outcome—people associate with innocence. I couldn't do it. I lowered myself to the couch and told her as much.

"You know why you can't?"

I watched the bow of her lip, keen to see if she could name what lingering virtue superseded my instinct for self-preservation.

"Because you're a misogynist. You think that little worm between your thighs means you know what's best for me. You pissant."

She had a point, but I didn't like being called names. That's what had gotten me into this mess to begin with. My father, in a fit of honesty, and before our family and the woman I'd nearly convinced I was worth loving, had revealed what he really thought of me. He'd been dancing around it all that week, saying my liberal arts education had made me lackadaisical, and that I was a fool to have gone tens of thousands of dollars into debt only to ruin myself for work. Rather than listing the dozens of jobs I'd applied for in the two weeks I'd been home, I asked how it was that he'd given my brother the money to start his tree service, yet he hadn't put a dollar into my education. "Delano is a good investment," he'd admitted, stopping short of calling me a bad one.

That night at his retirement party, though, inspired by the drinks and perhaps something trivial I'd said, he let loose a rant about my being his lesser son, calling me *defective*. So, perhaps to prove myself as capable as Delano, or perhaps to prove my father right, I retrieved an ax from his shed, entered the garden where he invested most of his postretirement labor, and went to work on its centerpiece, the ackee tree my brother had gifted him years before.

Chastity asked, "You think you control what happens to my body?"

I told her, "Of course not," but that I had a confession to make, one that would render me ineligible for further participation in her project. "Truth is, I'm a Black guy."

"Figures," she said, exasperated. "I don't actually care. It's just . . . my parents. Their rules are bullshit, but it's still their house." She explained that once, in high school, her older sister had brought a Black boy home for a study date and that night caught the beating of her life from their father. Just for bringing him inside.

"You're like the twelfth White woman to have told me that story," I said.

"I'm Latina," she said. "Brown."

"Point being, I have enough to bear. I don't want to know this stuff." But I couldn't seem to get up off her couch.

"The funny part is, Ravi wasn't even Black. He was South Asian."

"Hilarious," I agreed. But I felt sick with hatred. For her father, yes, but for all fathers, for their propensity for passing down the worst of themselves. How was it that her post hadn't read, *Sorry, no racists? Sorry, no child abusers?*

"If it motivates you," Chastity continued, "you're exactly who he wouldn't want helping me with this."

"Fortuitous. And I'm helping you with what, exactly?"

"Uh-uh," she said. "I'm in control. You don't get to ask me that."

Wondering if this was really about her father, or an art project, or if it had to do with deviancy she'd failed to locate in her sexual partners, I stood and told her I would try again. It's not easy slapping someone for the first time, even when they've asked you to. Even when they're paying you. "Look away," I pleaded.

"I want to see it coming."

"Fine." I patted her cheek with four fingers.

She looked at me as a kindergarten teacher might her slowest pupil. "You're going to have to do it harder than that."

My arm felt incapable, already missing the mass I'd built at my university's rec center. Incredible—the pace at which your body eats itself when left unfed. I readjusted her chin and inhaled deeply. On my second go at it, Chastity toppled over.

She didn't speak for a while, lying limp atop the couch, which frightened me. Her dark hair fanned over her face and shoulders. From underneath it I could hear clipped pants. Eventually, she said, "Good," her voice the offspring of astonishment and discordance. She pushed herself up, and when she brushed away her hair, a splotch the shape of Minnesota gleamed red from her chin to her cheekbone, but I doubted it would actually bruise. "That was good."

"All right, then."

"Do it again. Harder if you want." She scooted to the end of the couch and braced herself against the arm. "Hold on." She tied her hair back in a ponytail. "Okay."

I glanced down the hall toward the front door, wondering what it would take before she'd hand over my payment. I imagined I could have begged an old girlfriend from college to send money; enough of them had expressed ambivalence about their trust funds that this seemed a plausible path down which I might drag myself away from homelessness. But I'd sooner have hanged myself. The pity they'd cast my way over the course of four years—it was as though they'd already surmised how I'd wind up.

I couldn't trouble my mother: just weeks before graduating, I'd called from my Midwestern apartment to ask, in a tone I hadn't meant to sound accusatory, how she could leave Miami for Kingston when her children were here. "It's for me," she admitted, and she'd never sounded less motherly or more human. I could hear the packing tape unspooling as she continued filling boxes. "Look how long me spent taking care of men. Your father," she said, though they'd divorced more than fifteen years ago. "You boys. Who has ever taken care of me?" It was more truth than I'd been ready to hear. Though soon after, I vowed never again to be a burden to her.

And what if I simply rolled up my windows, parked in the unmitigated sunbeams, and waited?

I imagined, too, that I could have returned to my father's and begged him to take me in, despite his promising never to do so again, not after my outburst. Not after I'd assaulted his precious tree. But even if he did, his incessant disappointment, his *why can't you just*s and his *why aren't you more like*s and his *be a man*s assaulted my self-worth more than the hunger. And more than the hunger, and as much as the desperation and shame, the sleep deprivation bored new pathways in my brain, and I'd begun hearing voices and sensing entities that hovered in my periphery and then vanished as I turned to seize them.

I turned to Chastity, who sat solid against the couch's arm, expectant. I clutched her ponytail and angled her head back. Diamond studs twinkled in her earlobes. Her mouth opened and I saw beyond her white rabbit teeth down into the pink of her. I raised my palm and clapped her cheek.

"Harder," she said, her voice a grated whisper. The outline of my fingers surfaced before dissolving into her skin. She mouthed, *Harder*, and I tugged her ponytail to expose her unblemished cheek and clapped it. She blinked shut her eyes, nodding.

I straddled her, and she tensed, but did not push me away. Strange: what flooded my senses, pressed close, was the ripeness I'd carried in from the outside world. I rested my hand over her throat, then tapped her jaw. Saliva fell out of her mouth onto her lip and chin. I rubbed the spit away with my thumb and she gazed up at me, and her expression . . . the intimacy . . . I slapped her with certitude. She closed her eyes and nodded fiercely. Tears streaked her taut cheeks. I let go and stumbled to my feet.

As I stood waiting for her to demand more, she just sat there sobbing.

I began to ask if I'd gone further than she'd wanted, but my words came out: Do *me* now. I didn't know who put them there, but I felt jubilant with anticipation. Soon I'd connect with something enlivening that I hadn't before, or else something injurious that I had.

I'd found zero catharsis in striking my father's ackee tree— do you understand how difficult it is to fell a tree with an ax? I'd battered myself against it, spending myself, and still it towered. At my brother's reconciliation dinner, though, he reported that the tree's fruit had rotted overnight and it had yet to produce more. *Trauma* was the word he used. My brother is an arborist and so he feels qualified to use such a word. When he excused himself to the bathroom, my sister-in-law leaned over her plate to ask if I'd considered that my actions had hurt my father *and* my brother, but I doubt she or I expected my honest answer would be "Good."

Chastity sat firm in the grips of her release, so I went into the kitchen to make myself a sandwich and wait my turn.

You wouldn't believe the options they had on hand: prosciutto, chorizo, kielbasa, maple ham, honey turkey breast, dill pickles, pitted Castelvetrano olives, at least three types of mustard, including Dijon—and that's not to speak of the cheeses. Jesus Christ, the cheeses. That must be why I didn't hear them come in. Crouched in the refrigerator's bowels, I never stood a chance. Likely, they saw her, saw me, and two plus two equaled seven. The mother's heel hacked into my spine, sending me sprawling, but the dad's caught up rather impressively. His sole, cannonading against my temple, sparked fireworks in my retinas.

Even the little brother joined in.

It was elegant, almost, the way they worked in unison. If only my family had found me such a unifying force. I recognized it then, like petrichor, or some misplaced scent from childhood, not the familiar weight of existence crushing my lungs, but the awakening urge, the exquisite, racking compulsion to survive.

PESTILENCE

That first and only plot of American soil my parents purchased together was plagued, as was the house they built atop it. The millipedes blackened our front steps, made Mom tap-dance from car to welcome mat. They crept up pipes, bursting from bath drains at our most vulnerable moments, their dark bodies startling against the porcelain white.

When the crabs scuttled inland by the thousands, choking traffic on Old Cutler Road, only the foolhardy drove on. My father halted our station wagon, the sea of beige-and-blue crustaceans washing under us, resigning us to tardiness. From the back seat, Delano and I sat in silent reverence for the clack of claws on asphalt, witnessing pincers and shell-fragments puncturing car tires up ahead.

And when the locusts swarmed, we four crouched at the living room window, waiting.

Mom said it was the construction, that the onslaught of new development the eighties had ushered in had disturbed the animals and that the clearing of land sent them into a frenzy. Dad said it had always been this way but that people had not yet lived this deep in Cutler Ridge, our section of southeast Miami; that the crabs and locusts came in seasons; and that humans would need to acclimate to them. Delano said it was our job, the boys', to free our block of vermin.

We snuck lighters and matches, cans of Raid and Lysol, to blowtorch the millipedes and melt them to a slough. We prodded the crabs into Mom's gardening pail and plastic mop bucket with sticks and dried sugarcane stalks. We hovered over the buckets and bet against the crabs as they dragged one another down into mutual destruction.

Our neighbors made meals of them, but as they were blue and not the neatly plated red shellfish we recognized from restaurants' advertisements, we left our bucketfuls by the side of the house for days or weeks instead, letting the sun bake the shells to dry, brittle husks.

These crabs were easy pickings, except the one we chased through a quarter mile of field until—as though changing its nature by necessity, or as though to prove our misunderstanding of that nature—it escaped up the trunk of an oak.

The locusts we left alone, except for the three or four that stayed on after the swarm dispersed. We plucked shell-encased legs and wings from thoraxes and drowned them in bleach or iodine or whatever we could smuggle out the front door without our parents noticing. At times, we'd look up from our work to see strange boys—colorless or orange-speckled or similarly brown versions of ourselves—six- or ten-year-olds, crouching in pairs, or in triplicate, thusly occupied, and I wondered, *If all the world's boys are so engaged, will it not be long before we succeed in our duty?*

The locusts and crabs, and millipedes especially, decreased

from one year to the next, until their returns brought so few that we forgot they had ever covered our sidewalks and highways and skies.

———

We knew our house was cursed, not simply from the outside but from within. The animals we brought home met grisly deaths, no matter the care we took. Our Siamese fighting fish launched itself from its aquarium, as though the tank's water had been set to boil. Mom ladled it off the carpet with the square-rimmed net and thrust it back into its tank, jamming the lid down, but this seemed only to enrage the fish. We four gathered around as it rammed the aquarium's inner glass, beating its face to gristle.

The hamsters we discovered so: the astonished expression of the one protruding from its cage-mate's ruined jaw.

"Jesus, Joseph, and Mary," my father said when we carried the cage from Delano's bedroom into the kitchen.

"Maybe no pets for a while," Mom said, guarding her mouth with her palm.

I felt relieved, but Delano insisted, "If we name the next ones, they might treat each other humanely."

"They'll be hard enough to forget." Dad pointed to the cage. "Imagine if them had identities." Our father, like many of the Jamaican men my parents brought around, didn't believe in naming animals, not even the best of them. "Dog already 'ave name," he liked to say. "Dog named dog."

Our mother, though, had raised chickens and hogs growing up on the outskirts of Kingston, and she'd named every one of them, even after realizing what they were fated for. Mom said of our grandmother, "When Seema put her leather gloves on, you knew it was bye-bye, Betsy. Bye-bye, Henriette." She took the middle of a dish towel in her fists and twisted it sharply, a neck-breaking *grick* sound emanating from the depths of her throat.

"Me never did 'ave farm animal," Dad countered. He reached into the freezer and dumped a handful of ice into a tumbler, then placed the tumbler on the kitchen counter. "But me did hit me neighbor' goat one time." It was like that between my parents: one having always to best the other. Dad bit down on his lip, forcing the glee from his face. He tilted the neck of a rum bottle over his glass, continuing, "The goat run out in the road and me lick him down with Daddy's car. And me did think, the car mussee dent and mister goat mussee dead. But then mas goat stand up straight wit' him hoofs 'pon the car' bonnet and look 'pon me. Next thing me know, him turned to the whole of we neighbors and start bawl, 'Baheeeeeelp!'" Dad squished up his face, squealing in a shrill goat voice. "'Baheeeeeelp!' And me did take off, thinking, Mister goat going run tell Sheriff John Brown."

Such was his amusement that tears rounded my father's cheeks.

There's an alternate ending to his goat story, but on this occasion he punctuated it with unbridled laughter, and my mother slapped him with the dish towel, saying, "You're too cruel, man," but her eyes brimmed with love.

————

New plagues disturbed our neighborhood in subsequent years. We constructed slingshots and carried small stones to fight off the nighthawks. We poured salt on the slugs and frogs that seemed to fall with the rains from the sky. But to Mount Trashmore's sulfuric, skunk-squeezed stench we surrendered.

Mount Trashmore was the pride and shame of Cutler Ridge—at least that's how we viewed it. If we dragged Dad's ladder to the side of the house and ascended to the roof, through binoculars we could just make out the landfill's peak and its buzzard halo. The summer sun bored into Trashmore, releasing funk waves we choked on, and the hottest days left us no choice but to lift our shirt collars or hems to our noses and slog inside.

The nighthawks attacked us night and day but were most dangerous at dusk. They nested in the ground, camouflaged in the low-lying thicket that spread across the rocky terrain behind our town house. If we ambled too close, they'd burst from the dirt, gain adequate height, then dive-bomb us.

Once, Delano shot a nighthawk as it rose from its swooping attack. We gave chase, but it managed to lose us as it spiraled down into the expansive brush.

By then we had Double-O (short for 007) with us. His mom was a mutt, but his dad was pure Labrador. We ran him in the field, shouting, "Get it, boy," and "C'mon, Double, kill!," something I suspected worked only on TV until Double-O tore off into the briar.

I awaited the bird's blast back into sky as Double ruffled the surrounding bush, but he came skipping back, jaws clamped on a mass of meat and torn-up feathers. A line of the bird's blood dribbled down onto the V-shaped white patch that made Double's black fur look tuxedo-like.

Stern commands and tugging forced Double to eventually let go of his catch. When he did, the bird lay stiff and gnarled on the dusty gravel. "We killed it."

"What'd you think we were trying to do?" Delano asked.

He told me we'd better bury the bird, and I didn't stop to ask why we would bother; I had a vague sense that we were honoring the dead, that this life we'd taken was somehow different, more valuable than those of the insects and toads and crabs. To tear life down from the sky like that . . . or maybe I had begun growing into my conscience, and my guilt stood independent of what we'd killed.

We dug a shallow grave not far from where the nighthawk had first appeared. My brother suggested we look for its nest and eggs, to toss them into the hole, to wipe out its line and prevent future attacks, but I remember this with clarity: I had no stomach for it.

———

"When Daddy dies, I get the house," my brother told me while we were out walking Double. I can't remember if it was the time we killed the nighthawk or not. It couldn't have been long after, which means I'd have been ten or eleven, my brother around fourteen. Let's say our backs were bent in work, lowering the carcass into the earth, spreading dirt over the hole. Let's say the sun inched toward the horizon, sweat rolling from our pits down to our wrists and palms, when Delano called dibs.

I wondered why he would lay claim to a house we'd already agreed was doomed, but I said, "What about Mom?"

"Fine. When Daddy and Mummy die, I get it."

"Yeah, right!" I said, but I knew, even then, that he would. The way they fawned over my brother, the way he'd already inherited the best of what our parents had to offer, down to our father's eyes—eyes that strangers interrupted their day to gush over. How often I had stood outside the huddle, Delano enclosed by our parents and his random admirers. How often I'd wondered if I had actually disappeared.

"They'll leave the house to both of us," I insisted.

"That's not how it works," he said. "I'm the firstborn. That makes me the heir."

"You're not royalty, you moron." But who in this world of carefully constructed hierarchies wouldn't choose the blue-eyed brown boy to anoint? Who wouldn't assign him the higher value?

"Doesn't matter. It's how it works, Trelawnies." I'd entered a chubby stage, and as Delano had entered an evil one, he'd begun pluralizing my name to emphasize my size.

"Then what happens if you die?" I asked.

"Then it'll go to my son."

"You don't have a son."

"I will by the time I die."

"Then what do I get?"

"You, Trelawnies, get the shaft. You should be used to it by then." Seeing he had upset me, he added, "But you're still my brother, so if you're good, I might let you live here with me."

———

A plague can transmogrify, and in August of 1992 ours shifted into 175 mile-per-hour winds. We were three boys then, with our cousin Cukie in-house, while Aunty Daphne took her summer respite; three to battle the neighborhood plagues, three to plot our escape. We knew Andrew was coming for Florida, but the weather reports and the associated panic were not the first signs

of impending devastation. For one, our parents' arguments intensified that summer, bleeding through our bedroom walls.

Mom blamed the white rum, the nights Dad disappeared, then
reappeared reeking of debauchery. Dad claimed she'd become
too Americanized in her expectations of marriage. Delano told
us, the boys, to escape into the streets to find relief from their
bickering, but Mount Trashmore's fumes chased us back indoors.
That entire August the stench seeped into our pores and nostrils,
making our stomachs ache. We agreed—Delano and Cukie and
I—that Trashmore was no mere mountain but a volcano, gradu-
ally poisoning us, threatening to erupt.

The stink strangled our summer, but the morning before
Andrew's arrival the breeze felt miraculously soft and clean. We
drilled screws into plywood, safeguarding the windows, preparing to evacuate, and as we did, I asked, "What's it matter that we
live in the flood zone, when our house sits on such a high hill?"

Delano answered, "I bet we get an inch of rain like always. Or
else it misses us completely. What a crock."

Cukie asked, "Do hurricanes even exist?"

"Can we please, please, please get enough damage to delay
school by a week?" I pleaded.

We conferred over half-packed bags, choosing video game
consoles over comic card collections for our overnight at
Cukie's—he and Aunty Daphne lived farther inland. Cukie already had the best games and the best bedroom of any eleven-
year-old we knew, with a remote-controlled television and VCR
and a race car bed frame. Next door to his room, and down the
hall from his mother's, a third room outfitted with bunk beds and
trunks full of Cukie's overflow toys and board games solidified
the impression that only Cukie's playmates were ever welcome

to stay over. This would all be insufferable if it didn't first strike me as lonely, the two of them in that house.

Delano and I couldn't wait to spend the night there.

The only problem with evacuating was that Double-O had gotten loose the night before and had not yet returned. He'd taken to visiting his canine neighbors, the females; short of locking him indoors, we couldn't prevent his nightly excursions. But when we locked him in, Double's howls reached into our dreams, snatching us from sleep. Halfway through his second night of incarceration, my father relented, releasing him to the backyard, where he was silent, if absent.

One early summer evening, we boys had tailed Double and witnessed the full splendor of his escapades. It was something to see Double scale a fence, his front paws hooking chain links, his back paws tiptoeing to propel himself upward, his V-cut white patch exposed. I couldn't help exclaiming, "Double-O seven."

"Double-O seven," Cukie agreed.

It was then that we resolved to have Double-O neutered.

We made the appointment for the procedure, but as my father pulled into the vet's parking lot one Saturday afternoon in July, Delano in the front passenger seat, Double in the back seat trembling between Cukie and me, we began contemplating what it meant for Double to lose his testicles. I grappled silently with the weight of wiping out Double's line, and Cukie never voiced an opinion within earshot of an adult, but my brother expressed his concern this way: "I'd rather be dead than have my balls chopped off."

My father nodded. "It's what make a man a man. But it's you boys' decision. He's yours to look after."

I didn't know what was right in that moment, but I wanted to be like them, to partake in manhood as they did—no, that's not exactly it. I wanted to be *with* them, to be caught up in the love that linked the men of my family. I had begun feeling the weight of our age gap, Delano entering my father's world and leaving mine. So I threw my hands over my crotch, lowered and shook my head, as though too pained to discuss the situation. At that, Dad put the car in reverse and we headed home, agreeing to tell Mom that the vet's office had been inexplicably closed. It was perhaps the one time I'd felt such belonging.

What is that inimitable bond between certain fathers and certain sons?

Years later, Delano would try laying hands on our dad during an argument about his taking Dad's car without permission. He'd driven the car to homecoming. Not his high school's but FAMU's, eight hours north of us. Instead of returning home to my father's, he drove to Mom's house, my house, and let our father know he could retrieve his car there. I guess he figured he'd postpone his punishment, or maybe he just wanted witnesses. When our father arrived, and the words and excuses inevitably failed Delano, and Dad's chastisement became too much, he attempted to push our father out of his way. Dad easily won the tussle, pinning Delano against the living room wall, embracing him there, as though to say, *Not yet, not yet. You will grow to best me, and all that I am will be yours, but not now. Not yet.*

I'd risked Double's life for a fraction of that feeling. But in the pre-storm calm, as the boys scoured the neighborhood while Dad took the car out to search the streets beyond, I knew we'd made a terrible decision.

I made promises to God that afternoon, to the universe, to any power willing to accept my plea, that if we found Double, I'd have him neutered. I'd save him from the men in my family and from himself. But maybe that was the wrong promise to make. Perhaps instead I should have begun with atonement.

As we searched, I felt certain Double would trot out from under some bush, or from around some corner, his pink tongue dangling over his black jaw. When the sky turned dark, though, we abandoned the house and Cutler Ridge, heading inland.

"Don't fret," our mother said on the ride out. "Puss and dog know to shelter themselves in storm."

I braced myself, looking to the driver's seat, certain my father would contradict her, but for once he agreed, saying, "Animals can sense these things."

I understood anew that my father could change his nature, and that he would do so to protect me. I knew, too, that what he'd said was at least partially true. No Florida house could prevent trails of ants from marching in before a heavy rain. But where could Double-O hide? He was no insect.

===

The alternate ending to my father's goat tale goes as such: "The goat start bawling, 'Help.' And me know it then it must be in some rhatid agony. So me reverse the car to make sure me can aim for its head. Then me lick it down one time for good."

===

When the electricity at Aunty Daphne's house went, we knew Andrew would not join the slew of dud hurricanes we'd scoffed at. From Cukie's bedroom we watched a family of palms get wrenched from the yard, then thrust through the neighbor's walls. Like pins into a cushion. That's how the six of us wound up huddled in Aunty Daphne's walk-in closet.

I don't have to strain myself to describe what we'd discover in the light of the following day—the flattened houses, the overturned vehicles: you can find all that online. I recommend typing *Hurricane Andrew aftermath* into your favorite search engine, then clicking IMAGES to see what I saw the morning after. I'll say that when we finally located Cutler Ridge, then our block within it— these things were difficult with no road signs, few remaining landmarks, and many obstacles—little more than the skeletal frame and the squishy, rotting carpet remained of our home.

What the archived pictures can't convey is that a decomposing palm tree, one that's been ripped from the earth and left in the road to die, smells as pitiful as a rotting human. Or that even the inanimate innards of houses stink of loss, of soaked-through death post-storm, and after a day or so, this rot stifled not just Cutler Ridge but most of Miami.

You also mightn't have heard about the animals that escaped from MetroZoo and the various research facilities and exotic-animals dealers during Andrew, the teams of monkeys spotted jogging and swinging their way through wind-toppled suburbs to freedom. Conservative estimates put the number of these escapees in the hundreds, though some wildlife experts estimate that at least 2,500 monkeys got free. You can see them and their offspring peeking into backyards in certain Miami neighborhoods even to this day. And few Dade County residents haven't witnessed the parrots and parakeets and cockatiels now inhabiting Coral Reef Park and Tropical Park and beyond. Some cougars roamed free. Some might still.

So where we spent our youth ridding our block of species, choosing which, by their very nature, deserved to die, nature intervened and, in the course of hours, set loose new life to re-capture our neighborhoods.

But that's not what I want to talk about anymore. I want to talk about that night, crouched in the closet, when the wind howled like a god come down for vengeance. When I said, "I hope Double-O is okay."

And my mother held me gently in the dark and said, "Someone will have found him and taken him in." I imagined one of our neighbors ushering Double inside, pulling shut her door just in time to hunker down.

But my brother shifted anxiously beside me, as though he al-ready knew my father would respond, "Me didn't tell you? Me found it? Me didn't tell you?" His voice took the choppy lilt that it did when he'd been drinking his whites awhile. And though I couldn't have seen it, tucked deep within folds of blackness as we were, I can't help remembering a smirk on his face when he said, "Me didn't tell you me found the dog? Found it, dead in the street?"

SPLASHDOWN

1.

The summer he turned thirteen, Cukie Panton set out for the Florida Keys to meet his father for the first time. By then, Ox meant little more to Cukie than a syllable spat from his mother's lips. What he knew of Ox was that he was American—the catalyst for Cukie having been born in Baptist Hospital, right on Kendall Drive—and that Ox had stuck out the first two months of fatherhood, then bounced, leaving to Cukie the dried ink on his birth record that spelled out *Lennox Martin*.

More than a dozen years after this abrupt departure, Cukie's mom answered the phone to hear a remorseful Ox, saying he should know his boy. By this time Cukie felt ambivalent. It didn't help that Daphne Panton figured that the drink or else some brush with death must have resuscitated Ox's conscience to bring him calling. Perhaps Andrew had inspired Ox's reemergence, the hurricane having wiped away so much that would have to be rebuilt, not even a year ago. Whatever the affliction, Cukie's mother assumed it was ephemeral. The calls continued, though, and when plans grew specific, she told Cukie to pack his duffel and they departed Kendall for Smuggler's Key.

In summers past, they'd have followed U.S. 1 thirty short minutes south to Cutler Ridge, where Cukie would spend weeks with his cousins Trelawny and Delano. But Aunty Sanya and Uncle Topper had separated in recent months, dividing their sons and Cukie's nearest idea of a functioning family unit. His mother hadn't offered the *why* behind their separation when she relayed the news, but when she mentioned Uncle Topper now, she dropped the Uncle.

That his father lived within a two-hour drive was not lost on Cukie. "Me can't say he's a good man." His mother flexed her fingers over the steering wheel, eyes locked on the river of gravel rushing beneath them. "Every boy deserves to believe him father is good, but if each father were good, we'd be living in a different kind of world, you see me?"

Cukie nodded in response. Responding to adults and their questions sat atop the list of changes Cukie promised his mother he would make this summer, though these conversations felt like acid in his throat. His stomach tightened as he barreled toward an answer to the question that haunted his short life: *What kind of man abandons his son?*

Cukie preferred to focus on the water creeping up either side of the highway. Road and buildings fell away, replaced by an expanse of sea, prompting him to think of silver bodies gliding in the sun-speckled turquoise.

"Him says him changed," his mother continued. "Me pray

he's changed. And since me can't get you outside of your head, maybe he can."

Cukie imagined his body slicing through the sun-soaked ocean toward the horizon, the lapping crest breaks tingling along his spine. If he could picture himself as a dolphin, he would become one. And he'd had practice. He'd spent whole years imagining. He'd newly flunked seventh grade, due to what his mother called his *concentration problems*. She and his teachers had it wrong, though. Cukie focused too intently, more often on vivid worlds he built to hide within. All those times in class he stared blankly at the chalkboard, his mind a thousand miles away, his body unresponsive, till a teacher tramped to his seat to slam a textbook on his desk and jolt him back into his body, gasping.

Cukie felt something similar when his mother stomped the brake inside Blue Harbor Marina. "You see him there?" She pointed through the windshield at a figure loading a cooler onto a boat and insisted Cukie make his own introduction.

As Cukie approached the dock, he didn't spot much of himself in the man who was supposed to be his father. Standing barechested in sandals and board shorts, Ox looked more akin to his inanimate surroundings—every hair on his body having been sun-bleached and windblown—than to Cukie, except for that nose, pointed yet pressed close to his face like a stingray hovering above a patch of sand.

He'd never realized his nose, sharp and flat against his face as it was, had a lineage.

"Cukie?" Ox asked, and Cukie nodded, considering that Ox might have arranged to meet any number of his bastard children this afternoon. He had the impulse to turn back toward his mother's car, but Ox said, "You'd better follow me, then."

Cukie waved goodbye to his mother and trailed Ox to a tiki hut perched at the marina's north end. The hut's narrow bar faced the water; its back wall displayed an assortment of beer bottles standing proud like trophies. Dried-out palm fronds scarcely hid metal shingles reflecting the sun's blaze. Laminated card stock taped to the counter listed rates on charters and rental equipment prices. Each menu heading read *Slip 26 Charters*. Through an open doorway, rectangular wire cages sat one atop another, lining the storeroom's perimeter, surrounding stacks of beer cases. Cukie wondered why they hadn't met at Ox's home instead.

"This is just the side hustle," Ox explained. He swung a section of counter up on its hinge and stepped behind the bar. Cukie felt Ox's gaze follow his as he surveyed the tight space. His focus landed on the wall where Ox had tacked a now-faded poster. The woman staring out from it appeared to have just emerged from water, a red T-shirt soaked to translucence dripping against her frame, the word *JAMAICA* stretching across the curvature of her bust.

Cukie had studied this poster while waiting for his mother to purchase ackee and jackfruit at Jamaican groceries, and at restaurants, where it graced interior windows and walls, as commonplace as the black, green, and gold flag. The image had become one of the island's top signifiers, more iconic even than images of Jamaica's national heroes, Paul Bogle and Marcus Garvey. Its presence here comforted Cukie.

"This could've easily been your mother," Ox said, steadying himself against the bar, and Cukie said, "Huh?"

Ox flicked a finger at the poster's top left corner, where a heart had been drawn in black marker and, under it, an autograph.

"Me and Sintra have history." A grin spread above Ox's stubbly cleft chin.

Cukie dropped his eyes to the bar and thought, *Liar*. He picked at the sun-dried edge of the beer menu's tape with his pinky, letting his eyes lose focus over the dollar signs and numbers.

"It's a little-known fact," Ox said, and Cukie thought, *Please shut up*. "Sintra isn't even Jamaican. She's Trini." Ox laughed. "Picture that. The tourists flying down, not realizing they're on the wrong damn island."

Cukie ripped a strip of tape off Ox's bar top and began tearing it to pieces. He wondered what someone like Sintra could see in the redneck behind the counter. Toward the start of their drive, his mother had let on that she and Ox met on a flight out of Kingston, when she worked as a flight attendant for Air Jamaica. She didn't go so far as to reveal what he'd said to make her join him for dinner that evening.

Cukie returned his gaze to Sintra, hanging in Ox's tiki bar. Liar or not, Ox had now ruined her for him. Ox turned from the poster and examined him, jaw twisted, as though he'd found a baby in a basket on his doorstep.

"I got something special for you," he said, and he knelt to reach behind an icebox. Cukie thought he'd reemerge with two bottles of Budweiser, but he rose holding a square, netted hoop in one hand and a thin, wand-like stick in the other. "This here's your tickle stick and this here's your net."

Cukie waited for him to say more.

"It's mini season on lobster," Ox said, and Cukie nodded, silent. "It's time you learned to catch."

At Ox's urging, they went out on the *Belly Bloat* and anchored near a sandbar a mile offshore. They started with snorkeling; Cukie had never done it. Handing him his mask, Ox said, "Spit in it," and he spat in his own, then poked the saliva, smearing it on the lens to an even coat. Cukie did the same, eyebrows arched, forehead creased. "It's so your mask don't fog," Ox explained. "Amazing what bodily fluids are good for."

They swam until Cukie found his rhythm, breathing into his snorkel's mouthpiece. "Good," Ox said, climbing back aboard. "Now try it with these." He tossed Cukie the net and the tickle stick, and Cukie nearly sank himself trying to hold on to both.

"Float," Ox shouted. "Float, dammit."

Cukie didn't know how to respond to a stranger who was supposed to be his father yelling *float* while he sank. Several feet from his thrashing, the sea was calm as bottled water, and when he finally let go of the net, it bobbed on the surface.

Cukie relaxed his limbs and leaned into the water, imagining that beneath him a pair of cupped hands supported his body. He tilted his head back, sucking in slow breaths, making the water do the work of holding him up.

"Only a fool would drown himself," Ox yelled down from the *Belly Bloat*. "There's so much salt in these waters, a boy skinny as you should be walking on it." Cukie watched Ox glide about the deck. The ocean water matted his amber-tipped hair, turning it dark and heavy against his broad, tan chest, but he moved with a litheness he hadn't possessed on land.

The question loomed as Cukie watched his father—the one that always came when he thought of Ox: *What kind of man is he?*

Cukie fought the urge to sink to the ocean floor, to see if his father would rescue him.

Ox carried a mesh bag and a plastic gauge to the boat's edge, stepped up onto the gunwale, and dived in. He took the net, and the pair swam to the sandbar, where they could stand with the water's surface cutting below their thighs. Cukie ladled puddles of water in his palms and spilled it over his shoulders and neck to quell the sting of the beating sunrays.

"It's all about balance," Ox said, facing Cukie, squaring his hips. "It's a dance. Only there are more partners involved. There's the lobster, but she's not your main dance partner. Your stick and net, those are extensions of yourself. It's the ocean, the waves, which way the current's pulling. You learn to move with her, she'll never do you wrong."

Cukie nodded.

"You see a sea bug, what are you going to do?" Ox handed Cukie the net. "Show me. I'm the lobster." He patted his chest.

Cukie brought the net down on top of Ox, but Ox ducked and scurried to the side. Cukie tried again with increased intensity, but Ox fled in the opposite direction. Cukie swiped at him, trying to scoop him from the left, and Ox jumped backward. Cukie slapped the net against the face of the water, saying, "This is stupid."

"It won't work like that," Ox said, and he snatched the net from Cukie's hand. "You see a big ol' net coming down on top of you, what are you going to do?" He brought the net down over Cukie's head.

Cukie said, "Run away," and Ox pulled the net off him.

Ox snatched the tickle stick, saying, "You see a stick coming at your face." He poked the mask dangling from Cukie's neck. "What are you going to do?"

Cukie said, "I'm still running."

Ox poked him in the chest and Cukie stepped back, and Ox said, "Yeah, you are, but this time I know in which direction."

Cukie still wasn't convinced of Ox's method when they came upon a sea bug clinging to a hulking cut of limestone a hundred feet or so from where they'd been practicing. Cukie ducked under to watch, while Ox took the stick and net and went to work. He approached from the front, extending his net-holding arm, positioning the hoop behind the bug, partially against the stone's surface. He pointed the tickle stick at the bug's head, letting the current pull him slowly toward it till the stick's tip touched antennae and the bug shot backward into the net. Ox flipped the net, open end up, and brought it out of the water.

Cukie viewed the net with no small level of repulsion.

Ox extracted the lobster, allowing it to kick air. "Don't that look tasty?" he asked, and Cukie scrunched his face, saying, "What kind of lobster is that?" Its outer core held hints of yellow and tan but was otherwise cockroach-colored. Its feelers shifted away, then back toward each other, as though searching out a signal. Like a bug. Like a prehistoric palmetto with a fantail and extra legs.

Ox explained it was a spiny lobster, the kind native to Florida's coast. Like crabs and shrimp, lobsters were rarely red before you cooked them. And warm-water lobsters didn't have pincers like the ones up north. He showed Cukie how to measure the carapace with the gauge to make sure it was within regulation. "Three inches or longer," Ox said. "The body, never the tail."

During this conversation, Cukie learned about Ox's job as a trap fisherman during season. "There are eight days until Splashdown. That's when we drop our cages. You're going to learn to trap," Ox said. "We'll start you building and baiting. Before long, you'll be pulling in hauls yourself."

Cukie let his fingertips twirl along the water's surface. His eyes followed the ripples his fingers created. "I have to work?"

"Your mother told me about your skylarking. You're old enough to learn a trade."

Cukie drew a circle in the water, digging deeper till his finger formed a miniature whirlpool.

"It's something you'll be able to fall back on when you're older."

Cukie raised his finger from the swirling water and watched how long the ripple lasted.

═══

That night, father and son returned to the tiki bar, the back end of which Ox had converted into an apartment with a shower stall, a toilet, and a kitchenette. Over a supper of broiled lobster tails, Ox explained the next morning's agenda: trap construction. "Make certain you sleep," he warned. "We start early."

While Cukie brushed his teeth, Ox set out a second cot between the kitchenette and a maze of stacked beer crates and broken lobster traps. *It's like camping*, Cukie reasoned, laying his head on his cot that night. Except he couldn't see the stars, only the thick skin of night trapped within the tiki hut, only the pitched ceiling beyond.

And in the predawn, as Ox ripped him from his dreams to start the day, Cukie thought, *It's like the military. It's like torture.*

Cukie expected he'd hate trap building, but the work lubricated his interactions with Ox that first week. If, hunched over a corroded cage, pliers in his grip, Ox said, "I reckon your mama's still mad about . . . everything," Cukie could respond, "We need more wire. I'll run to the supply shop." If, bent shoulder-deep in a trap's throat, Ox asked, "What exactly is it you keep fantasizing about?" Cukie might shake himself present enough to lie: "What it'd be like? Getting caught up in a trap?"

It wasn't a week, though, before the ache in his arms made Cukie feel Ox owed him something, made him brave enough to collect. He wrapped himself in his bedsheet after dinner and revealed what he'd spent so many days wondering. "Where've you been all these years?"

Ox lowered himself to his cot and kept quiet a full minute. "Been here awhile. Before that, all over."

Cukie nodded, then recognized that he hadn't come away with any kind of answer. "All over where, though?"

"Spent about a decade steering yachts up the coast of South America. Throughout the West Indies. Anywhere anyone paid me to take them."

"Fun," Cukie said, barely audible, and Ox moved his head in denial.

"It wasn't as glamorous as it sounds," he wanted Cukie to know. The sea was unpredictable, as were the men who'd employed him as their captain. He'd worked for unscrupulous men, men he hoped never to set eyes on in this lifetime. "They'd direct me to some pier, and I never knew what they would ask me to pilot. Nor what they had me transporting."

As Cukie listened, Ox slipped into strange accents that wrapped around the names of ports he'd swiftly exited from. His recollections presented uncontextualized brutality. "Seen a man brighten from brown to beige, punctured and drained over a beach in Bimini. One woman, she simply vanished a day out to sea from Mobay." That night, Ox spoke the language of dreams, of the impossibly venturesome, and of implausible, inevitable violence.

═══

The pair awoke early the morning of Splashdown, dropping the first of their traps when the sun's apex broke the horizon as a fiery pinpoint. The cages would soak and attract lobsters for a week before season opened and they returned to harvest them.

In the days between Splashdown and season, Ox resumed escorting tourists on diving excursions while Cukie manned the tiki bar.

His first morning alone in Smuggler's Key, Cukie felt an undeniable urge he hadn't felt since he was seven years old, searching through his mother's drawers for signs of a father long gone. Now his father had reappeared in the flesh, and Cukie couldn't yet tell what kind of man he was.

In the lull of the marina's foot traffic, Cukie found himself in the storeroom, staring down at the closed lid of the plastic bin that served as Ox's dresser. He lowered himself to his knees and peeled the bin's lid off tenderly, as though expecting to locate the tattered map to his father's soul. At the bottom of his mother's bedside table, he'd once found a picture of her lying in her hospital bed, cradling him on what appeared to be the day he was born. A man Cukie guessed was Ox leaned over them, hands placed gently on his mother's shoulders, only his face had been cut out of the photograph.

Cukie swept his hand across the bottom of the bin but found

no corresponding photos or remnants of the past. He lifted one of Ox's folded shirts to his nose, inhaling. If he could detect goodness, or remorsefulness, or deceit, what would they smell like? In the shirt's cotton fibers, Cukie smelled only what the surrounding air carried: the pungency of the sea.

=====

The next afternoon, the marina's manager, Happy, saddled up to the tiki bar. The sun had lightened his yacht club blazer by several shades. Sweat congealed in his neck beard, and Cukie thought he resembled a shipwrecked captain.

"You must be Ox's calf," Happy said, resting a Styrofoam coffee cup on the bar top before extending his sweaty hand. "A certain semblance gives you away."

"Cukie," he said, returning the handshake.

"You're a little young to be tending bar, no?" Happy placed a clipboard on the counter and uncapped his pen, as though to begin recording their exchange. "Your dad ever hear of child labor laws?"

"I haven't served you anything," Cukie said.

"No need to get defensive." Happy performed a chuckle—one meant to deflate tension, or contribute more, Cukie could not tell. "Learn to take a joke."

Behind Happy, boats swayed in their slips, and Cukie wondered how long before his father would return.

"They pay me to be a bit of a prick," Happy said, raising the clipboard and placing it down again. "But not to worry. I'm told I do a piss-poor job."

"I wouldn't sell yourself short," Cukie said.

Happy paused a beat, then allowed himself a genuine laugh. "Your father's son all right." He lifted the cup and the clipboard, making to move on, but stopped to say, "I've known your father a long while. Before his trapping racket, even." Happy watched Cukie expectantly, as though waiting for this information to alter Cukie's estimation of him. "Known him for ages."

"That makes one of us," Cukie said.

Happy frowned and raised the cup to his lips.

"What is it you know about him?" Cukie asked. "My father?"

"That's a question." Happy paused to choose his words carefully. "Here's a thing. You might find it useful. Long as I've known him, Ox never let the truth get in the way of a good story."

===

When season opened, Ox and Cukie searched out their pots using GPS, spotting the cages by the bright buoys they'd tethered to them. As they bagged their catch and reset the traps, Ox told Cukie, "A wise man keeps his overhead low and reinvests his profits." And "A man doesn't follow trapping laws because he's afraid he'll get caught. It's about integrity. It's about doing right by your neighbors and respecting the sea that ensures your livelihood."

Trapping, Cukie came to understand, had centered Ox. It was his faith. All that was necessary for Ox to be good, then, Cukie considered, was for Ox to be a good fisherman. It was a thought that eased his mind when anger surfaced over his abandonment.

At the end of each day's harvest, they sold the lobsters to a market not far from Blue Harbor.

At the close of summer, before Cukie reunited with his mother in the marina's parking lot, Ox handed him a cash-filled envelope. As Ox paid him what amounted to a small fortune in the hands of a teenager, he looked Cukie in the eyes and said, "Good work, son."

———

Cukie brought his summer work ethic home, no longer tethered to the question of where in the world he might locate his father. He possessed the answer: Two hours south. Smuggler's Key.

On visits to Aunty Sanya's, Cukie set the table for dinner and started on the dishes afterward without having been asked. His aunt usually shooed him away from the sink, then yelled for Trelawny to come out from his room and take over. Trelawny did so begrudgingly, muttering, "Thanks, suck-up," as he passed Cukie in the kitchen.

Growing up, Cukie had envied Trelawny's access to his father. Now he wondered what Uncle Topper had taught Trelawny that left him content to lock himself in his room, wasting hour after hour playing video games.

Cukie committed to the idea that he'd make his hours count, focusing them on his schoolwork and helping his mother around the house.

Toward the end of the school year, Cukie's academic counselor summoned him to her office to inform him that, provided he did well on his final exams, he'd proved ready to join his original class and enter high school in the fall. Before school let out, his father phoned. "I expect you'll be coming down again?" he said, and Cukie said, "I expect I will."

———

The summer Cukie turned fourteen, he and Ox fell into a rhythm, as though their months apart had been mere hours. As they worked, they spoke little of the past and much about whether Cukie might like to work with Ox full-time, once he finished high school. "I think I might," Cukie said with measured enthusiasm. Together they imagined ways in which they could expand, and Cukie began to see himself as Ox's partner and, maybe, the heir to his trapping business.

Come Splashdown, Cukie took the *Belly Bloat*'s steering wheel as Ox directed him out of Blue Harbor Marina to where they'd drop their cages. By sundown, their traps were at sea, and the next morning Ox again left Cukie in charge of Slip 26.

One afternoon, while Cukie sat repairing a trap in the storeroom, he heard Happy's voice out front, followed by his father's.

"It's perfect," Happy was saying. "Near genius."

"Then do it yourself," Ox broke in. "Leave me out of it."

"You're already in it. Why do you think we let you set up shop here in the first place?"

"Can't you let me live?"

"I'd like to, friend, I would," Happy insisted. "But middle management doesn't get a say in these things. The decision's already been made."

Cukie heard the sound of flesh beating wood and he crept out to see. Happy was already hustling away. Ox stood behind the bar, rubbing his palm.

"What was that all about?"

Ox shook his head. "You heard the saying about arguing with fools?"

Cukie wanted to ask what sort of trouble Ox was in, but said, "True as ever," and Ox grinned.

"When did you get such a smart mouth?" From his expression, Ox genuinely wanted to know.

═══

At the start of the ninth grade, Cukie noticed how his classmates and teachers appeared newly attentive when he spoke, though he noticed, too, how their eyes fell and lingered on his chest, and how frequently their hands, as of their own will, reached for his triceps and biceps. He hadn't fully perceived how hoisting cages had transformed his body till he saw himself through the gaze of others; until Lianne, his middle school crush, asked him to homecoming; until his PE teacher invited him to try out for the football team; until one night, as she passed him in the hall, his mother grasped his wrist and said, "But my god. You've become a man."

Through his father's instruction, Cukie had raised himself out of his daydreams and into the world.

═══

The summer Cukie turned fifteen, after long days out on the water, he'd follow Ox to the marina's south end, where Happy and other fishermen gathered to decompress over beers. Cukie would sit at the water's edge, leaning back against a pillar, silently listening to the men's stories. On one such night a fisherman named Roy asked no one in particular, "You think Smuggler's named itself that to attract tourists? You know what Miami was built on, right?"

Happy interrupted, "You're confusing your centuries. It got its name in pirate days. Blackbeard's time."

"It's not drug runners you should be worried about," Ox

said. "It's trap thieves. I once caught a guy emptying my pots the day before season opened. Tell you what: I put sixteen shots in that motherfucker's hull. Had a young couple with me I'd taken diving, otherwise I'd have spared his boat and shot him instead. Coast Guard had the nerve to confiscate my rifle."

Cukie hadn't heard this story before and wanted to ask his father to elaborate, but another fisherman took the conversation in a different direction.

On some of these summer nights, Happy's daughter would ride her bike to the marina and join them. Her dad called her Genie, though she told people to call her Genevieve, and Cukie assumed she hung around because she lacked age-appropriate companionship. Adolescence clung about her in her baggy, grass-stained jeans and unkempt hair, though she was a year older than Cukie. Cukie knew he liked her when, one night, while Ox and Happy and several other fishermen circled the base of the dock telling jokes, she bravely stepped in and said:

"A sailor and a marine are pissing in side-by-side urinals." Genevieve stood with her legs wide and held her soda bottle out from her crotch, making *wsshhh*ing sounds. "The marine washes his hands after, but the sailor doesn't. The marine says to the sailor, 'In the marines, they teach us to wash our hands after a piss.' The sailor says, 'Yeah? Well, in the navy they teach us not to piss on our hands.'"

The fishermen erupted in laughter, from the display of foolery more than the joke. Cukie had never been brave enough to speak up in these gatherings, not unless he was invited to answer a question, but Genevieve took the spotlight with a confidence that stunned him.

On another such night, during Cukie's fourth summer at the

marina, while Happy was in a particularly drunken uproar, Genevieve turned her attention to Cukie, lazily circling him on her bicycle as the pair drifted back toward the tiki hut.

"What kind of name is Cukie?" she asked, one foot on the pedal, one leg extended to the ground like a kickstand.

"Same kind as Genie," he said.

"Do you have soft filling inside? You're kind of an Oreo, aren't you?"

Cukie found his admiration for her declining. "How's this genie thing work? Do I have to rub you to wish you'd shut up?"

"Depends. Where would you rub me?"

Cukie's heartbeat quickened. "Your mouth."

Genevieve lowered the bike to the gravel and stepped close. She took his hand and brought her mouth down over his thumb. It was just his thumb, he'd remind himself in the hours to follow. But the sensation felt like his entire body rubbed against her lips and tongue, and he tingled in such a way that he hardly realized when she removed his finger from her mouth. She stooped to lift her bicycle and asked, "You ever get breaks, Cukie?" Her hypnotic circling continued. "You ever get over to Smuggler's beach?"

"I could if I wanted."

"Saturday? At six? Want to?"

Cukie nodded, and Genie said, "Bye, Cukie," before pedaling into the dusk.

———

That Saturday, Cukie sat waiting for Genie, watching the tangerine sun dripping down the sky. He was supposed to be watching the tiki bar while Ox was out fishing with a group of tourists. If he left now, he might beat Ox home and he'd never be the wiser. Cukie sifted his fingers through the sand, wondering whether she had stood him up intentionally. The public beach was a thin strip, truncated so that either end was visible no matter one's position. They couldn't have missed each other.

What's bad about getting stood up, Cukie considered, is knowing how little you are worth in the eyes of the person who left you waiting. Worse, though, is understanding that in your own estimation, you must not be worth all that much, either, because while they thought so little about you, you continued to wait.

Cukie couldn't imagine confronting Genie about it. The only reasonable thing to do was to pretend it had never happened. If she came by the tiki bar again, he would force a smile, as though he, too, had forgotten they had planned to meet. Because the only way getting stood up can get worse is if you admit that it hurt you.

Cukie raised himself to leave and saw Genie approaching, holding herself at the elbows, chin tucked, as though traveling against a gale. As she neared, Cukie saw her tear-spattered cheeks.

"What's going on?" He lifted his hands to take her in his arms, but dug them into his pockets instead.

"Dad didn't come home last night. The police won't even look for him until another day passes. Something's wrong. Have you seen him?"

"No," Cukie said, glancing down at the sand. He hadn't seen him today, but he didn't offer up that he had seen him the day before, headed out on the *Belly Bloat* with Ox. Instinctively, he knew to cast his father, and by extension himself, as far as possible from whatever trouble loomed. "I bet he's somewhere sleeping off a hangover."

Genie stared back coldly. "He wouldn't just not come home. My father wouldn't do that to me."

Right then Cukie understood the difference between them.

———

Cukie forced his mind blank on the walk home. Not until he spotted the *Belly Bloat* parked in her slip did he consider whether Happy or Ox had looked worried or angry or afraid the day before. He entered the storeroom and found Ox hunched over, inspecting an assortment of fishing rods. Ox said, "Where've you been? It's not like you to abandon your responsibilities like this."

Cukie crossed the room and lowered himself onto his cot. He didn't speak until Ox stopped fussing with the rods and neared. "Do you know what happened to Happy?" Cukie said in a half whisper.

"What are you asking me?" Ox said.

"Happy. He's missing."

"What's that have to do with me?"

"You two went out on the water yesterday. No one's seen him since."

"You're mistaken," Ox said, adding, "I haven't heard from Happy in days," and Cukie said, "I saw you."

Ox leaned over and snatched Cukie's shoulder. Cukie winced and grabbed his father's hand, and Ox squeezed harder, dropping his face close to Cukie's. "Listen here. I won't have some bastard child accusing me." Ox released Cukie and returned to the fishing rods.

No words passed between father and son for the remainder of the night. And in the morning, as Ox pulled the *Belly Bloat* out of slip 26, Cukie tore through his clothes bin, stripping it bare, stomping the container to sharp plastic shards, before hitching a ride back to Miami.

2.

His baby boy had emerged slippery and screaming into the world when the panic began blooming inside Cukie. They'd agreed on Julius, after Lianne's grandfather, and once Julius had been wiped clean, swaddled in a hospital blanket, handed to Lianne—exhausted, red-faced in spite of her brown skin—she'd had the wherewithal, after minutes of staring, of breathing him in, to spin Julius toward Cukie, saying, "Look. Your nose." But Cukie had already recognized it, like an arrowhead glued to a sapling.

Of the anxieties Cukie had brought into the delivery room, passing down his least cherished feature had not been one. He had, of course, considered whose face he'd eventually come to see in his son's, his or Lianne's, or some near-even split, or else neither, though Cukie figured that would reveal itself over years, months at the earliest. Among his anxieties: he had recently dreamed that Baptist's staff had misplaced Julius in a ward of in-distinguishable newborns—as all newborns, to him, had been indistinguishable up till this point—and that Julius would never be recovered with any certainty. Chief among his anxieties had been the money, that there wasn't any.

Now, though, his boy appeared fated, as he himself had been fated, to see his father everywhere he saw himself.

Lianne lifted Julius for Cukie to take, and Cukie edged toward the door, saying, "I'll be back."

"You'll be back?" Cukie heard Lianne ask, though he was

already making his way down the hall, dropping his scrubs on the hospital floor.

======

It wasn't until Cukie saw his boy's face that he knew he would have to do something drastic to save his family from destitution. He's just turned off U.S. 1 onto the bridge that will lift him over the hem of the Atlantic, and after a mile or so, land him in the midst of Smuggler's Key for the first time in four years. Every once in a while he takes his sight off the asphalt in front of him and pushes it over the aluminum rail to search out fishing vessels down in the water. Not seeing many, he thinks there's still time.

His headlights are becoming unnecessary as night recedes, his truck's nose already dipping toward Smuggler's. He's rehearsing greetings for when he pulls up to his father's tiki bar. *Hey, Pop*, or *Remember me, deadbeat?* He's got to play it cool, though. To humble himself. He practices the words: *Do you have work for me? Work I can fall back on?*

Smuggler's has changed very little since Cukie's last visit, and this comforts him as he pulls the truck along the narrow highway toward the marina. In the residential area, enough of the yards are still more sand than grass, more shipyard than driveway; rowboats and kayaks lean against manatee-shaped mailboxes and over porch railings. The ocean glows aqua behind the houses on either side of the road, creating dual panoramas.

When Cukie reaches Blue Harbor he jams the brake, halting the truck just inside the marina's entryway. He recognizes the shipyard over on the south end and the docks straight ahead of him. But over to the right, the north end has been transformed.

Along the waterfront a restaurant occupies the majority of the space. There's no sign of Slip 26 Charters.

Cukie removes his foot from the brake and lets the automatic transmission pull him toward the docks. Fishing crews are loading boats up ahead. Stacks of cages sit beside bait drums, and men rush to get their vessels stocked for the day's voyage. Cukie guides the truck parallel to the water's edge, kills the engine, and jumps out, peering down the coastline in either direction. No tiki bar in sight.

He paces the docks, seeing his father everywhere and nowhere at once. Ox, with grayed hair, baits cages. Ox, plus forty pounds, inspects buoys. Ox, withered by the sun's oppression, yells down at a teenage version of Ox.

The morning sun is already melting everything to a chowder of dead fish and salt water. The heat mats Cukie's hair to his scalp. If he inhales hard he can taste his sour flesh in the soup, and the more he does this the more he realizes he is not cooking but rotting.

Cukie stops inspecting the men. None of them is Ox, nor are any of their vessels the *Belly Bloat*.

He trudges in the direction of the restaurant, but he does not look at it. It is an eyesore, an affront to his past, however unfavorably he looks upon that past. Instead, he surveys the docks. Many of the slips are empty. But as he draws closer to where the tiki bar should be, he sees that his father's slip, slip 26, is occupied not by the *Belly Bloat* but by a sleek blue cigarette boat.

This absence nearly topples Cukie. He is convinced that his father has met utter ruin, and he is surprised by how the thought sickens him. Slip 26's business line might still be worth trying, but Cukie lost track of that years ago. It was likely written in one of his mother's address books, boxed up with her belongings, but Cukie stopped paying the storage fees on her unit six months after she passed.

Before she was even gone, Cukie had begun cultivating the idea that he had not done enough to save his mother. After the surgery and the radiation and the chemo failed, he sat quietly at his mother's side in the too-small office at the Miami Cancer Institute as her oncologist explained, yet again, how her cancer had progressed. Cukie said nothing and did nothing because this man in a white coat said there was nothing more to do.

After her funeral, what astounded Cukie was not his guilt or his sense of innate weakness; what astounded him was the feeling that he had been abandoned for the final time.

Soon thereafter life degraded into a struggle to keep the house his mother left him from going into foreclosure.

Lianne had kept Cukie afloat with the word *we*—*we've* got this, Cukie, and *we'll* figure this out, and *we'll* make it through—even when he knew he alone was drowning. She'd moved in, halving the mortgage, but you can't bartend on South Beach with a volleyball under your shirt—that's how her manager had put it to her. And deliverymen can't use company vehicles to run errands for their pregnant girlfriends—that's how his supervisor put it to him. So they've both been out of work for weeks now.

What strikes Cukie as most pressing is that you can't raise a baby in a home that's been repossessed by the bank. And if he can't fall back on his fishing experience, if he can't depend on his father for this final safety net, he's not sure what he's going to do.

Cukie ascends the ramp to the restaurant's covered deck, where wooden booths surround a varnished bar. At the top of the ramp, a chalkboard announces *Splashdown Specials*.

Cukie hasn't eaten for hours, and when he takes a seat at the bar, he realizes he's exhausted from being up all night at the hospital. He sees no servers, no other customers. To the right of the bar, the door to the kitchen is propped open, and he can hear faucets running and dishes moving around in a tub. Intermittent drafts of cool air exit the kitchen, sending shivers along the circumference of the sweat beads on his skin.

As he scans the bar area, looking for the yellow pages or white pages, a woman emerges from the kitchen. "What can I get you?" she asks.

Cukie doesn't recognize her yet, as he's scarcely glanced at her face. What he stares at as he says, "The tiki bar, Slip 26, the one that was here before this restaurant: Do you know what happened to the owner?" is her taut, round stomach, stretching her shirt to the brink. He catches her eyes in time to see her lids drop by several degrees.

"Genevieve?" Cukie says. He forces a smile and nods toward her center. "Had a little one today myself."

Genie nods and says, "Hang on."

She darts through the kitchen door, closing it behind her. Before long Cukie can hear her shouting with a man, but he can't make out what is being said over the sound of spraying water.

His phone buzzes in his pocket as he awaits her return. Cukie does not want to speak to anyone. He wants to focus, which is growing increasingly difficult. A single buzz signals that a message has been left. It's a text from Lianne: *You couldn't even sign it?*

It occurs to Cukie, perhaps not for the first time, but for the first time that he's willing to acknowledge, that it appears as though he has run out on Lianne and his son, that his prompt departure from the hospital was an act of cowardice.

Not cowardice, he assures himself. Panic. He starts to type a reply message: *I'll be back soon.* But he's interrupted when Genie returns.

"You were asking about your dad? I haven't seen him," she says. "Not for a while now." She takes out a rag and begins wiping down the bar. "God, Cukie, how long's it been?"

"When'd the tiki bar close?" he asks, feeling light-headed.

"Couple years back." Genie studies her hand's brusque, circular rotations. "You still in Miami?"

"Maybe Happy would know—"

"Daddy's dead," she says. She glances up, not quite meeting his eyes, but somewhere just below. "We never found him."

Cukie stifles the urge to say, *Oh, right*, and says, "I'm sorry, Genie," instead.

Genie purses her lips and runs her tongue over her teeth. "I can give you some water for the road, if you're not staying to eat."

Cukie nods, but Genie doesn't move. Her jaw is tensed. Her hands cradle her belly. Behind her the back wall is a mirror. Bottles line the shelf in front of it. The mirror is angled so the top end juts forward slightly toward the counter, toward Cukie. In the reflection Cukie can see the stacked dish racks, and beside that, the sink filled with murky green liquid. To the left of the sink is the tap, and adjacent to the tap there's a stainless steel freezer. Taped to the freezer is a faded poster. It's a picture of a woman, dripping in a red T-shirt, the word *JAMAICA* flipped backward across her chest. And in the reflection, in the top right corner of the poster, above a scribbled signature, Cukie can just make out a heart.

=

When Cukie bursts into the restaurant's back office, it isn't quite surprise he reads on Ox's face so much as regret.

Nearly an hour later Cukie is out on his father's speedboat heading for open water. He still hasn't eaten, but the ocean breeze and the sporadic splash of salt water on his face is waking him some. He wants to ask Ox everything: What happened to the *Belly Bloat*, the fishing? How'd he come by this apparent wealth? And why would Genie lie for him, and why lie at all? But Ox insisted they take a ride out on the boat, first thing. To have alone time, man to man. "Like the days of yore," Ox said with the detached enthusiasm of a car salesman.

The wind is in Cukie's ears now, and the motor is roaring besides, so his questions will have to wait. Plus, even though Cukie feels compelled to ask, he suspects he knows an answer or two.

Ox stops the boat about forty minutes off the coast. He pours cognac into two short glasses, handing one to Cukie.

"It's a little early, no?"

Ox says, "Nonsense," and tilts back a mouthful. "So what brings you down to paradise?"

Cukie sits in one of the camel leather seats and takes a sip. The cognac burns in his empty stomach. "I knocked my girl up," he says.

Ox laughs. "You didn't come all the way down to discuss the ins and outs of ins and outs, did you?" He straightens his face a bit. "I suppose it's too late for that now. For either of us," he adds.

"Whose baby is Genie having?" Cukie feels sick at his words, and sicker at the denial his father does not offer. "I guess I don't have to tell you you're old enough to be her father."

"Genie's an adult," Ox says. "Same as you." He shoots

the remainder of his brandy. "And how about this girlfriend of yours? She far along?"

"She had it. Today. A boy."

"And you're here." Ox removes a flat wooden box from the cubby and opens the lid, offering Cukie his choice of cigars. Cukie declines. Ox removes one, along with a silver cigar cutter. He snips the cap. "Well, congratulations. Born on Splashdown. That's got to be some luck." He removes a gold lighter from his pocket, flips it open, and waves the flame over the foot, taking short, sucking pulls off the head till it's lit. "Is it fatherly advice you came for?"

Cukie considers this a moment, then asks, "How'd you do it?" In the silence that follows he grows fearful that Ox will misinterpret the question, and before he can lose his nerve he says, "I mean, how'd you live with yourself? How does a man abandon his child like that?"

Ox stares back, unfazed. "The past is the past," he says.

"And now you've got another on the way," Cukie says. "Not a boy, I hope."

Ox says, "I'll do better by him. That what you're needing to hear?" He glances out over the water.

Cukie follows his gaze to the short, choppy waves surrounding them. He wants to steady his mind, temper his words, but Ox's cool demeanor is kindling to a lifetime of pent-up resentment. "Looks like you've done better by yourself," Cukie says, waving a hand around the deck. "You've never been particularly good with sons, though. Maybe if Genie births a sea bug, or a made-up bullshit story." Cukie searches Ox's face to see what he's provoked in him, but there's nothing there.

"What did you come here for?"

Cukie takes another sip. "You still have the *Belly Bloat*?"

Ox shakes his head. "I told you, I'm done trapping."

The brown liquid swirls in Cukie's glass. He thinks he feels his phone buzz. There's no reception out here, but his cell displays a second text from Lianne, received over an hour ago: *You didn't even sign it.*

The reply he'd drafted remains unsent.

"You came down to fish?" A plume of smoke veils Ox's face. "If you need work, I can always use a busboy."

Cukie laughs bitterly. "That's what you offer me?"

"You above it?" Ox finally looks offended. "What is it you *think* I owe you?"

Cukie considers what he owes to Julius: more than passivity and inaction; more than minimum-wage provision. He owes him everything he can give, everything he can take.

"Happy never turned up, huh?" Cukie says. "I told Genie I never saw him the day he went missing. What's that worth? Turning your son into the liar you are?"

"Careful, boy. Don't let your anger make you say something you'll regret."

"I'm thinking ten," Cukie says, and Ox grunts, "Hmm?"

"You want to know what I came for? Ten grand. Call it back pay on the child support you skipped out on. Call it blackmail if that suits you better. Ten thousand. Today. Or I'll tell everyone I saw you two headed out to sea that day. But I'll start with Genie. Let's see if the past is the past then."

Ox takes a long drag off the cigar and lets it out slow. "Ten?" he says, and the word billows, expanding in the smoke cloud. "Is that all?"

Cukie's head seems to nod of its own volition.

"You really are something stupid, you know that?" Ox throws

the cigar overboard. "You think I killed Happy? My oldest friend?"

"If you didn't, I think you know who did. I know you two had some shady business going. But at this point," Cukie says, "I only care what Genie's going to think. If you want to save your family, I'm going to need you to save mine."

Ox doesn't respond and instead begins pacing the deck. After a while, he says, in a softer voice than Cukie has ever heard Ox use, "You know I never knew my own daddy. He visited us at my grandma's house once when I was nine or ten, but I can only ever remember the back of his head." Ox stops pacing and looks at Cukie in a way Cukie thinks Ox never has before. "It never really bothered me. His not being there."

Cukie says, "I didn't come here for stories."

Ox nods. "I'll give you the money," he says brusquely. "The minute you set foot on land. But I want you to do something for me. I want you to see why I came back that day and Happy didn't. I want you to see the cost of saving your family."

Ox starts the motor and drives the boat another twenty minutes out, glancing down at the screen, mapping their coordinates. He slows, and Cukie follows his pointing finger to an orange-and-black buoy bobbing on the water's surface. Ox cuts the engine, steering the boat so it rides up close to the buoy. He takes a diving mask from the boat's cubby and flings it at Cukie.

"Here. I don't have any diving flags, and it's five years for molesting a trap now, so I suggest you hurry." He produces a flashlight and holds it out to Cukie.

Cukie clasps the mask in both hands but refuses the flashlight. "What is it?"

"Your ten grand," Ox says. "You want to know how I came

up in the world? You want the truth about your old man? See for yourself." He extends the flashlight. "You're going to need this, son."

Cukie looks out over the water, at the buoy, bright against the blue-green waves.

He strips to his boxers and puts the mask on, then takes Ox's flashlight. The water sends a sobering shiver through Cukie's body as he penetrates the surface. He holds his breath and dives, using the buoy line as his guide. It's cold below, despite how hot it is up top. Cukie's not used to the pressure that's forcing itself against his ears, though he's not far under. He turns the light on and aims it down the line. The traps sit atop the surface of a reef, close enough to reach, if he can hold his breath like he once could. He returns to the surface and swims so he's right above the nearest cage. He steadies his breathing, preparing to take enough air in. The waves slam him, so he has to time it right. He inhales deeply and dives, kicking as he descends, shining the light against the trap directly below. The light's beam bounces off the siding's plastic links. As he nears, he sees the lobsters piled one on top of another. He shines the spotlight against the next pot down the line. Also full.

It's the morning of Splashdown. The pots should be empty.

He reaches and tries to open the trap, but it has been sealed shut, so he slips his fingers through the mesh to pinch one of the lobsters by the tail, pulling it toward him. The lobster floats, stiff-legged. He braces his feet against the trap and latches on to the mesh with the hand holding the flashlight. With his free hand, he nabs the lobster's tail, then jerks it as hard as he can. Its legs catch against the cage, then begin snapping off as Cukie pulls back. He loses hold of the flashlight; it somersaults toward the ocean floor. He wraps a second hand around the tail and yanks it through the link, out of the cage, then kicks furiously to return to the surface. The lobster's shell is cold and hard, though cracked in several places. All but one of its legs have broken off and there is a nickel-sized gap in its underbelly, exposing a patch of white. Cukie pokes the white and feels a smooth plasticity over it. He presses both thumbs into the gap and rips the shell open, the shell slicing his hands as he does so. Inside, a clear plastic pouch contains white powder.

Cukie breaks the surface, dropping the lobster shell. The motor runs. The speedboat is farther from the buoy than when he went under.

"See anything?" Ox yells from the deck, and Cukie nods, panting. He holds up the plastic pouch.

"Happy's idea. But our friends in charge didn't think him up to the task. If I hadn't convinced them I was, neither one of us would have come back that day."

Cukie swims toward Ox. As he nears, Ox leans on the throttle so the boat pulls several yards away. He steps to the stern and looks down on Cukie. The motor idles. Cukie stares back, paddling in place. He hears Ox say, "I'm sorry, son," but it might just be the confluence of the motor, the waves, and Cukie's exhaustion.

In a moment, Ox will pull away, leaving a strip of wake as he disappears into the horizon, and Cukie, finally understanding the man his father is, will set his thoughts on Lianne's texts and how he might survive in her and Julius's imaginations. But right now, behind Ox, the sun is still making its ascent. If Cukie reaches out, he can almost touch his father's shadow on the water.

INDEPENDENT LIVING

f you asked me, *What do you do for a living?* I might admit I
hunt elderly people. I wrangle them, force them into stiff,
scratchy chairs before interrogating them. I get out of them
whether they have a job or a niece who sends them checks every
month, and whether they've acquired a cat. I figure out if they
smoke and if they do so inside their apartments. I coerce them
into signing forms, not least among them the Independent Living
Agreement, which states that if you, as a renter at Silver Towers,
cannot care for yourself or hire the necessary help, then you can
no longer reside here. I chase down tenants. Currently, I'm chasing the fastest.

Carlos Rodriguez is always running. Dude's wiry, with skin
like beef jerky from the neck down, but from the way he hurtles
past his Silver Towers neighbors, you might guess he was a high
school track star. When I'd catch him in the building's elevator—
back when I could catch him—I'd watch his feet in full bounce,
sneakers flopping up like fish blown ashore in a storm. His knees
would jerk forward in his khakis, right-left-right-left-right, as

he watched the little yellow light descend from four to three to two, and as I'd begin to mention that his annual recertification was approaching, he'd sprint out the elevator doors, flashing over his shoulder a youthful, though somewhat rotten, smile.

======

If you ask Silver Towers' property manager, he'll tell you I'm the administrative assistant at this federally subsidized senior housing scheme. And that I've been assisting for just over a year now. I'd been a month on the job, though, when our assistant property manager—the original resident wrangler—went MIA, and I've been covering her workload, without a proper promotion, ever since.

The property manager's job is not so much to chase tenants as it is to squeeze from them every cent the Department of Housing and Urban Development will allow him to, and he does this through rent increases—increases justified by the findings of my interrogations and the paperwork I process.

Paperwork means, *Tell me what you're worth, so I can see if you're lying to me.* It means, *Tell me, and I'll tell you if you can still live here.* I could tell you about verification forms faxed to our residents' banks and their employers—their assets and income determining how much rent we can legally charge them. But that's not what you'll want to hear about. You'll want to know how I came to spend my nights tucked into the building's various crevices, scurrying through darkened halls like an Ocean Drive alley rat. We'll get there.

Here's the important part: My manager says that if we get rent increases to a high enough bracket by the end of the fiscal year, he'll convince our head office to reapprove the assistant property manager position and promote me. As the APM, I'd be able to move out of my car and rent my own apartment; I could live like a fully formed twenty-first-century North American human. I need this.

———

The downside of being the face of rent increases in a low-income development is that the residents wish you dead. Not a month goes by that I don't receive hate mail. It arrives in the form of letters, mailed to us from our tenants' family members: *How can you raise my mother's rent? You want her to starve?* the letters ask. *If you're really NON-profit, how come you're so damn greedy?*

There lies the largest misconception people have about government-subsidized housing. People erroneously figure it's in our interest to charge the elderly as little rent as possible. In reality Silver Towers' mission is threefold: increase the property's value, maintain high occupancy, and keep rents climbing.

It's not just the rent hikes that anger our tenants' next of kin, though. One letter actually read, *My father shouldn't have died alone. How could you let him?* How could *I* let him.

But the ones that really stick are the handwritten notes.

The last one, retrieved from our office's drop box about a week ago, simply read, *die.* That its author penciled it in lowercase letters makes me feel worse about it somehow. Had it read *DIE!!!!* I'd have attributed the message to rage, which is passing, unsustainable. But *die,* to me, seems cool-headed. The sender appeared to have given it ample thought.

Often I'm spared the brunt of the insult because the notes

are terribly misspelled, illegible, or not written in English at all. Not long ago, though, we received a sheet of construction paper displaying a message that circumvented language barriers and literacy deficits. The note featured a stick figure hanging in a noose. One stick arm reached up to clench the vividly rendered rope the character swung from. An arrow pointed toward the figure's head, the word *tú* written at the other end. I turned the paper over and saw *El Jefe* written on the back.

Oh, thank god, I thought. I handed the paper to my manager and said, "It's for you."

It might be hyperbole to say I identify with my tenants, most of whom are asylum seekers and refugees, but I can empathize well enough. My parents came to the U.S. not for economic advancement but to escape the violence the U.S. government funded in Jamaica throughout the 1970s as part of its war on socialism. But when I say *Jamaica* to non-Jamaicans, no one thinks of CIA operatives, or puppet prime ministers, or historical continuity. Instead, they break into free association, as if they'd been tossed into a rap cypher: *Bob Marley, irie, ganja, poor people, Sandals, 'ey mon!* At best, they believe our history began the moment they purchased their all-inclusive vacation package.

Of course, the difference between exiles and my parents—in fact, the difference between *me* and my parents—is that my parents have a homeland to which they can return.

Just weeks before I came home from college last year, my mother said to hell with Miami, with this whole damn country— the rat race, all of it—let the bank foreclose on her house, and dipped back to Jamaica. She says she can finally breathe now. She feels freed by the privilege of relative racelessness. In 2009, Kingston's murder rate reached the highest ever on record, and my mom returned there so she could finally feel safe.

It was my father's address I wrote on my résumé and job applications. I didn't last three weeks at his house before the beef got too thick to choke down, so I moved into my Raider, parked in whichever lot I could find, the few left without security officers or meters, moving it incrementally to keep gas costs low and to keep from getting towed. The day I finally interviewed for this job, I filled a fast-food-restaurant ketchup cup with hand soap and washed myself at a South Beach shower station, the one just a block over. I aired my suit on the seawall, waiting for the sun to bake my drawers dry.

You might guess the best thing about transitioning back to a paycheck is the food security, the dignity of work, or the promise of upward mobility, but it's none of these things. The best thing about a job is having a toilet on which to sit and unload your twisted, clogged-up colon without having to fake like you're planning to buy that Double McFuckery with fries.

———

The residents, you'll see, if ever you visit, have been through this kind of hustle—worse, if I had to guess. You see it on their faces, in the congealed grimaces and winces. They've been drained, decimated by poverty, in conjunction with aging. The ones who are alone in their final years are pitiful. The ones who still hold familial obligations are damned. This brings me back to dude I was telling you about earlier. Carlos. Carlos is among the damned.

Carlos, whose recertification is due for processing, spends much of what's left of his time caring for his invalid wife. I suspect she's the reason he's always on the move. On his way out of the building, there's a lightness in his step, optimism in the swing of his limbs. But when he sprints in, back from work or whatever errands he's run, you can see the worry in his eyes, the tension constricting the muscles in his jaw, the look of someone certain he's left his burner lit under an empty frying pan. Imagine carrying that stress every day for years. Consider what that does to a person.

We've never established a protocol for processing catatonic spouses, never bothered with terms like *power of attorney*, so last year I allowed him to take blank copies of the Independent Living Agreement and the rest of the recert forms to his apartment to have his wife cosign them. Of course he came back after too short a period, her signatures closely matching his. I didn't press the issue.

This year, when I reminded him about our appointment, he said his wife was not doing well.

"Still, we have to get this done in December."

"Late December," he said. He flashed his crooked, gray-brown teeth, a book's worth of spent matches, before fleeing down the hall. His signature red baseball cap sprang up and down as he sidestepped his neighbors, a child's bouncy ball bounding through week-old snow.

⸻

I've always liked Carlos—let me just put that out there. Maybe it's his demeanor in spite of his financial and familial woes. The corners of his lips, much like his cap's brim, are aiming ever up-ward. He's perpetually draped in an oversize navy polo, WAL-GREENS stitched on the breast, the bagginess adding to his impression of youthfulness, as if he were planning to grow into his older brother's shirt.

Excluding the elevator, Carlos will halt in the hall outside my second-floor office for exactly one thing: his Hawaiian Punch fix.

The building's vending machines are stationed between the second-floor restrooms and the elevators. One offers your main-stream brands of canned liquid sugar rush—Crap, Diet Crap, Orange Crap, Iced Crap, and even Malta, which suggests our vendors do understand our demographic. More mysterious is the second vending machine, the straight-up nineties throwback, the dedicated Hawaiian Punch dispenser.

The machine glows blue and red around the mischievous il-lustrated figure, jumping yet frozen in the center of the enlarged can pictured on the front. The character also sports a red hat above his blue-and-white-striped shirt. Carlos, the sole patron of this dispenser, as far as I can tell, will pause to purchase a can, slurp back the red, syrupy liquid, and once he's refueled, will dash back into action. If you were to catch sight of this ritual in your periphery, you might think the sudden blue-and-red burst from the backlit box's center was the character finally escaping the confines of the machine.

———

In addition to standing out for his youthful quirks, Carlos is no-table for being one of the building's few fluent English speakers, employees included. Since I took this job, I've had to cultivate what I like to call Leasing Spanish, Spanish being the predominant language spoken here, Russian the distant second.

I get the building's engineers to fulfill maintenance requests through hand gestures and miming and our mutually limited though ever-expanding knowledge of one another's languages. *Una problema con la puerta en apartamento #512*, I'll write on the work order, when a tenant complains of a squeaky door. The original complaint itself will have been acted out for me, with the tenant making screeching sounds as he opens and closes my office door.

When my ninth-grade Spanish comes up short, I break down and call El Jefe to come help translate. He, of course, thinks this a monumental waste of his time, but I'm supposed to be helping him with his English, so he'll generally acquiesce.

Truthfully, our trade-off is a sham, because dude speaks English about as well as any community college grad in Miami-Dade County. Every now and again he'll disfigure an idiom, saying, "For better or for worst," and I'm supposed to correct him. I did at first, but I've begun to believe he goes out of his way to exaggerate his English deficiency to appear foreign, or local, depending how you look at it.

Over the course of a year, El Jefe's English has deteriorated rapidly, a political move to gain influence with the Cuban community's older generation, I suspect. He insists he belongs to this community, but he's admitted, too, that his almond skin, his full lips, his too-round nose, and his tight curls are viewed among many of his brethren with distrust and contempt.

"¿Eres Dominicano?" I've heard about a dozen of our Cuban residents ask him. When they ask, I see the hurt drowning the corners of his eyes.

"¡Dominicano mi pinga!" he answers. "¡Soy Cubano!"

"They act like there's no color back on the island," El Jefe once told me. "They act like Africa doesn't pump through Cuba's veins."

The absurdity of such pronounced colorism is, in his view, topped only by the fact that, despite my twenty-odd years in Miami, I still haven't learned Spanish. "How do you even get by? How do you talk to your neighbors?"

"I'm from Cutler Ridge," I explain. "Which they now call Cutler Bay." To his blank expression I add, "Many of our rapist colonizers spoke English."

That he needs English-language tutoring is what's unfathomable. I suggested that perhaps he's just bad with grammar, so he took our lessons to the next level. He'll say, "What's the word for," and point at something unbelievable, like a pencil sharpener or the sole of his shoe, and I'll say, "Tip whittler," or "Foot bottom."

Last time, when he pointed at the AC vent and started, "Cómo se dice—" I asked, "Dude, weren't you born in the U.S.?"

"Yeah, but I grew up in Hialeah," he told me.

"That's in America, though, no? I mean, didn't they teach you English in school?"

"Have you been to Hialeah?" he asked. "Even the stop signs say ALTO."

———

Like El Jefe, Carlos is interested in ethnic and racial distinctions, language proficiency, and such. One memorable exchange of ours began when he hurried into the office and slung himself into the seat facing me, and said, "I see you and I can tell you are mulatto. Am I right?"

"We don't say *mulatto* in this country," I corrected him.

"I'm from this country," he corrected me back. "And I can tell you no' one of these Negroes. I have a nephew." And to complete the sentence, he dragged his index finger across the skin of his wrist, then aimed it my way. "Love," he said, and he spread his arms wide and shrugged, repeating *love* as though the word might explicate and exculpate what he'd otherwise deemed incomprehensible. I thought he would say more, but he just winked and skipped out of the office.

Had he stayed, I would not have bothered explaining that I *am* one of these Negroes or that by many Americans' estimation, so is he.

Carlos has been incrementally prepping me for his random, if specific, expressions of prejudice for some time now. "I'm Puerto Rican," he likes to remind me. Nearly every conversation we have includes this bit. "I'm no' going yell at you, *Learn Spanish.* I'm no' one of these Cubans."

The Cubans and the Russians who split the building's population beef furtively, rarely inviting my participation. The factions cling together like true mafiosi. Carlos Rodriguez sticks to himself. He has to. No one can keep up with him.

———

I see less and less of Carlos as we get to mid-December. I'll hear the tumble and catch of a can in the machine, peep a flash of red flying past the office's entrance; by the time I step out into the hallway, he's ghost. When I go up to his eighth-floor apartment and knock on his door, no one answers. I tried sliding the recert forms under his apartment's door, hoping he'd sign and drop them back at the office, but the gap underneath stays blocked by a mat or a towel or some other implement of subterfuge.

Most of the December recertifications have wrapped smoothly, which is good because next month is our big audit. Federal audits mean the bosses are on edge, which means I've got double the workload, purging and combing through files and updating documents. El Jefe has spent most of the month working from our head office in preparation for this audit, so I'm practically running things solo over here.

Since Carlos is the last tenant who hasn't filled out his paperwork, I've had time enough to scrutinize his file and realize he has good reason for avoiding me: on last year's Employment Verification form, Carlos's signature is at the bottom, and on the line that asks, *Are you currently employed?* Carlos wrote, *No*.

This contradicts the several mornings a week I see him in his uniform, running in the direction of the Walgreens over on Fifth and Jefferson. *Could he be newly employed?* you might naturally ask, *if* Carlos hadn't worn the same blue work shirt nearly every day since I started here over a year ago. Why didn't I notice this discrepancy during his last lease signing? Maybe I was too busy figuring out the job. But since I've gotten that down, I've had time to learn our tenants' names and faces and routines.

I know Alvaro and Leonardo Fernandez run dominoes daily in the cafeteria, where the Little Havana Meal Program offers free lunch, and I know Vladimir and Saskia hold down the front stoop from noon till 3:00 p.m. And I know Carlos is a fiend for that red liquid crack, so the odds of catching up to him are in my favor.

═══

When next I spot him, I run up on Carlos right as he drops a quarter into the vending machine's slot. He looks up at me reluctantly, then down to his curled, coin-carrying fist, then to the vending machine, like he could cry. The machine's digital screen flashes INSERT 00.75.

"How's work?" I ask him, examining his polo.

"Oh, no, I no' work there anymore." With his free hand he pinches the shirt near the WALGREENS insignia, as if to subtract it from his personage.

"No?" I ask. But he is down the hall, heading for the stairwell, before I can further interrogate him. I nearly run after Carlos, then stop. *You're not a cop*, I remind myself. *You make $8.20 an hour*. I press the machine's coin-return button and pocket Carlos's quarter.

═══

Christmas brings extra mail in the leasing office's drop box, and as I check it, I see that the bribes have started rolling in. Last Christmas, my first here, I thought the envelopes stuffed with cards stuffed with cash were signs of holiday cheer, but soon I realized that the envelopes came exclusively from tenants with December and January recertifications. I recognized, eventually, that considering the dictatorships so many of my tenants had escaped, these offerings were vestiges of the survival tactics they'd acquired in the old country.

My manager requires that I report this money to him, and initially I did, given that none of the envelopes that first year were addressed to me, while some indicated they were meant for *El Jefe* and others simply read *oficina*. He took the cards and propped them up in the hallway-facing window in his office, so the residents could see he appreciated their gesture. The money he claims to have returned.

This year, the Christmas cards have taken on more careful designations. Many of the envelopes still read *El Jefe*, while a more or less equal number are addressed to me. They don't actually read *Trelawny*, of course. They're addressed to *Secretary* or *Secretario*. Either way, I place the cards on my desk and pocket the cash. Did I tell you how much I make? Besides, these offerings make no difference in whether rents go up, which, almost certainly, they will.

Keeping the money does not make me a bad employee, nor does it suggest that I shouldn't be promoted—let's be clear. Allowing poverty to inhibit my ability to perform my job duties: that would make me a bad employee.

I'm ripping through the stack of envelopes on my desk, pondering my responsibility to report Carlos to the manager, when a manila card catches my eye. I pick it up, wondering if cash or a rent check might fall out. When I open it, the card is empty, except for the carefully hand-drawn penis shooting across the inner fold. The back of this card does not specify the intended recipient. An arrow points to the head, and at the end of the arrow a single word is written: *tú*.

———

It would be easy to prove. A quick phone call. Walgreens is a few blocks away. I could walk there and see for myself. If Carlos is employed, his income might just account for the rent hike needed to spark my promotion. You see, I like Carlos, but, by leaps and bounds, I like myself more.

When I get back from lunch, I fax an Employment Verification form to the store to see what happens. The space on the form for the tenant's authorizing signature is blank, but I send it anyway.

———

Milda Perez is a different kind of problem. Milda is a May recert, which means that, since there's no benefit to enduring her dementia, I avoid her at all costs. She's the Towers' tiniest, most audible resident, and she's the only one who might keep up with Carlos, if she didn't primarily move in circles.

Milda should not live alone, yet she does, so she loses the keys to her apartment several times a month and leaves duplicate rent checks in our office's drop box. El Jefe claims that this is enough to put her in violation of the Independent Living Agreement—"How long before she burns down the building?" he says—but she's avoided eviction thanks to a nephew who has donated benches for the building's front entrance and dining tables for the cafeteria: anything to keep her from living with him.

Milda will peek in my doorway, watching me tabulate rent payments or type up our building's newsletter. When I look up, she'll dart over to the elevator, press the CALL button, then dash to the cafeteria's entrance and peer through the glass double doors. After flitting past the maintenance staff's office and the social worker's office and the restrooms, she'll stomp into my office in a fit. I might manage to pick out bits and pieces of her frantic

Spanish before she runs out in frustration. A few minutes later, though, she'll run back in and tell me in near-perfect English that the air conditioner in the dining room is blowing too cold, or the elevator is taking too long, or the mailman hasn't yet arrived.

Today Milda shows up a little after eleven o'clock. I know the time without checking my watch, because the walkers clacking from the elevators toward the dining room have already quieted, and a steady hum—cut by dominoes smacking tabletops—emanates from the end of the hall. Milda waits for the phone to start ringing, for a fax to begin spitting out of the machine, before her mouth gets working. I pluck the fax off the floor, wave it at her, then grab the phone.

Milda stands just beyond the threshold, murmuring something I don't think I could make out if she were speaking English.

"Silver Towers," I say into the phone.

El Jefe, on the other end, says, "You sure you want a promotion, welcoming calls that way?"

"Sure I do. It's a beautiful day at Silver Towers. A busy one, too."

"How're the recerts coming?"

"One left."

"Get it done this week," he says. "I hear this auditor's a bulldog."

Milda approaches, as if forging against a barrage of waves. She increases her volume as she nears, her face wet, her eyes humungous behind her glasses.

I've missed the last several things my manager has told me, so I say, "Yeah, it's just that I can't seem to track down the tenant in eight-oh-two, Carlos Rodriguez. He's the last one." I cover the receiver with my palm and say, "What's the matter, Milda?"

She stops midway between the door and my desk, mixing words with elongated breaths.

"Dime en inglés," I say.

El Jefe says, "Make sure there are no surprises with his income and bank statements." I glance at the fax in my hand; it's the returned verification form from Walgreens. The form is blank, except that right below the line where Carlos's signature should have gone, the words *Authorizing Signature* have been circled. Without his signature, Carlos's employer has no legal obligation to admit that he works there. As though he were staring over my shoulder, El Jefe says, "Take his signature off one of last year's forms. It's not rocket scientist."

I follow Milda out into the hall. We make it halfway to the cafeteria before she stops to stare through the window that looks out on Collins Avenue. I'm not sure if she's forgotten her destination or if this is it, so I follow her gaze. A crowd has gathered on the sidewalk in front of the building. It's December; locals pass quickly through the crowd wearing jackets and Ugg boots, but it's also seventy degrees out, so the dawdlers are mostly sandal-clad and tank top–draped.

"Mira, chico," Milda says, staring down at the street.

Traffic has halted on both sides of the gathering. Pandemoniac horn blasts rise above the buzzing people. I'm wondering which celebrity is disrupting our day with her presence, or else whose inebriation ignited a fistfight, but I can't seem to locate the source of the spectacle.

What I spot is Carlos's red cap and his signature gait as he turns onto Collins from Fifth Street, approaching from the direction of Walgreens. To his chest he holds a bouquet of roses and baby's breath, and the word that springs to mind is *love*. As he skirts the crowd, I wonder if he used his employee discount and if Mrs. Rodriguez can still appreciate flowers or the sentiment behind them. But Carlos continues north on Collins, never once glancing at Silver Towers.

"Look," Milda says, raising her hand horizontally, palm down. "He went over." She brings her hand into a vertical dive.

I press my forehead to the glass and search between the tanned necks and shoulders of onlookers until finally I see the sprawl of asphalt interrupted by pink-tinged body fragments.

"It's better this way, chico," Milda says, sniffling. "He had the cancer."

———

Silver Towers' waitlist for residency is five years long, but officially, the waitlist is closed. Do we keep this list in an electronic database or anything so efficient? Is it encrypted with up-to-date security features? In fact, our list takes the form of four ragtag composition notebooks, which we house in a drawer in the supply closet.

When a tenant does a ten-story belly flop onto Collins Avenue, leaving a permanent pink stain and a vacant apartment, the name of the game becomes turnover, and the composition books come out of the closet. Since the late Mr. Leibnitz was paid up through the end of December, we have till January 1 to find a new tenant before we start losing money on the empty unit. Every day that an apartment goes unrented draws a red flag with Head Office. Too many of those and the whole staff gets replaced, from

El Jefe on down. This, he reminds me monthly, is how he and our former assistant manager got their jobs in the first place, and how I got mine.

As to the efficiency of the waiting list: I call the number next to the first name in the book that isn't crossed out. If no one picks up after that initial set of ring-a-lings, I'm on to the next name. If a waitlister picks up but can't meet our fast-approaching move-in date, she gets scratched off the list completely, as per El Jefe's protocol. She begs me not to do this. She says, "Just call when *next* one opens. I'm ready *then*." But I don't make the rules, even if she has my sympathy.

It usually takes eight to ten calls before anyone even picks up. They'll see Silver Towers' number on their caller ID and call back, though, often after it's too late, at which time I tell them it was just a courtesy call to let them know they're still on the list. The truth—that their trip to the grocery store or the pharmacy or the loo cost them their rightful opportunity to move in here— would just break their hearts.

The fallibility of our waitlist procedures gets ticking on the dome when, just hours after Leibnitz's suicide, a woman in her late forties strides into the office, inquiring about the possibility of etching her name in composition book number one. It's her age that distinguishes her from our other applicants, true, but before I examine the relative smoothness of her face, it's her movements that strike me. Her hips lead her thick body forward, as though she were performing a belly dance.

I round my desk to greet her and she introduces herself as Nikolina. Nikolina smiles when she speaks, as though passing along a joke or a piece of good news to an old friend. There's a sparkle in her eyes, which distracts from her shallow crow's-feet.

Nikolina's blouse exposes a deep valley of cleavage, speckled with coffee-colored sunspots and delicate stretch marks. She asks about the waitlist. I find I'm disappointed to have to tell her it is closed.

She doesn't flinch when I say this, but responds in an accent I take to be Eastern European, "Surely there is something that can be done." She steps closer, adding, "I'm desperate."

"Maybe you don't realize, but this is elderly housing. You wouldn't qualify either way."

"I have disability. This makes me eligible."

A HUD provision states that people with qualifying disabilities are eligible for residency here, regardless of age. It's obvious she knows the system; the nature of her disability is less so.

"But still, the waitlist is closed," I say. "And if it weren't, there'd be a five-year wait."

"Please." She raises her hand and rests it on my forearm. "Help me."

I pull out of her reach and look toward the entrance, to the empty hallway beyond. Most of the residents are up in their apartments this late in the afternoon. "There's nothing I can do for you. Have you tried Alton Gardens?"

"Here," she says. "It needs to be here." She lowers her voice. "I have thirteen hundred dollars I can give you."

"I can't take your money." I say it quickly, as though I'm insulted by her suggestion. But within a breath my mind has divvied up and allocated every dollar.

She steps closer, taking my arms in her grasp. "I could give you something else." She pauses, eyes darting back and forth over my desk, as though assessing what someone like me needs most in the world. "You're too skinny," she says. "Allow me to cook for you." She's near enough that I can see my reflection in her dark, unblinking eyes: a clear sign that she's inappropriately close and that I should push her away. I ask myself, staring back from her pupils: *What kind of employee are you? And just what kind of man?*

———

There are perks that come with this job, perks that go beyond a toilet and my unofficial Christmas bonuses. For starters, Silver Towers pays for my parking space in the public garage across the street. This means no meters or meter maid dodging, no PARK-ING FOR CUSTOMERS ONLY signs, and no tow-away zones. El Jefe parks in the residents' lot, which takes up most of the Tow-ers' ground floor, so the risk of his catching me sleeping in my car is slim to none.

More important, when the weather dips into the forties at night during a cold front and my car becomes unbearable, there's a spare apartment on the second floor, two doors down from the leasing office. Technically, this space is the break room, used by all Silver Towers' employees, from the social worker to El Jefe himself, but it's also a model apartment, a showroom with a kitchen and a TV and a working shower. When you lock yourself inside at night, after everyone has gone for the day, the apart-ment's homeliness becomes more apparent. And though the only furniture in the bedroom is a conference table, the floral-print couch in the living area isn't as stiff as it first appears.

When my weather app buzzes with an *Early Morning Frost* alert, an hour or so after Nikolina's proposition, I don't even bother going to my car.

I close the office and meander along Ocean Drive, browsing

window displays and sidewalk signs promoting happy hours. Half-clad bodies push past on either side, squeezing between me and the storefronts and the sidewalk diners. On the street, a white McLaren continually speeds north, only to crawl back south again, but few are paying it the attention the driver desires.

The beach doesn't really pop off till later in the night, which makes right now a buyers' market and everything's on special. The bouncer at Wet Willie's, a hulking mass of muscle, nods at me as I pass—surprising, because South Beach bouncers are known to toss men through windows sooner than make unsolicited eye contact. Up ahead, two of Mango's dancers, a bare-chested roider type and a woman whose high ponytail sweeps the backs of her thighs, have wandered out front to perform Miami; they gyrate, shaking their flesh against anyone feeling froggy enough to join them.

I fight the urge to swipe a finger along either of the dancers' leopard-print costumes to see if they're textured, and it reminds me how long it's been since I've been touched.

As I pass restaurant entrances, hostesses spring at me, their menus aimed at my chest like spades. They're impossibly beautiful, these hostesses, displaying phenotypes that, according to American media outlets, should not coexist. Bronze and brass-colored flesh make aqua eyes glow like jewels in their faces. Tight blond coils spiral out above plush brown lips. Pale, broad noses create backdrops for sprinklings of orange-brown freckles. All manner and mix of racial ambiguity guards the entryways to these establishments, which boast French or Italian or Mediterranean cuisine. These gatekeepers' images should be plastered over magazine covers and billboards, but their bodies, their hips and thighs and backsides, are more robust than mainstream fashion mags and ad execs know what to do with, the sole reason the hoi polloi are allowed to stand this close to them.

American men, Southerners and Midwesterners, especially, stop to ask where these young women are from. More often, they drunkenly slur, "What are you?" To which the hostesses smile and name their country of origin. These dickheads are just that for asking, but I linger when they do, because I also want to know.

The hostesses are hired to lure the uninitiated into dining at these beachfront establishments, restaurants that provide the lowest quality food for the highest possible price. If business is slow, they'll part their lips for you, expose their teeth and gums, and flutter their eyelashes, as though your patronage were their one wish in life. When business is a-boom, these girls remain tight-lipped and stare around you, unless you look a lot like money.

They're hungry for diners now, though, so even in my frumpy work polo, I'll do. I nearly succumb to one before crossing the street and wandering onto the sand to sit barefoot, awaiting the sky's gradual fade from indigo to black.

In the past, when loneliness ravaged my better judgment, I've hit up Mango's or the Clevelander, where I nurse ten-dollar Heinekens and flirt with tourists (never the dancers—waste of time), especially the Americans who think every light brown thing in Miami is exotic. If they ask if you're Cuban, say yes. If they ask if you're Brazilian or Puerto Rican or Cape Verdean, say yes to that, too. Anything they ask, just nod along; be the surface onto which they can project their colonial desires and they'll take you back to their suite at the Fontainebleau or the Shore Club or the hotel on Fisher Island, where the necessity for security clearances and aquatic transport will transform you from a fling into a captive audience. But at least there will be a bed.

=====

The guard stationed at the Towers' security desk sees me re-enter. It's inevitable. But we contract our security officers from a company that rotates them out often enough that word of my nightly returns seems unlikely to make it back to El Jefe. Just in case, I prepare to tell him about the audit and the necessity of working late, but from the expression on his face—unadulterated indifference—I know he won't ask for more than a glance at my credentials.

When I flash my badge, he answers, in the same Haitian accent they all answer in, "Okay, my friend."

In the elevator, instead of heading to the second-floor offices, I hit the button for ten, intent on stretching my stiff, achy body over a mattress. The hallway is dim up on ten, but I know the layout and find Leibnitz's apartment with no trouble. Once I'm in, the process is always the same: I scout out dinner by the light of my phone and the open refrigerator. I eat only from unopened containers and sniff-test everything, expiration dates be damned. Tonight, it's canned tuna on toast, no mayo, since the thought of Leibnitz's hand dipping into the mayonnaise jar turns my stomach.

Keeping the lights off has the added benefit of my not seeing portraits of the deceased staring down on my depravity. In the dark, if I can ignore the fragrance of gradual decay, I can pretend I'm home.

After dinner, I flick the TV on and keep the volume low, in

case a neighbor hears voices, ventures into the hall, and decides to knock. These tenants, you see, are curious, to put it mildly.

At some point in my tenure, a group of the building's Russians petitioned to evict their Cuban neighbor, whose daughter they'd clocked crashing with her for over a week. There are limits and restrictions on such visitations, but still. If they'd do that to one another, imagine what they'd do to he who raises rents. Or he who *announces* rent hikes, to be more accurate.

This night, I'm especially lucky: since Leibnitz's illness left him mostly bed-bound, he'd moved his television into the bedroom—a no-no for most tenants of his generation.

Reclined in the slow-flickering beam of television images, I scroll through my contacts and search for a friend to text with. For a moment, I consider texting my brother to see if his offer to move in with him—now that his wife up and left—still stands. His invitation had arrived with brotherly advice: *People amount to their actions and you've been acting like a bum.*

I took no offense but clarified, *I identify as dispossessed.*

I went on to explain that the last time I crashed at his place, it took me an hour to get to work in the morning and two hours to get back. That's fifteen hours a week in traffic. That's over a month of my life per year sacrificed to Miami-Dade's highways. To say nothing of the literal cost of fueling such excursions.

But my real hesitation is this: Delano rents our childhood home from my father, and I'll be damned if I'll give him a second opportunity to strip the roof from over me. I suppose that when my father dies and my brother inherits the Cutler Bay town house and the house in Palmetto Bay, I'll eventually wind up as his tenant. Some siblings have predetermined roles, and mine is to be shit on.

Delano's agreed to keep my vagabondage from our mother, at least, and for that I am grateful.

If my mother were to call, as she has a knack for doing at times such as these, I'd have to whisper into the phone about how great things are going: Living in the heart of South Beach! Opportunities for career advancement! I'd ramble off whatever assortment of bullfuckery I could pull from my ass. The truth would be harder for her to hear than it is for me to live. It would break her to know that her son has joined the nouveau hobo class.

In the past, I'd message Lauren, whom I'd met on the sand when she asked if I'd put down *Sula* to join her at Frisbee, and who recently admitted, I like you, Trelawny. But I just can't date a homeless guy. So we haven't spoken since.

I decide to text a former classmate, Caitlyn, who still has another semester at university before she finishes her master's. The afternoon she suggested we start sleeping together, she made me agree that I could never meet her parents, which was as much about their being Chinese as it was about my being Black, she assured me, so my housing status thwarts little in relation to our future prospects. She asks me if anything interesting happened at work, so I tell her about Mr. Leibnitz's suicide.

That's terrible, she writes. *Did you know him?*

Intimately. I know he paid $150 for rent.

Jesus. And he killed himself?

I start telling her about Carlos and his elusiveness. About how he's costing me my promotion.

Since when do you want a career in housing? she texts back. *I thought this was just your day job. What about applying to grad school? What about art?*

I'm already doing the work, I respond. *I might as well get paid for it.*

I guess, she texts. *Just don't become some grandpa-abusing suit. Christ, Trelawny.*

To win back her favor, I tell her that I'm close to earning my teacher's certificate through a course I've been taking online. I fit it in on my lunch break and after work, using my office desktop. The course cost me every penny that isn't reserved for my dollar-menu dinners, my car insurance, and my phone. This I don't mention.

One has to have multiple hustles to survive in this economy, I type, though Caitlyn, to my knowledge, has never held a job.

She texts back, *K-12? ROFL. They will eat you alive.*

The subject of the conversation rotates, as usual, to when she can come visit. *I want to see your glamorous South Beach lifestyle. Plus I need to escape the snowpocalypse.*

Too bad you have to spend winter break with your family. I leave out that if she stayed with me, she'd have to squat in the home of the recently departed.

Let's lock it down, she types. *Spring break?*

I type, *Tired. Sleep time.* Then I turn the volume up on this documentary about poachers killing black rhinos in Africa. The poachers make boatloads smuggling rhino horns into Asia, Vietnam being the largest market for the contraband. Some buyers keep the horn intact, to symbolize status, but more frequently they grind down the horn and ingest it as medicine. Rhino horn is rumored to be a cure-all; cancer patients are among the most enthusiastic consumers. Of course, ingested rhino horn cures fuck all, but the poaching continues.

When I see these rhinos, not the ones that have been killed

outright but those that were tranquilized and are struggling to awaken with their faces crudely hacked to a red gaping wound, I want to avenge them. I want to fly to Zimbabwe and stake out the most vulnerable of what remains of the species. And when the poachers arrive, I want to hack off their noses.

Yet somehow I fall asleep envisioning myself at a party, at a mansion on the beach. The host offers me a glimpse of his horn. Not a rhino's horn but a unicorn's, likely the last in existence. Except it's no longer a horn at all but a powdery heap, amassed on a silver serving tray. Women and men in shimmering garb have queued up to snort lines of the unicorn.

I wonder, so far removed from the brutal annihilation of this once-majestic being, with the whispered promise of everlasting health, would I do it? If given the opportunity, would you?

———

I shower, then clear the apartment before 7:00 a.m., leaving behind as little evidence as possible. The maintenance guys will be by to empty the place, to throw the family portraits, the mattress, the couch, and the leftover milk in the dumpster. Leibnitz's emergency contact said what most emergency contacts say: "Does it look like he left anything valuable? Ah, fuck, just toss it all."

In some cases, when a tenant dies, a family member will arrange to see if there's anything worth salvaging: a watch or a necklace or a ring. If it'll fit in their pockets and holds monetary or sentimental value, these sons and granddaughters and nephews will carry it home with them. If it's larger than an armful, they let it ride to the dumpster.

I pack a to-go bag, taking the back stairs out so the morning guard will see me enter, upon my return, for the first time. When I'm done eating, I still have a half hour to kill, so I walk over to Walgreens. I pick up a stick of deodorant, some toothpaste, and a toothbrush, then wander the aisles, searching for Carlos. The store is empty except for the pharmacist and the teenager working the front register.

"I thought Carlos was on today," I tell him.

"Who that?" the kid shouts. He flops onto his elbows, knocking my purchases back toward me. His jaw winds in tight circles, but he's not chewing, as I'd first suspected. More likely he's been up all night rolling. His sunglasses' white arms rest over his pink ears, and the lenses wrap around the back of his closely shaved head.

"Rodriguez." I raise my voice to match his. "Carlos Rodriguez."

The kid shrugs. "That your uncle, bro? Tío Carlito?" He laughs.

"Lanky old cat. Red cap? Works here."

"I might know who you mean. He work the photo lab?"

"Might just." The lights above the empty photo center are dimmed. "What time's that open?"

"Never, bro. The machine broke down five months ago."

I push the deodorant toward him with my forefinger. "If you see him," I say, "tell him his mulatto nephew is looking for him."

———

Adding a name to the waitlist is both simple and tricky. If I add it to the end of the list, in that glaringly blank space beneath what should be the final waitlister, the next time the boss looks at it, he'll recognize that this name was not penned in his hand.

Adding a name to the top of the list is also tricky.

The names aren't numbered, but they're clustered so tightly that it is impossible to write anything new in between them. Simply writing a name to the side of these others will draw the auditor's attention, and I'm not trying to go to the Fed. My best bet is to hold off till it's time to call her in for the application, then act as though one of the already-scratched-off names belongs to her.

———

It's nighttime when Nikolina returns to the building to meet me. I let her in through the door that connects the parking lot with the back stairway, the one that opens only from the inside. When she steps in, she carries no grocery bags, which is confusing because she's here to cook me dinner, "no strings," as she put it.

On floor two, we step out into the dim hallway. I wouldn't dare bring her up to Leibnitz's apartment, where we might easily be spotted together, but since there are no apartments on the second floor, the break room will do. The door to the stairwell shuts, tucking us into relative darkness. All is quiet except for the hum of the vending machines up ahead. I pull Nikolina past the Hawaiian Punch dispenser toward the red glow of the RESTROOMS sign at the far end of the hall, just across from the break room entrance.

We slip inside and Nikolina's head gets to swiveling. Before she can locate the light switch, I pull her into the living area and onto the couch.

"Why are you here?" I ask her. "Are you sure you want to be here?"

She lifts her palms to clamp my face uncomfortably. "Boy," she says in a brusque voice, "life is not wants and diswants. There

are only dos and won't-dos. For a spot on your list, I will do this."
She hands me a bank envelope. "Six fifty," she says. "The other
half when I sign lease."

It's too dark to count the money, so I slip the envelope into
my pocket. "Fine," I say. Her bribery has taken on a quality of
meanness that puts me further on edge.

She seems a woman capable of anything, and this thought,
not for the first time, sparks my paranoia. "Open your bag," I
say. "I want to make sure you're not recording this." I search her
handbag, pulling from it a comb, a compact mirror, several tubes
of lipstick and eyeliner. I empty it out onto the coffee table, then
say, "Tell me why living here is so important to you."

She seems to search my face, but in the dark it's impossible
to tell. "I've given you my money," she says. "Don't ask for any
more of me."

———

I flip open the waitlist and, for a half hour, stare at the names cast
in the early-morning sunlight. I could call Nikolina to come in
straightaway to fill out the application to take Leibnitz's apartment. In a sense, I could have had her fill out the application
before she left.

But I don't call her. I pick up the phone and begin dialing applicants, starting with the first name on the list.

———

In the evening, between the workday's end and my return to the
break room, I wander the storefronts of Washington Avenue, all

the way down to Lincoln Road. White Christmas lights swathe the palms between the shops. Red ribbons and bows wrap around palm trunks with no detectable sense of irony. Next week is Christmas, and whom do I have to buy gifts for but myself?

The throng of shoppers provides an even more diverse backdrop of languages than my building; French and Arabic and Japanese join Spanish and the myriad variations of English spoken in the crowd. Young Black dudes keep trying to sell me their rap albums as I walk the mall. They're approaching everyone, but when they see me, their eyes brim over with hope and they abandon the tourists, judging me a more appropriate target.

"Support home team," one says, when I don't pause to hear his spiel.

It's important not to make eye contact with these peddlers or else they'll never leave you alone. I make the mistake of saying, "Next time," which this young entrepreneur takes as encouragement.

He bounds in front of me, cutting off my stride. In one hand he holds his box of CDs. In the other, headphones. "All I ask is that you check it out, my dude."

I pluck a CD from the box and bring it close to examine its cover. The quality of the image is impressive, high-def. The artist sits shirtless on the hood of a candy-green vert, an old-school Caddy, his lips peeled to expose gold fronts, his grip exhibiting a Jesus piece linked to the end of his elephantine chain. The kid might be twenty. Could he have paid for these adornments by hawking CDs on the mall, or was even the pictured grill borrowed? And if it was borrowed, or even if he's a dopeboy as Miami rap culture demands that he claim to be, the support system he must have in place! Of the two of us, who *really* needs my ten dollars? I set the CD back in the box. "Try me when you drop your jazz album," I say, then step around him.

"Uncle Tom—ass sellout," he says to my back.

I bypass the maxis and sparkling cocktail dresses and tutus draped over porcelain mannequins in window displays boasting COUTURE and find a shop that mass-produces fast fashion for the young hipster demographic. A skinny White girl seated cross-legged on the ground obstructs the shop's entrance, stirring a heavy bowl of red paste with her hands. I wonder if she's captured this two-by-two slab of concrete and if she intends to grow old here. A smattering of onlookers surrounds her. I want to shout at them to leave the girl alone, to say, *We don't have the luxury of going mad in private*, but then I spot the dollar bills crumpled in the overturned fedora to her right and realize this is a performance. "And he did this to me," she's saying. "He did it!"

I duck through the assemblage into the store, feeling I've escaped something horrific.

I shuffle through racks of T-shirts and jeans, a bit lost, before wandering into the home decor section, setting my eyes on a display of record players. They're the kind that are neatly tucked into a carrying case and that can convert vinyl recordings to digital files. A rack marked RE-MASTERED ALBUMS displays Nina Simone and Nat King Cole and Billie Holiday. I pat the envelope in my pocket for reassurance, then walk the record player and all three albums to the register. It's more than twice what I wanted to spend, but it's exactly the kind of purchase that will make my future apartment homey. As soon as my promotion comes through. I pull out the envelope to pay and find myself wondering if Nikolina enjoys listening to records, if she appreciates the fullness of their sound.

===

"Why it is we don't meet at your apartment?" Nikolina asks on her second visit to the break room. We sit on the sofa, holding our bowls, spooning the stew she's fixed into our mouths at markedly different paces. "Don't choke," she's already warned, with the sincerity of someone worried about her investment. She asks now, "It's because you live very far away?"

She's set me up to tell her my go-to line about the Cutler Bay town house and its distance from here, the one I give tourists who would prefer not to take me back to their shared hotel rooms, the one that failed to hold up with Lauren. But my arrangement with Nikolina is born of such corruption that I feel I can tell her the truth. "I'm between homes at the moment."

She looks at me as though she does not understand, but then nods and says, "It's difficult, youth." On the kitchen counter and on the coffee table, I've set out candles, which Nikolina has mistaken for a romantic gesture. One she clearly does not appreciate. I've already explained the need to keep the lights off, and since she did the cooking before she arrived, we needed only to heat it on the stove. Still, she sits at the very edge of the couch and keeps one eye on me, as though she suspects I might pounce on her.

Against the glare of South Beach beaming through the sliding-glass doors that let out onto the balcony, I can see the silhouette of my record player set up on the floor. But when I placed the needle down on "Sinnerman," even with the volume low, the staccato piano chords quickened my heartbeat and I felt my chest being stomped in, so I promptly turned it off.

It's for the best. It's risky enough just allowing the aroma of our dinner to seep into the hall, even if there's no reason anyone should visit this floor at this hour. Nikolina had suggested we meet at eight, but I made her come at eleven-thirty.

She's prepared beef goulash and poured me Russian wine, and the two roil in my stomach. When she called this afternoon to ask about the apartment, I reminded her that she still owed me dinner. But I hadn't considered how my body would reject nourishment after so long.

Nikolina is dressed similarly to how she was dressed when we first met: the plunging neckline, the mouthwateringly sweet perfume. When I can restrain myself no longer, I ask, "Have you done this before?" The thoughts had poked at my mind all day: That there's conduct befitting survivors that my parents and my professors were unwilling or unable to teach me. That I'd be housed by now had I learned to live by the rules of ruthlessness. And that if I understood these rules and that this is how the world actually operates, I could carry on with a clear enough conscience. "Is this how you get your way? Bribes and . . ."

"And?"

"You know." She gives no indication that she does know, so I say, "Manipulating men."

She lifts a spoonful to her lips and says, "You always take advantage of poor, vulnerable women? Do the viejas remove their dentures and suck your cock for a deposit? This is your way?"

"Of course not."

"Why 'of course not' with you, but for me, I have to play whore?" She inserts her spoonful.

"I'm trying to understand how you live." My voice sounds whiny and childish, so I clear my throat.

"Why I am here?" she asks in a softer tone. "Tell me. You're handsome." This part she says as an accusation. "You must have girlfriend younger than me."

"I'm homeless," I say, and something inside me uncoils. "Who would want me?"

She pretends I haven't spoken and continues, "If it's money alone, you'd take only this. But no. It's power you want to experience. Am I right?"

"The meal you promised. A conversation. Nothing more."

"You want the thrill of recklessness, too," she says. "To brush flame. That's your youth."

"Go on."

She rests the back of her head against the couch cushion. "When I will move in? I know there is vacancy."

"How could you know that?"

"The jumper. He was all over news."

"You better not have told anyone about this. I could go to prison. We both could."

"I am careful," she says.

"You think they'll blackmail me. But just wait. They'll expect something out of you soon enough."

"Don't change subject."

"The jumper's apartment is taken."

"How taken?"

"*Taken* taken. An applicant was already approved for it when we made our arrangement."

She raises her head and shifts her body so that she faces me. The couch rocks under her weight, sending tonight's dinner swishing around in my belly. "Don't fuck with me," Nikolina says.

"Why do you need to live here so badly? You get evicted or

something?" Her eyes veer sideways, I think, though it's difficult to see in the candlelight.

"I have friend with bad heart in building," she says. "I need to be close."

"What's her name? Maybe I can keep an eye on her for you."

She stares into my center, unwilling to give me anything.

"I've been thinking about the rest of the money," I say, hoping to lighten the mood. "You'll probably need it for move-in costs."

"I will pay you money," Nikolina says. "After that, I will owe you nothing."

"Suit yourself." I rest my bowl on the coffee table and head for the break room's toilet. I turn on the faucet to drown out the sound and sit with my head cradled in my forearms. When I come out after what feels like thirty minutes, the apartment is empty. Nikolina's handbag sits on the kitchen counter. I pull open the front door to find her standing in the hall.

"What are you doing?" I shout in as hushed a voice as I can manage.

She tilts her head my way. "I came out only to pee." Her hand lifts toward the ladies' room across the hall. "I'm sorry." But she's not speaking to me.

The outline of a man breaks the barrier of black at the far edge of the vending machine's radiance. His head is a balloon, smooth and faceless. A second passes in which I expect him to say something aggressive or else turn away, but he just stands very still in the shadows.

"It's nothing," Nikolina says. "Only dinner."

When the metallic clatter of coins rains down on the linoleum floor, I hook Nikolina's wrist and tug her into the break room, locking the door behind us.

"Did you see who it was?" I whisper. "Did he say anything to you?" I collect our bowls and rush them to the sink. "Help me clear up. Don't just stand there."

She falls onto the couch and drops her head into her hands.

"Okay, okay," I say, kneeling in front of her. "Just think. Was it security? Did you hear a radio or see a badge?"

"It wasn't security."

"How can you tell? Look at me."

"It wasn't security!" she shouts.

"Okay." I pat her shoulder. "We're okay then. We just need to get out of here." I close the record player and shove it behind the couch. Then I crack open the door and peek out. The hall, the expanse of dark between the vending machines and the exit sign, appears empty.

———

I'm forging Carlos Rodriguez's signature when Milda scampers into the office. I'm tracing it, to be precise. I'm exhausted. The late-night drive to Nikolina's and back, plus the paranoia . . . From the passenger seat, Nikolina would only give me directions to her complex. Wouldn't say a word otherwise. Went so far as to make me drop her at the corner, like I was going to see where she lives and stalk her or something. Before she opened the car door to exit, I almost commented on how close she lives to Silver Towers: twenty short blocks at most.

But to hell with it. Nothing is so clear as this: I fucked up.

The car was too chilly to sleep in. I just sat, rubbing my arms, waiting for the sun to rise and burn through the cold front.

It's difficult to describe this feeling of impending doom

hanging over me. I don't know which direction it will arrive from or in what form, but I have no doubt it's coming: obliteration. Some tenant will stroll in and demand a payoff. El Jefe might call me into his office in a couple days to tell me he knows what I've done. Will I just be fired or will charges be brought against me? At the very least, I'll lose my parking space, my access to a toilet.

I pull up my brother's number in my phone and type, *Would it still be cool if* . . . before backing out of my messages.

In the light of this sobering morning, I realize how much work I've neglected over the past several days, since I met Nikolina; that, if nothing else, my promotion seems as far away as ever.

When Milda chirps, "Ven, chico," I don't even try to hide my act of fraud. "Chico, ven!"

"What is it this time, Milda? Tell me."

She clutches my arm and begins to pull me out of my seat. I allow her to drag me into the hall, but when she presses the elevator's call button, I lose patience. "Can you tell me in English? I know you can."

She shakes her head.

Down the hall, the social worker's door is closed and the WILL RETURN AT clock is posted. The maintenance office is closed, too. I was so terrified to return to the building that I somehow managed to be the first employee on-site.

Strewn across the floor, from the vending machines to the wall opposite, are quarters and nickels and dimes. I turn and start back toward the leasing office.

Milda squeals.

"Un momento, señora," I shout over my shoulder. I grab the master key to Milda's apartment. As I pass my desk, I see Carlos's file next to the form I originally faxed to Walgreens. I realign last year's Employment Verification under this year's and finish tracing over the thin copy paper. I stick the form in the fax machine and redial the store before locking the office behind me.

Milda and I step into the elevator. She presses the button for the eighth floor—surprising, since the many times we've made this ride it's been to let her into her seventh-floor apartment. She speaks hushed Spanish, rubbing her hands together, watching the light as it moves up the columns of numbers. I catch the words *emergencia* and *enfermo*.

"¿Quién?" I ask her. She doesn't tell me who, but continues to wring her hands until the ascending light finally arrives at eight.

The elevator doors slide open. I follow Milda toward an open entryway at the end of the hall. She whimpers as we get near. She puts her hand over her face and points, urging me to continue without her.

I cross the threshold, finding the apartment's kitchenette dusky, empty. Sunlight peeks around the edges of the drawn curtains.

"Hello!" I shout. "¡Hola! Is everything okay?"

In the living room, a woman sits on the sofa that's pressed against the left wall. I don't immediately recognize her, except that she looks like the others—gray-white hair, liver-spotted skin. Her hands sit leaden in her lap, eyes planted on the wall ahead of her. There's no indication that she has heard or seen me, or even that she is breathing.

I begin to approach her, then see.

At the foot of the couch, khaki pants appear deflated over twiggy legs, and above that, a dark-colored polo. The torso seems to be missing, except for the hunched shoulders, which hold the arms parallel. My eyes come to rest on a baseball cap pulled low over the eyes.

This is Carlos Rodriguez's apartment. This is Carlos.

Rustling sounds from down the hall. A paramedic emerges from the bedroom carrying a baby blue sheet. It's not until she covers Carlos's body and head that I fully grasp what I am seeing. She sits, placing her gloved hand on Mrs. Rodriguez's shoulder.

The faint ding of the elevator rips through the silence, and I take a step backward, then another, until I'm out in the hallway, where it is again possible to breathe. I can't see Carlos from out here, only his doorway, only his kitchenette beyond, yet I can't seem to turn away from him. Wheels squeak. Two more first responders maneuver a gurney into the apartment.

Milda hasn't moved. "I didn't understand," I say to her.

She nods.

I head down to the office so I can call El Jefe to let him know we've lost another one. I get him on the line and ask, "What should we do about Mrs. Rodriguez?"

"Call the next person on the waitlist," he tells me. "She can't live here by herself." I think about the Independent Living Agreement. I vaguely hear my manager say, "This isn't a nursery home."

I hang up and call Nikolina.

When she picks up, her voice cracks, like maybe I've woken her. "Good news," I say, but from the way I say it, I know it is not. She starts to wail, so I say, "Listen, don't sweat last night." My words are of no consolation. "Listen, listen, listen," I repeat until she's quieted some. "An apartment opened up."

"I don't want!" she screams. "You don't get? It was him. It was for him I did this."

"Him?" I say. When I suggest we meet so I can return her

money, she hangs up on me. I drop the phone's receiver into its cradle, stunned not as much by our brief conversation as by the immense quiet that follows.

A slip of paper shoots into the office from under the closed door. I dash from my desk, but when I peek out, the hallway is empty. Who other than Carlos could move so swiftly? Who could have let Nikolina know?

I lift the paper, expecting that it will contain the demand. For what, I'm not sure. But when I flip the paper over it reveals only a hand-drawn horse. No, a donkey. The arrow points to the donkey's backside. Written at the tail end of the arrow, in English this time: *you*.

An hour hasn't passed since I returned to the office when I hear a fax coming in. It's from Walgreens. Carlos is their employee, according to the fax. At least he was. His start date was years ago. His hourly wage times hours worked adds up to not very much, but it's enough that we could charge his wife back rent. Given her impending eviction, we could realistically expect to use this information to keep her security deposit, which, for El Jefe, would be plenty.

I imagine him waving the fax like a gift certificate to be exchanged for some new blinds or a new light fixture or a new something that might increase the property's value. This would please Head Office. El Jefe might fulfill his promise to promote me. The signature validating this document is forged, of course, but who's left to call me out on it?

What I really wonder is this: Was it the running that killed

Carlos—the distance from the Towers to Walgreens to Nikolina's and back? Or was it that moment in the dark sliver of hallway, in the dead of night, when he finally stood still?

I put the fax aside and open up my teacher's certificate course on my office computer and work on it until my manager walks in. "They're dropping like cats and dogs," he says.

I fold up the fax with the drawing of the donkey and walk them to the shredder.

IF HE SUSPECTED HE'D GET SOMEONE KILLED THIS MORNING, DELANO WOULD NEVER LEAVE HIS COUCH

ut Delano is not clairvoyant. The closest he comes to a premonition is when, in the dream he is suffering through, his father says, *A storm's coming. Fool as you are, you can see that.* Delano forces his brain to escape into the waking world, but his TV insists: "Key West residents are expected to begin evacuating as early as this evening as Hurricane Irene continues to gather strength over the Atlantic."

The anchors discuss flood predictions as the camera cuts to a digitized map of Florida. The peninsula is altered by a translucent cone, which curves from the northern coast of Puerto Rico up past Hispaniola and Cuba to Miami. As the producers zoom in on Greater Miami, Delano imagines he can pinpoint his Cutler Bay town house and his body, stretched across the sofa.

He mutes the television and the front door rattles. A gruff voice bellows his name from outside, but it's not his father. It's Nordic, his erstwhile business partner, shouting, "Rise and shine!" To the right of the door, rose-gold light penetrates the kitchen's blinds—it's daybreak. He considers lying still until Nordic gives up, but there's no telling how long he will yell from the front porch, and the last thing Delano needs is for Nordic to wake his brother, Trelawny, whose hobby of late is judging Delano's failures. He stands, the room sways, and for a moment he's back in his dream: Delano is onstage, performing at Piranha, only he's forgotten the lyrics and his father is heckling him from the crowd, reminding him that *musician* is not a real occupation, and that Delano has sons of his own to support, and that Delano is outrageously late on the rent he owes him.

He blinks away the image, hobbles to the door, unlatches it, pushes. Nordic looms on the doorstep, bouncing in place. His jeans are tucked into shin-high boots, kneepads above that, weight belt at his waist. His beard juts out like broken spaghetti yet to be boiled. If wings emerged from his hard hat, he would be Thor. Odin, maybe. "The early bird catches the worm," Nordic says.

"Then what's the early worm catch?"

Nordic drags his knuckles across his chin. "Depends what type of hole he's digging in." He follows Delano back to the living room, launching into the conversation that has spanned the past year: how to resurrect their tree service. "This hurricane is it," he says. "That big break we need."

Delano lies back on the couch. *Shakespeare's Comedies* rests on the floor beside him, fenced in by a row of upright High Life bottles. He realizes that Trelawny likely left for work, and wonders if he needed the book to teach today.

Nordic hovers, slap-boxing his words as they exit his mouth. "This hurricane's got folks running dog-mad. We need to jump on this, Delano. We clear Lakes by the Bay by sundown, we might just earn ourselves a contract." He mashes his fist into his palm. "The whole property is ripe for a trimming."

Delano hates restraining Nordic's zeal but says, "What makes today different from all the times we tried before?"

The last time they went after the Lakes contract, Tina, the property manager, began scheduling weekly lunches to discuss their servicing her property. She made clear that Nordic's presence agitated her, so Delano went alone to her office, and Tina would drive him to Applebee's or Olive Garden in her Lexus RX. On the way, she'd fondle his locks, enumerating the times she'd seen his performances, telling him how much she loved reggae, pronouncing it "raygay," saying she kept an ounce or so at the crib if ever he wanted to pop by and blaze.

Delano regretted that she knew about his band at all and evaded her questions about his upcoming gigs. He learned to tie his dreads back and hide them under a tam before seeing Tina.

At the restaurant she'd chat him up, slapping his thigh, patting closer to his crotch with each glass of Crown she downed, till he'd ask about the bid and she'd seize his forearm, bring her pink face within inches of his, and say in a husky whisper, "These things take time."

On their final lunch Tina grew brazen, emboldened by the restaurant's two-for-one special, and as they arrived back at her SUV she slipped her fingers between Delano's legs from behind and cupped his genitals. Delano whirled to escape her and his elbow cracked against her cheekbone. She unclenched him, nearly toppling. Instinctively, he reached to catch her, but she steadied herself, and as she did, her lips eased into a disconcerted grin.

All that time he'd put into getting the contract—all the proposals and lunches, and the fingers, always creeping over his body. "I would rather starve," he told her.

Her smile deflated. The sun cut his skin for the entire hour-long walk to retrieve his truck from her office.

Thinking on it now, Delano wonders why he didn't suck it up and sleep with her. He doubts there's a property manager in Miami who doesn't expect some sort of kickback. He would like to believe he doesn't need a reason to have refused her, but it occurs to him that a year ago he was still hoping Shelly-Anne hadn't left him for good.

He never told anyone the details of what happened that day, and he doesn't plan to now. He knows Nordic would ask, *What kind of man turns down sex?* He would belittle Delano as his amusement turned to outrage. This deal could have kept them afloat while the economy was tanking, when so many of their contracts were expiring without renewal.

Nordic had returned to bouncing at a watering hole out near the Everglades. He didn't profess to hate the work, weaning men from their bloodthirstiness, maiming men's bodies. Nordic hated that the job took him away from his daughters' bedtime reading.

"Say Tina gives us the contract," Delano says, "or even a day's work. How you think the two of us can clear so many trees before this storm hits? This isn't some rinky-dink complex. Lakes is neighborhoods within neighborhoods. A veritable labyrinth."

"A veritable gold mine," Nordic counters, gesticulating overhead. "We'll get ourselves a crew. We'll recruit some laborers from down at the Depot."

"You charging them on your Home Depot card?"

Nordic shrugs.

"How much cash you have?"

Nordic looks to his boots, shamefaced. "I would've had the cash, Del, but Eliana, you know how she is. She went in the account, took a couple grand out, and bought the runts a shit-load of American Girl dolls and OshKosh. The rest she went 'n' wired her family in Bogotá, and, hell, that's money I just can't get back."

Delano lifts *Shakespeare's Comedies* and rests its open pages over his face. He wonders if Brandon, his and Shelly-Anne's firstborn, started the guitar lessons Delano bought him for his birthday, or if she even gave Brandon the card he sent. When he first called to ask about it, Shelly said, "Of course you get him lessons out in West Covina. Of course you buy something that's going to strip hours from my life." Delano had spent weeks researching affordable instructors in the L.A. area. Covina seemed close enough on the map. "And who gets a four-year-old guitar lessons?" Shelly asked. "The boy can't sit still five minutes."

"You start them early," Delano answered. He explained that he'd recently begun giving lessons to a four-year-old. Of course, he'd taken on anyone Guitar Center sent his way, irrespective of how likely the prospective students were to pick up his lessons. "If you hadn't left, I'd teach Brandon myself."

"Fi what? So he can grow up to be like you?" Shelly laughed. "Why you couldn't just come take him and Hadyn to Disney-land?" Delano still couldn't believe she'd named their second son Hadyn. He'd wanted to name him something powerful, like Zion or Judah, but *Hadyn* had already been written on the birth record by the time it was handed to him to sign.

At this point he wishes they could just speak to each other with civility. But the anger in her voice always makes him defensive. "Who said you could take my pickney to California indefinitely?" Delano had asked. "Me going get a lawyer, Shelly. Me going sue your kidnapping ass." He'd been threatening this for months now, though they both knew he'd never have the money for a lawsuit. Rich-people threats just sound pathetic, impotent, in the mouths of the poor.

"We need this," Nordic says, drawing Delano out of his reverie. "Even a day's work on a neighborhood that size can get us back on track."

"We need cash, Nordic. Up front." Delano's voice sounds muffled against the pages of the book, and this comforts him. Since Shelly took his children, his entire life has felt distorted—populated by phantom limbs, things and people who should be present but are not. Of late, further distortion makes him feel closer to wholly inverted. NotDelano. NegativeDelano. "If we don't have the money after running your 'crew' through hell and back, you'd better hide the chain saws before telling them."

"Maybe we could pawn something we're not using right now," Nordic says.

"You have something to pawn?"

"I'm thinking your Fender, maybe. And your amps. That's got to be worth—"

"Forget it," Delano says.

"We'd get it back after."

"How much is OshKosh going for? Maybe let's pawn that."

Delano hears Nordic land heavily in the armchair beside the couch, hears him mumble, "Well, I just thought . . ."

No unaltered plan of Nordic's will ever work out, and Delano's not about to gamble his guitar on one of his schemes. To pull this off they would need an experienced crew; they would need to somehow convince Tina to give them the job; and on top of all that they would need a working bucket truck—theirs is still in the shop for nonpayment on the last set of repairs.

In the silence of Nordic's wallowing, Delano hears Shelly laughing at him from somewhere within the couch cushions. Before the split, he'd recorded her laugh and set it as his ringtone, and he's been unable to change it since he dropped his flip phone and smashed its inner screen. In the context of their current relationship, her voice sounds mocking and cruel.

He fishes the phone from between the cushions and sees his father's number scroll across its outer display. "We could get Mikey and his crew on board," Delano says.

"Mikey?" Delano can hear Nordic's lips smacking over something. "*Crackhead* Mikey? Last time I set eyes on ol' midnight Mike, you were trying to hit him with an ax handle."

The last job they did together, Mikey cut into a tree wrong and nearly crushed Delano underneath it. It's also true he's an addict. But if their plan is to work, they'll have to prey on people's desperation. It's the end of the month, and knowing Mikey, he's already fed his addiction with next month's rent money, so there'll be incentive for him to work, even for a guy who once tried to bludgeon him.

Then there's Tina. She'll never in a million years give them a long-term contract, but the threat of being sued over some homeowner's Benz getting crushed by a fallen tree limb during the storm might supersede her bruised ego. The bigger companies are likely busy doing city jobs, and the not-so-big companies that are any good at staying in business will have to tend to their contracts first. If they're lucky, Tina might not view a one-day gig as much of a win for them.

"You sure Tina doesn't already have someone?"

"I drove by on the way over and nobody's there now. I can tell you that much."

Delano removes the book from his face. Nordic's just finished rolling a white-boy. "Then all we need is the bucket."

A flicker of excitement dances across Nordic's face. He explodes out of the armchair. "I'll pop over to Rusty's and tell that son-bitch he either gives us our goddamn bucket truck or I'll rip his head off!"

This is a bad idea. On matters of violence, Nordic doesn't speak in metaphor, and Rusty doesn't open his yard unless he's locked and loaded.

"I'll deal with Rusty. I need you to get over to the Lakes office before it opens and wait for Tina." Delano stands, feeling some of Nordic's electricity pulsing through him. "This is important. Make Tina understand how serious this hurricane is. They're saying it's a category three?"

Nordic's nodding, tongue out, like a dog awaiting his treat.

"Tell her it's a four—going to be here tomorrow. I don't care what the news says. The dump is closed tomorrow, so it's decision time. She wants to decide at noon; noon's too late. Tell her it's now." Delano snaps his fingers. "Now or never. And listen."

Nordic stops panting. He tucks the spliff behind his ear.

"Be firm on our pricing—no, up the rate ten percent. If she complains, that means she's giving in. If she complains, you tell her to suck out herself." Delano is down the hall getting his gear before Nordic can answer, but he knows he's listening, because he hasn't heard the lighter flick.

═══

"Hurricane-force gales are expected to touch down in Miami-Dade in just a little over thirty-six hours, if Irene stays its course . . ."

Delano is in the passenger seat of Nordic's dually, on the way to Rusty's Repair, when he starts feeling it—like he's swallowed a fishing weight, a sinker that's still on the line. It's a pendulum in his stomach, scraping his insides. They've left Cutler Bay, heading southwest through Goulds, flying past churches and Church's Chicken, and he's supposed to convince a guy he hasn't paid in two months that he should give him his truck back.

Nordic can always tell when Delano's lost enthusiasm for an idea. He clicks off the radio, then slaps a massive hand across Delano's chest. "You got this. That pig-porking prick says you can't have the truck, tell him two hundred eighty pounds of Swampbilly is coming for his ass." Nordic cracks a Popeye smile, teeth adjoined at one end, the other clamped over an invisible pipe. "And I's hungry!"

Delano croaks, half belch, half laugh.

"I know what you need." Nordic thrusts his arm behind his seat and flings his backpack into Delano's lap. "Small pocket."

Delano opens it, figuring he'll find a flask or a tallboy, but finds a sandwich wrapped in plastic and a green apple.

"I want you to take that apple, and the minute you sense he's not gon' give you the truck, I want you to bite into that green little fucker."

"Fi what?"

"Trust me. The second he stops taking you seriously, chomp into that sour apple, and give him the condescendingest face he ever saw. It'll sour you up good, like you'll flip if he doesn't give it to you."

Delano sucks his teeth and lowers the backpack to the floor.

"It's that you get the jitters sometimes, Del. And you know well as I do, if I go in there, ain't but one of us coming out alive. But you can't go in acting like him not giving it to us is a option. 'Cause it ain't a option. We got mouths to feed, gosh darn it." He says the last part under his breath. Delano wants desperately to believe what Nordic believes, that because they want or need a thing, they should have it.

They pull up to Rusty's yard, and Delano hops out. At the driver's-side window, Nordic hangs his head over his arm and asks, "Should I pass by Mikey on the way to the Lakes?"

"He might take off if he sees me coming," Delano agrees.

"Don't forget this." Nordic tosses Delano the apple. "Give him hell," he says, and revs the engine before tearing down the road.

When the dually turns the corner at the end of the block, Delano remembers that his brother's book, which he'd intended to drop at Palmetto Prep, is still in Nordic's truck. He feels certain Trelawny needed it to teach today. It occurs to him that his brother may have planned to pick it up on his lunch break, and now it will have gone missing. And isn't that the way of things? You try to make a situation better, only to make it worse. Better to do nothing.

———

Delano once considered himself an optimist, someone who controlled his own fate. Before the 2008 recession, life had mostly gone his way. He'd dodged the horrors of desk work and student loans—in fact, he'd avoided college altogether—the groveling for jobs and promotions, the humbling himself to those people arbitrarily ranked as his superiors, all the things that soured life, that turned life into drudgery. He'd started working for a tree service in high school before borrowing money from his father for start-up costs and partnering with Nordic, who'd been in the business for years. He took night classes to get certified as an arborist and loved that so few people knew what an arborist did, so he could explain, "I'm a tree doctor." He took pride in being his own boss—Shelly, he believes, once took pride in that, too. Neither she nor their kids would ever see him bow, humiliate himself for some sadistic supervisor.

At least, that's what Delano had believed. At some point toward the end, before he realized it was the end, when the work had all but dried up and he returned home day after day with no new clients, Shelly said, "Couldn't you just get a job? At least till things pick up back?"

"I could gig more," he'd told her. "Maybe it's time I focus on the music." Performing wasn't steady either at that point, but at least his shows left him with walking-around money. And since Delano's father owned the house they lived in, he took care of getting them extensions on the rent—he counted that as one of his contributions. Shelly's marketing job at Sony Music would have to cover the rest. Maybe if he redirected all his energy toward promoting his band, the Zioneers, Shelly would stop being cagey with her industry connections.

Then Shelly was calling from her mother's house in California to say she'd transferred offices and wouldn't be returning. Even then he couldn't grasp just how far a turn his fortune had taken, asking, "When should I expect the boys?"

Shelly said, "If I abandoned my children, you think it's you I'd trust to take care of them?" He hadn't asked her to elaborate, but she'd added, "You're not a provider, Delano. You're a liability."

He palms the apple now, then hits the buzzer at Rusty's gate.

Rusty's yard is a fortress, a tract of fenced-off land in a neighborhood with few or no property codes. Across the road from him sit squat bungalows—hot pinks and purples you'd expect to see beachside in the Bahamas. Their yards are one matte sprawl of concrete, hosting a Chevy on blocks, loose wheels, and a tricycle with absentee handlebars—an arsenal of debris for the storm to launch.

The air is electric in the still before a hurricane, and now a cool breeze raises Delano's arm hairs. The curtain of humidity that hangs over South Florida is lifting. A storm *is* coming and Delano finds an odd sense of euphoria in accepting this fact. He's never seen men so content as when they have to abandon the menial tasks put on them by their nine-to-fives to come home and board up their houses, to leave what does not matter to protect what does. The farce of daily life is put on pause. The weather transcends small talk: *Could this be the next Andrew?* Andrew's name is always invoked—South Florida's Christ-event, its marker for before and after.

He's seen the relief of abandoned ambitions, too; dreams left half-chased in the face of survival. Imminent disaster brings simplicity: Run through a checklist dictated by channel 7 news—canned food, water, matches, candles, batteries, flashlights, portable radio. Are the windows boarded up; is the bathtub filled? Relax, then. Crack a beer. Relish the fact that you did all you could, and should the worst transpire, come Monday, you might not have an office to return to. The roof you slave to keep over your family's head, the problems and the expectations, the dreams deferred, the rent and back rent and your landlord father—all of it might just have blown away.

He hits the buzzer again.

There's movement in the yard. Hounds bark, shoes crunch over grass, the eye slot above the gate's handle slides open. The sun is catching against Rusty's orange eyelashes. Behind their stillness, Rusty's mental clockwork is ticking toward a decision.

"Rusty!" Delano sends one syllable low, the other high, in a voice they use in beer and chips commercials during the Super Bowl, when they try to make the twenty-one-to-thirty-five-year-old suburban male demographic seem dumber and happier than it could ever hope to be. "It's me! Delano."

"I know who you are," Rusty says, his eyes unwavering. "What I want to know is whether you possess the nerve to show up at my gate without my money."

Delano raises the apple to his chin, then lowers it. He slips "Yeah" under "I came to bail ol' girl out of lockup."

Rusty hesitates for a moment. "About fucking time," he says.

The eye slot shuts. Keys jingle. A chain clangs against the gate. Rusty rolls the gate open a crack, and Delano scooches in. He follows Rusty across his dying lawn, through a maze of blue-collar small-business vehicles. There's a powder-pink ice cream truck replete with an airbrushed Mickey Mouse, except this is not your typical copyright-infringement job. This Mickey's face is chocolate brown—an urban, friendlier Mickey for the Black youth of Miami.

They pass a short yellow school bus and several vans used for private busing before the lawn service vehicles appear alongside riding mowers and trailer hitches. Delano wonders how many of these Rusty will have to move to create a path large enough for his truck to make it to the front gate.

Inside Rusty's garage, his desk sits amid mounds of metal scrap and grainy stains in the concrete. The garage doors are rolled up on both sides, and there, nestled in the far corner of the backyard, is Delano's bucket truck.

Rusty motions for him to sit in the miniature orange chair in front of the desk, while Rusty plops into a black BarcaLounger on the opposite side. He produces a ledger from a drawer, along with the keys to the truck, and slams them on the desktop with brutish force.

Half of Delano's ass fits in the kiddie-sized chair, so he rotates from one cheek to the next. "What, did you rob a nursery school?"

Rusty stops flipping through his ledger and points a pen at Delano. "You worry about the furniture in your own rathole, or wherever you people come from." He scribbles something in the book. "I'm not the thief. I pay off my debts. On time."

Delano raises his hands, palms forward. "Relax yourself, Rusty. Nobody's a thief. I'm here, aren't I?"

Rusty slumps in his seat. "I should've scrapped that piece-of-shit cherry picker a month ago. You want me to relax?"

"What's better?" Delano asks. "You work with us here and there and keep customers loyal, or you do us dirty and lose our business forever?"

Rusty says, "Your half-wit partner has been failing to build a legitimate business since before you probably had a green card. He's been failing to pay me on time for half as long. He picks up some"—he gestures toward Delano—"*arborist*, and that's supposed to convince somebody he's legit? Listen closely," Rusty says. "I don't give a shit if I ever see the likes of you dead-beats again." He tears a white sheet out of the ledger and flings it toward Delano. "Just gimme my money, and poof." His hand mimes Delano's vanishing into thin air.

The invoice hangs off the edge of the desk, displaying the total owed, but the writing—the numbers—are all blurry. Delano says, "You wan' sling insults, yeah? Look here, you bumbarasclat pussyclat boy. I have a job lined up, and they're waiting for the truck so we can do the job, so we can get paid, so we can pay you."

"Do the job so you can pay me?" He rolls the sentence over his tongue, alternating stresses. "Do the job *so* you can pay me?"

Shelly-Anne laughs from his pocket, and as Delano pulls out his phone to silence her, he sees his father's text message scroll across the outer display: *We need to figure out something with this rent. You need to call me.*

"Are you telling me . . . ," Rusty says. "And you expect . . ."

Delano slips the phone into his pocket and lifts the apple to his mouth, crunching into it, feeling his cheeks pucker inward. He tucks the chewed bits into his cheeks with his tongue and tries to speak without spitting it back on himself. "The only way we can pay you," he says, "is if we do this job."

Rusty dabs a finger across his nose. He opens the desk's top drawer and places his hand inside it. "Leave," he says.

"Just hear me out." Wads of apple drop into Delano's lap.

"Get the hell out of here!"

Delano stands and takes a few steps toward the exit before hearing the drawer closing, before hearing the jerk of released pressure off the BarcaLounger as Rusty rises to follow him out.

When Delano reaches the gate, he rolls it open, thinking of a last-ditch argument. What if Rusty undid the work? Stupid, not just because it would involve Rusty doing more work, but because they brought the truck in when its arm malfunctioned and nearly ejected Delano. He'd managed to latch onto the branch he was pruning—otherwise he'd have been flung from two stories up. He takes a final chomp on the apple as his phone buzzes again. A text message from Nordic: *It's all lined up, bud! U get the truck?*

Delano looks over his shoulder: Rusty is only a few yards behind.

Delano lifts the padlock off the chain hanging from the gate's inner handle. He turns and watches Rusty's eyes widen as he raises the lock, balancing it off the tip of his index finger. He balls the lock into his fist, brings both hands together, and cocks back for a Hail Mary.

Rusty says, "Boy, you better not," but he's already rushing past Delano to follow the object's ascension, its trajectory toward the bungalows. As Rusty reaches the threshold he stops, realizing, perhaps, that what Delano threw was not the lock but the apple core. Delano sends his size-eleven boot into Rusty's ass, knocking him to the dirt patch outside the gate.

He slides the gate shut and gets the padlock clasped over the chained handles just as the wood thumps and trembles. "Just hear me out," Delano says, and waits for Rusty to respond or else heave himself against the gate again. Instead, a chunk of cedar erupts from the gate, a bullet whizzing into the yard, striking something metal.

Delano throws himself under a rust-eaten pickup, thinking, *I'll wait here till it's safe again*, before realizing this is a terrible idea, perhaps his worst today. He clutches two patches of grass and drags himself over the ground, out the other side of the truck. He's having a difficult time standing. His legs are gelatin, crushed pig bone and boiled cow hoof, and he's about to die for a 1982 bucket truck that nearly killed him once already.

Above, against a powder-pink backdrop of sky, chocolate Mickey stares down at Delano like a god. In his benevolent, wide-eyed levity, Mickey maintains a stiff-lipped smile, performing a ventriloquist's trick. In a voice that sounds much like Delano's, he whispers, "Run."

Delano springs into the junkyard maze, banging his body against side mirrors and fenders, passing a taxi and the lawn mowers, and finally he's back in Rusty's garage. Another shot goes off, but the sound is no closer than before. The lock. He's trying to shoot the lock, Delano thinks. He slows, careful not to slip on the grease streaks coating the garage floor.

On the desk, a rabbit foot keychain rests atop the open ledger. He scoops up the keys, looking down at the yellow merchant's carbon copy of the invoice Nordic signed. He rips it out and crumples it, along with the white customer copy still hanging off the desk's edge, into his pocket, then heads out back.

Behind the garage, the dogs thrash in their cages; a blurred cyclone of tan and black fur; rottweilers or Dobermans or some ill mix of man-eater. The bucket truck is backed into the yard's far-right corner. Delano has no idea how he is going to get the truck out. He hasn't thought that far ahead. To his left, there's a clear path of grass for a hundred or so feet, before a rusted-out Chrysler blocks much of the path forward.

He pulls the truck's door open.

He could climb onto the truck, use its height to hop over the fence, and leave Rusty searching his yard for him for the next two hours. He'd lose the bucket that way, but he'd be back to the safety of his couch by lunch. Then? More dodging his father? More wondering when he'll ever see his kids?

He clambers into the driver's seat, sticks the key in the ignition, turns it. She coughs twice, then roars to life, drowning the dogs' growls beneath the squeal of loose belts and the kick of the motor. Beyond the Chrysler: another two hundred feet before the yard hits the fence. There should be a street on the other side. If he can plow through the Chrysler's tail, he can ram down the fence. *The bucket's a tank*, he tells himself.

He yanks the door shut, shifts into drive, jams down on the gas pedal. The truck jerks forward. Rusty sprints out from the garage. He shouts something, but the truck tears into the Chrysler's tail at twenty-five miles per hour. The bucket hesitates against the car, then the Chrysler fishtails out of the way. *Push it.* Thirty, thirty-five miles per hour. The truck's fender rams the fence and it rives in two, somersaulting over his windshield, crunching beneath his tires. Delano spins the steering wheel right and the truck's tires roll free of the fence post panel, debris left in a gray, empty road.

———

"I got it," Delano tells Nordic over the phone. He leaves out the part about Rusty or the police maybe being after him. He's crossing back over U.S. 1, same way he came. "Mikey and them geared up?"

"That's the only thing," Nordic says. "You're gonna need to swing by Mikey's. He says you're gonna need to apologize."

Delano spots Sandy's coming up on his left. The Zioneers had a four-month residency there before it all went to shit. They covered reggae hits, from Bob to Beres to Barrington, with Delano singing lead, but Camille, his co-vocalist and bassist, along with their keyboard player, wanted to play more originals than their contract allowed. Two months in, Sandy's manager, Paulo, called to inform Delano that Camille had showed up at the bar aiming to renegotiate their agreement. "I thought we had an understanding," Paulo said over the phone. "Get your people under control or I'm going to have to go in a new direction."

"We can' be puppets all we life," Camille said when Delano confronted her at their next rehearsal.

"That's ego talking," Delano told her.

"H'ego?" Delano remembers Camille adding the *h* every time. "Is me 'ave the h'ego h'over ya so, mister front man?" He had attributed much of the band's stage presence to Camille's size— often surpassing his six feet two inches, depending on her choice of heels—but during their confrontation the word *imposing* took on new connotations.

"Was Hendrix a puppet when he covered 'All Along the Watchtower'?" Delano asked. "When he did 'Hey Joe'?"

"So now the man think he's Hendrix," Camille said.

Delano argued that to ruin a good thing before it got good was ass-backward. Truthfully, he didn't feel like a puppet singing songs written and performed by the masters. He felt like a vessel. He kept to himself that he flat out needed the money, that losing this job would be his undoing.

The band resolved to play out the rest of their contract at Sandy's, but the next several performances were uneven. Camille wasn't feeling it and it showed. Paulo noticed, too, and he replaced them with a band that played funk. The Zioneers split after that, though Delano promised his drummer, Busha, that they'd rebuild with new members. That was over a year ago now. For the first time today he says the words aloud: "I'm supposed to be a performer."

Realizing he is still on the phone with Nordic, Delano asks, "Do you know what I just went through?"

"We all got to eat that pie sometimes," Nordic says.

Delano snaps shut the phone, then reaches into his pocket for what he hopes is the only evidence that Rusty ever worked on their bucket truck. He makes certain to tear both copies of Rusty's invoice to bits before tossing them out the window: white and yellow flakes catching in the wind.

———

"I'm a man like you're a man," Mikey is saying through the black bars guarding his driveway.

"Sure," Delano says, staring into the remarkable brightness of the whites of Mikey's eyes.

"There was no need," Mikey says. "Totally uncalled-for."

"You're right. I'm not saying you're not right." Delano grips one of the bars, growing impatient. The bucket is pulled up on the side of the street, running. A series of dents have disfigured the fender and hood, though the truck looks otherwise undamaged. "But don't forget, Mikey, you nearly killed me."

"I don't even very much know about that. I mean, accidents happen." He leans in, peering up the street, as though he also stole something. "I almost had to drop one on you."

"You did drop one on me. That's what I'm saying."

"A dime," Mikey clarifies. "To Po 9." He shakes his head to emphasize. "That's near worth compensating."

"You do a job tweaked out your mind, almost kill me, and I owe you compensation?" It would have been easy to reduce Mikey to a junkie fuckup if they hadn't gone to junior high and high school together. Instead, Delano sees in Mikey what he sees in himself: limitless wasted potential.

"I can't say if I was tweaked or not," Mikey says. "But I'm thinking it affected me. The violence. I'm thinking PTSD."

"You must be high right now."

"Nope," he says.

"Hear me nuh, Mikey. I can't stand up here and talk fuckery all morning. You want compensation? Work. That's what I'm offering."

Mikey looks around uneasily. "You can cash out today?"

Delano doesn't want to tell a lie, and maybe it's not one, so he says, "Just you. The rest of them will have to wait till the job pays. You tell them what you want."

Mikey nods, looking back at the house.

"Who've you got with you?" Delano asks.

"Peanut, Jesus, Jorge. Rob's back there, but he might not be in any condition."

"I thought Rob caught a body?"

"That's White Rob. That nigga'll never see the light of day," Mikey says. "I'm talking 'bout Black Rob."

"Oh," Delano says. "Well, go wake him nuh. If you can drag him out the house, then he can help lug branches."

———

Amazing, Delano is thinking when they make it over to Lakes by the Bay in two truckloads. He can see Nordic's dually parked in front of the leasing office, so he pulls onto the grass and directs Mikey to park his truck half a block up the street. The crew seems mostly sober, mostly itching for a fix. Delano instructs the men to get started on the trees over on the adjacent street, then heads toward the office. Nordic is in his truck eating his sandwich when Delano yanks open the passenger door.

"What'd Tina say, exactly?"

"Wants you to ask for it," Nordic says, looking straight ahead through the windshield.

"Rass, Nordic."

Nordic scoots across the seat and pats Delano's shoulder. "I already gave her the rundown. Alls you gotta do is smooth things over. She's waiting on you. Here." Nordic hands Delano what's left of his joint and says, "This ought to mellow you."

There have been select times in history when the seemingly impossible has been accomplished through mere necessity. Delano tells himself this as he enters the office, only he can't think of a single example beyond this morning's incidents. He shuffles toward Tina, who sits behind her desk, sneering. Her multitiered bun, with its burgundy streaks and its red and blue and green scrunchies, reminds Delano of one of Brandon's first toys, a set of stackable rings from Fisher-Price.

When he's certain he can bear the silence no longer, he says, "Nordic said you need me to sign the paperwork?"

"Nordic said no such thing," Tina responds.

"If you're busy, I can come back when we're finished."

"Let me be clear," Tina says. "If you boys touch one leaf, I'm calling the po-lice."

"*Tiii-naaaaa*," he says, massaging her name. "You mad?"

"Why would I be? Could it be the bruise you left on my face last time I saw you? Think on it while you pack up and get from the property."

Delano sighs like a whipped dog and drops his chin to his chest. He can tell Tina takes this sign of resignation to mean he will leave, but instead he slumps down into one of the two chairs facing her. "I fucked up," he says. "I say the wrong thing sometimes, and sometimes even the right things come out twisted." He aims to appear sorrowful and pitiful, but when he looks Tina in the eyes, his own start to water, and he realizes the emotion is real. He can't close the tap.

The corner of Tina's mouth drifts toward the edge of her face, her lips parted. The expression is that of someone watching a grown man vomit on himself.

"Tina," he says, "I always liked you."

Tina's laugh is forced. "How dumb do I look to you?"

"No, listen, I did. Not because you have this job, or a fancy car." He jabs his thumb toward the parking lot. "Not because you have anything, but because you earned these things."

Tina blinks down at her desk, as if involuntarily remembering a set of trials she's endured. She asks, "So?"

"So I wanted that. I wanted to earn the Lakes contract. You took that from me."

"I took it?"

He nods. "The minute you made it about something other than business. Our bid was the best for this property and you know it. But none of that mattered once you compromised the dynamic. You know what this meant to me? Do you have any idea?"

Tina says, "You'll say anything. That's how desperate you are."

"Maybe," Delano says. "Maybe this is ugly enough to be truth I'm speaking. It doesn't make you feel any type of way but sick, does it?"

"Give me one good reason I should help you."

"I'm not asking for a favor. If you don't want a long-term arrangement, fine. But this storm's coming. It's coming and we're the ones who're here. Let's deal." Delano sticks his knuckle into the corner of his eye, wiping away the wet.

She asks, "You tell your partner what happened? You go out and laugh about it with all your boys?"

"I'm sorry if I bruised you, Tina. But you can't go around grabbing . . . let's just call it what it is: assault."

Tina looks horrified. "Is that what you think it was?"

"You mean aside from sexual harassment?"

"I thought we were having fun," she says.

"Look, I don't mean to throw phrases out like I'm planning to press charges or call your corporate office or sue or anything like that." Delano can already hear the saws going, but he says, "If we're going to do this, if anyone's going to, they'll need to start right away, Tina. Like right now."

Tina bites her lip. "I didn't mean to . . . harass you." And before Delano can say, *Yeah, you did*, Tina adds, "Just this once. For real. Just today. And not a dollar over your original pricing."

Outside, the saws are going and Mikey is rising in a sky so blue that the bucket containing him looks like a cloud. Peanut and Jesus have their spikes in, shimmying up trees farther down the street, and Rob is hauling what they're dropping over to Mikey's truck bed. Nordic hangs halfway out of the bucket truck's driver's-side door, directing Jorge on something.

Delano scans the block, searching for Rusty, the cops, but the road is empty. If they can finish this job, they'll be flush enough to pay Rusty back for his gate, his work on the truck, and a little extra, Delano thinks, so there's no hard feelings. Then he'll pay back his father—not everything at once, but this month's rent and next month's. And he'll need to book a flight to Los Angeles to see his sons.

A vaguely familiar sensation starts creeping up, an emotion akin to joy, but he beats it down, fearing he has gotten away with something. Still an idea slips through, despite his efforts to contain it. An idea that he controls his destiny.

Mikey's up top with the chain saw, dropping branches, when the bucket's arm starts gyrating. Mikey doesn't notice at first that it's not the truck moving but the arm, of its own will. Delano yells for Nordic to kill the engine, but his voice is lost under the saws. He calls Mikey's name, but the truck's arm is already catapulting the bucket to its apex, windmilling Mikey and his screaming chain saw into a hemorrhaging street.

———

Delano is onstage at Piranha, cradled within its spotlight. To his left, on a blue screen, white words fill with yellow as they scroll, but having no need for the lyrics, he stares into the spotlight and wails into a microphone. The instrumentals of "Three Little Birds" blare from the speakers on either side of the stage. Bodies sway in the dim, shallow crowd. When the song ends, he stumbles offstage through the weak applause and back-pats and lands at the far end of the bar, where his brother's book reserves his seat. He doesn't recall how he got here, doesn't know how much time has elapsed, but he's certain school has let out by now. The regulars have been tipping beer into his mug each time they order another pitcher.

Camille, all six feet two inches of her, straddles the stool beside him and says, "You've never sung it so sad. Rough day?"

Delano thinks about the patrolman who questioned him while the paramedics scraped Mikey off the street, the one who informed him that they were impounding the bucket truck and that he'd better get a lawyer. He thinks again about how he destroyed his only evidence that Rusty was supposed to have fixed the truck. "I've never felt better," Delano tells Camille.

"Let me buy you a beer," she says. "So there's no bad blood between us." Her hair was dark the last time he saw her. With her cornrows popping blond against her glistening, rich brown skin, Camille looks to Delano like a celestial being come down to smite him. "Me no hear nothing more 'bout your music," she says. "You mussee busy with your tree service? Business take off so?"

Delano says, "I'm recently retired," and Camille laughs.

"You're too young to retire. You must mean you're transitioning."

"If you're buying that drink, buy it nuh. You don't know a storm's on the way?"

This, too, Camille finds funny. "How long you been in here?

The hurricane turned. It's missing us completely. That ought to cheer you up."

Delano lowers his forehead onto the bar.

Camille flags the bartender to order him a Heineken. "Me back working with Busha, you know?" she says, and Delano thinks, *Here we go.*

"Our new singer's a songwriter, too. A true artist."

Delano faces Camille to allow her the pleasure of annihilating him head-on.

"But every now and then when we're onstage," she continues, "I look over and it's you I expect to see."

"Nice of you to say." He raises his bottle in appreciation, then guzzles it.

"We're playing out on Ocean Drive tomorrow night. You should come check us."

Delano sees tomorrow and the next day and the next with startling clarity. He'll hardly leave his bedroom for fear of what he'll have to endure: court appearances and threats of imprisonment, his father's intensified attempts to collect, increasingly convoluted communications with Shelly-Anne, and, worst of all, the deficiency—the love he can't project across three thousand miles to his children, the love that can't serve as a beacon to call his family back to him. You can't project love while burying yourself. You can't emit love while flickering out, evaporating into the ether. And he must tuck himself away from the envelopes that will arrive with official seals and the knocks that will start at his front door and reverberate throughout the house to the base of his spine, and he'll try to escape his regrets, too, his trauma, his guilt, Mikey, though they'll find him, at the bottom of empties, in the embers of each spliff drag. He'll hide to the point of hunger, which won't be far off, since he'll hardly have money to feed himself now. And when the hunger becomes intolerable, when it muddles his thoughts and rearranges the dimensions of his face, and when he can't recognize himself in his bathroom mirror, finally, he'll emerge to sell himself to the first available boss, and when he feels it, the gratitude, that is when he will be wholly inverted. A phantasm Delano.

The DJ announces that Delano is next in the queue, though he can't recall submitting another song. Camille winks and says, "Special request." He could ignore the DJ, though they're too familiar, and Delano has too much presence to blend into this thin crowd, to make it seem as though he's left. He considers actually leaving, beginning to vanish, but he knows himself well enough not to pretend he could walk away from a beckoning microphone, even now. He lingers, remembering his purest, most concentrated self, and decides he'll latch on to that version for the fleeting moments he can. He stands and begins taking gradual steps toward the stage. If he can create a deep enough impression of this Delano, like tracing his name until what lies beneath bears the indent, perhaps at some point he'll find his way back.

IF I SURVIVE YOU

This is a version of how it ends: Your father stands below you on the algae-stained steps of your childhood home, muttering, "He's killing me." He says this of your brother, your delinquent roommate. His sideburns flicker like crows' wings as hot air sifts Mount Trashmore's stench through the sloping yard. It's 2012, December—late in the year for the landfill's funk to carry on the wind, plating Cutler Bay in putridity. You suspect your brother hasn't paid rent in years, testing the limits of his position as family favorite, but now your father tells you, "Me can't pay mortgage here *and* on my house."

You want to remind him that "here" is *also* his house, and that, as you've faithfully paid your share of rent since moving back in two years ago, doesn't he mean to say, *I can't pay one and a half mortgages?*

Instead you say, "So?" adding, "Kick him out." You're surprised at how quickly guilt flips your stomach inside out. Delano is, after all, the person who took you in to this house when living out of your car became untenable after your father kicked you out of his Palmetto Bay residence. Though he's stopped confiding in you, it's clear that your brother has been consumed by depression, to say nothing of his external troubles, which arrive, in part, via mail from the county clerk's office. Last year, one of his workers died in a freak accident, and a civil suit soon followed. He's still waiting to learn if his liability insurance will cover that. For these reasons, he has your sympathy. Still, your brother, of late, seems intent on destroying what's yours—your home, your relationships, your mental stability. So *Kick him out* is not wholly unreasonable.

Your father seems not to notice that you've spoken at all, and says, "What if you buy the house from me?" which sounds to you a lot like *What if this became exclusively your problem?* He quickly follows with an exact cash price. It's a small sum for a house, you admit. More than fair. Too reasonable, really: $11,698 even.

"No, thanks."

It's the obvious answer. Why else would it fall from your mouth with so little assistance from your brain? You suspect there's a host of ills pushing the town house along the path toward condemnation, but the layman's diagnosis is this: your childhood home is sinking.

The west end dips into the hill below; ivy tendrils hooked to its face are dragging it into some hellmouth. Near the east end, a fissure runs a foot down the exterior wall. Your father has hung an unvarnished birdhouse with wooden chimes to veil the aperture.

If the homeowners' association hasn't yet mailed you warning letters about addressing the house's gradual submersion— that is, if neither your brother nor your father has been hiding notices from the association, or the county housing authority, or the state, or whoever takes an interest in seeing that houses don't sink forever into the earth—it has less to do with the genius of the birdhouse and more to do with the coconut and mango and ackee orchard Delano transplanted into the sloping yard last year, as one of the final acts of his now-defunct tree service.

Through the summer and fall, torrential rains helped the orchard grow dense, jungle-esque, blocking the view of your house from the road, but this has not prevented the family next door from whispering, "Sucio," when they see you out on the sidewalk. The word is at times accompanied by *puta* or *putas*, depending, but the last time the father-mother-pickney amalgam passed you on the steps and bounced "Las sucias putas negras," between them in not quite a whisper, you aimed your forefinger at the father's raised unibrow and said, "Run go suck out yourself nuh, pussyhole," because why pretend language has a thing to do with understanding one another?

Still, you can't help but wonder if they have a point.

Your girl Jelly moved in this past September and has already come to loathe living here, due in no small part to your brother's antics; his insistence that you not clear the ivy that's ripping into the roof; his 3:00 a.m. sing-alongs with strays he rescues from this or that shithole bar; the dish towers he constructs on the kitchen counter and stovetop and in the sink.

Just last night you discovered Jelly near the microwave staring down one of these towers, hand extended, fingers inches from a mug wedged into the tower's upper quarter. She finally let her empty hand drop to her side, and, on seeing you, said, "I guess I'll just drink from a bowl. Like a dog."

Of the many motivations prompting *No, thanks*, the simplest is this: $11,698 is more money than you have ever possessed at once in your thirty-two years; more than double, almost qua-druple, the money you've accumulated at a given time. In your checking account, there's $987. In your wallet, there's a twenty. You have no savings, nothing stashed in the mattress, nothing buried in the backyard, no investments to cash in, and nothing to borrow against.

As the hot wind rakes your father like a dead palm frond, you tell him you won't buy his house. But as hours pass, then days, the idea spreads moss-like in your mind.

———

You won't buy your father's house, you decide, but in the week following his proposition, you find yourself probing the pos-sibility with others. You ask your brother. You don't actually say, *Should I buy Dad's house and kick you and your fuckery to the curb?* You say, "I've been thinking about the future." You've set down your briefcase—plump with your students' midyear pa-pers. It's 4:00 p.m.

Your brother stands before the stove, dashing minced garlic and shredded cheese and thyme onto the open face of an omelet. He somehow looks precious in his tattered bathrobe. He's gotten mawga over the last year, seemingly subsisting off gas station eggs and Miller High Life. You offered to put him in touch with your school's music department, but he prefers to teach private guitar lessons so he never has to leave the house. You're impressed to see the counter clear of dishes, aside from a cutting board, a mix-ing bowl, a fork, and a serrated knife. A lemony tang emanates from the peninsula of counter separating you, and on it there rests a single opened envelope. You hope this signals Delano's emergence from many months of ratchetness. "And how's your future look, my youth?" His lips arc into a grin as he turns to you to say, "It's bright, eey?"

Delano jerks the dented frying pan to and fro, the egg sailing over the sizzling olive oil. His locks sway across the small of his back. From the den you hear guitar strings being plucked languidly into melody. You doubt he'd be so bold as to give a lesson in his bathrobe, so you know it's Sadie, the latest calamity Delano has brought home, your de facto third roommate.

Sadie is perhaps the worst woman your brother has brought through the front door, because, despite appearing to have her own life in order, she's done nothing but encourage Delano's slackness, and you've been quietly waiting for him to realize he can do better than someone quite so okay with his not doing better. You lean across the counter and crane your neck to confirm her presence. As she sees you, disbelief surfaces on her face, as though you're the guest she'd expected to be gone weeks ago.

You'd save this conversation for when you and Delano are alone, but, of late, he has clung to Sadie like deodorant caked under her armpits. "Jelly and I are getting pretty serious," you tell your brother. "I think this one might last."

Delano turns from the frying pan. "Is marriage you talking?"

"Not marriage," you say. "Potential co-homeownership."

The melody halts and Sadie clears her throat. Delano glances her way, then yours. "I've been meaning to talk to you about that," he says. "Sadie and I have news, too."

You don your best *Are you fucking kidding me* face, but Delano has already turned back to the stove. "The letter came today," he continues. "They settled the suit against me. Insurance is taking care of everything. I have a new lease on life, bredren, and I'm not wasting it."

"Congratulations. But what's that have to do with Sadie?"

"You must hear us rehearsing deep into the night? It's the band we're starting back."

"The band!" you say, trying but failing to conceal your relief.

Delano nods. "We're going to need more space for practice, though. We're thinking . . ." He pauses to flip closed the omelet. Perhaps he flips the omelet closed in order to pause. "We're thinking we need your bedroom for rehearsal space." He pinches the burner dial and rotates it off. "The den we'll convert into a bedroom for the boys."

"Boys?" You lean across the counter for a second look at Sadie. "She's pregnant?"

"Brandon and Hadyn," he clarifies. "You forget you're an uncle?" He tilts the pan, sliding the omelet onto a plate, and places the steaming plate on the counter between you. "I'm going sue Shelly-Anne for joint custody. You understand?"

You let his question hang unanswered. There should be a word for the expression someone makes to communicate *You're really going to make me spell this out?* as well as the corresponding *You think I'd make fucking me over easier for you?*

"I been letting you live here two years now," Delano finally says. "And I think that's plenty time."

"Letting?" you respond. "You've been?"

He shrugs. "Is lie me a lie?"

"You think this is more your home than mine?"

"How isn't it?" he asks.

You consider the logic he's used to come by this conclusion

and how he came to live here in the first place. Simply put: Your father chose Delano. He chose him when your parents bisected your family unit the year you turned thirteen. And later, when your father built the new house, with the two-car garage and the pool and the bay windows, the town house went to Delano by default.

Still, this house cradles your preadolescent memories: the lost baby teeth, the young skin scraped onto the interior walls and molding, the floor rushing down on your head when you tumbled from your private reading nook—the linen closet's top shelf. Dried though it may be, your blood is caked into the foundation of this house. Your DNA is intermixed with its bones.

Also: "Who do you think's kept the roof over your head these last two years?"

"Who built the roof?" Delano responds. "After Andrew?"

You raise your voice to ensure Sadie hears. "I didn't want to have to say this, but Dad told me to kick you out." Though it's more of an interpretation than a fact.

Delano grins angrily. "You sure it's not you he meant? Don't he kicked you out once already?"

You lower your voice and say, "Not from here." When your father did, in fact, put you out, and you moved into your car, you deteriorated in the ways one can while still waking up on the right side of the dirt. So why should you care if Delano captures this house and throws your father into financial ruin?

Delano says, "You can't kick a man from his own home. House man built. House him grow up in. I been here what, thirty years? A few late payments can't change that."

"A couple dozen at least."

"No matter." He opens a drawer, takes out a knife and fork, and places them on either side of his plate.

"You're basically squatting," you say softly. "We both grew up here. So what's that have to do with anything?"

Delano shakes his head. "You only think it's here you grew up. The house you grew up in doesn't exist. It washed away in ninety-two." He picks up the knife and fork, angling them at the omelet. "I'm going need you out, T."

You slip your fingers underneath his warm, moist egg, lift it, and bash it against the counter. It spits its innards onto your brother's midsection, onto your crotch.

"Soon," Delano says.

"We'll see," you say, before heading down the hall to your bedroom, though you have no idea what the next days will bring.

———

You will buy your father's house, you decide, so the question becomes: How? "How much money do you have in savings?" you ask Jelly.

"Savings?" she responds. "Who am I, Warren Buffett?"

"How much do you think your parents would lend you?"

"To chain myself to a sinking ship?"

You wonder if you're the ship in this metaphor. Still, your bedroom floor slants Jelly, italicizing her. You resist the urge to catch her by the shoulders, straighten. "We could start building our future together here. At a bargain."

"Bargain-basement romance," Jelly says. "That's what you offer me." But then she goes silent and looks to the ceiling, as though doing the calculations. Her mouth parts as she tilts her head. She's already the type of fine that makes friends and strangers, men and women alike, congratulate you before planting seeds of doubt in hopes of swiping her for themselves. But when Jelly is still, she resembles the subject of a Renaissance painting: Botticelli's Venus, if Venus spent her weekends sunbathing at Nikki Beach.

You first got to know Jelly at work, when Palmetto Prep's Caribbean Club members decided the Latin American students and those from the Anglophone Caribbean could no longer operate under the same banner. As the club's faculty adviser, Jelly asked if you'd help her cohost a club event meant to help the students find common interests. "For balance. So there's no perceived bias in favor of the Latino kids," she'd said. The club event was a hit, in that instead of locating any such common ground, the Jamaican and Trini and Guyanese students announced their intention to found a separate West Indian club, with you as their inaugural adviser.

Your several afternoons spent in cafés, delineating how your Jamaican American experience related to her Cuban American experience, brought exactly two people together. "We connected over cultural difference," Jelly likes to joke with people. At least she did before she moved in here.

Now, lowering her chin, Jelly admits to you, "My parents probably would loan me money for a house." She adds, "If I promised I was leaving you."

———

You pick up your father's phone call. "I'll buy your house," you tell him. "But I'm going to need time."

"Well," he says, "price goes up the longer you take."

"By how much?"

"Significantly," he says. "I was hoping to have it by January. The money. By the second, if possible."

"In what world would that be possible?"

"It's not much I'm asking," he says. "For a house? You know how much house cost?"

"It's not much," you agree. "But it might as well be a billion dollars."

"I guess I'll find another buyer, then," he says. "But I figured you boys would want to keep it in the family."

"That's thoughtful," you say. "I see now that you are a thoughtful, family-oriented man."

"Don't start with your foolishness, boy."

You bristle at his tone, identical to his tone that summer night when he told you to leave. "I'll find the money," you say, having no idea how. "But I need you to do something for me."

"Mm-hmm?" he grunts. He's listening, however skeptically.

You could say any number of things now that you have his attention—have it because he wants something from you in return, perhaps for the first time in your life. You might demand that he tell you where he was, those nights you cradled your distraught mother in your ten-year-old arms, as Delano and you passed the phone back and forth, calling everyone in your mother's address book because you hadn't seen him in days. You might ask if it was laziness that made him choose Delano when your parents split, the mere fact of his being older meaning there would be less parenting left to do. Or if he saw himself in Delano, in his duplicated eyes. But answers in the mouths of the untrustworthy are worthless, so you say, "I need you to tell Delano he'll have to leave."

Your father, on the other end of the line, chews his thoughts for a while before saying, "That's not something I can do."

———

You email Bob, your head of faculty, to inquire about the possibility of the charter school advancing your spring-term salary.

Rather than replying to your email, Bob responds in the subject line of a separate message. The subject heading: *OUT OF THE QUESTION AND A NOTE OF CAUTION.* Bob's cautionary note begins:

> *It's come to our attention that you are straining the boundaries of the Palmetto Preparatory code of dress. While we appreciate the sharpness with which you generally present yourself to our students, we've noticed, too, how your hair's growth has continued without intervention, and we feel that this sets a rather lewd example for the young men of PP— particularly the AAs.*
>
> *We fear this is a slippery slope.*
>
> *We fear an outbreak of unmitigated naps and pant sagging.*
>
> *We fear bedlam.*

The email ends, *Take action before classes resume in January.*

"AAs?" Jelly says, when you stomp into the bedroom to show her Bob's email.

"Presumably? African Americans."

"Is he allowed to say 'naps'?"

"I'll consult my Black-guy handbook."

"Why do you even want this house?" Jelly asks. "It's sinking. Or hadn't you noticed?" She pushes your laptop aside and resumes studying her lunar tide calendar. She'd asked that you clear the room so she could spend the afternoon grading papers, but of late she's been preoccupied with the idea that the world is ending, that the next of Miami's rain-free floods will expand to swallow the earth. "The tides are coming up and your house is going down, my friend."

You sidestep her cynicism to fully consider her question. You want this house because it's your turn to have it. Even if Delano denies your right to it. *Because* he denies your right to it. You want Jelly to feel safe here, atop this hill, the way she felt when you first asked her to leave her parents' house and move in. But you don't say this. You say, "Why should I have to cut my hair to teach?"

"Maybe it is time." Jelly sits up on the bed and reaches for one of your curls, yanking, not so hard that it hurts, but hard enough that the coil does not retract. It dangles at your collarbone. You grasp Jelly's outstretched hand and pin it to the mattress before she can ruin a second coil. The loosened strands you take to tickle Jelly's nose till she crinkles it like she might sneeze in your face.

Sweeping the strands back into your bed of curls, you say, "It's barely longer than Bob's. Just because he can slick his hair back—"

"Yeah, but it's different, isn't it?"

"How you mean?" When Jelly returns a blank stare, you employ a tactic that works with your twelfth graders. "Say more."

"I mean . . ." Jelly pushes herself to her feet, as though her words might flow freer through her unkinked body, and when they don't, she flops back onto the mattress. "You don't make it easy for me to bring you home, you know?"

"Because of my hair?"

"Jesus, don't play stupid, Trelawny." Jelly's chin quivers, the message she's transmitting weighing more than her mouth can carry. "You know how it is. It's hard enough, my having a Black boyfriend. You don't have to rub it in their faces."

"How thoughtless of me."

"It's not that they hate you. My mother even said how handsome you were, just the other day. Like this mulatto boy she'd crushed on back in Cuba when she was a girl. Her words. The mulatto part. That's progress."

You wonder which part is supposed to be progress: her mother seeing you as handsome, or her seeing you as mulatto.

"It's just that every time I visit, she reminds me, 'If you have his babies they'll never have blue eyes.'"

"Has anyone in your family ever had blue eyes?"

Jelly shrugs. "It's possible."

You don't remind her that your mother might have registered the same complaint, or that your father's and brother's and nephews' irises are light enough to perpetually drown in the surrounding whiteness. "The sacrifice," you say. "They might name a church after you."

She lowers her chin, examining her cuticles. "They're my family," she says, with an assuredness that makes you nauseated. "They may not be perfect, but they're the parents I've got. Who else can I depend on? Who else can I go to when your crazy brother puts us out?"

"So you think shaving my head will help them accept me?"

"Maybe not," Jelly says, "but it might. You can try, though, can't you? If you loved me," she says, "you'd try."

———

You do what you do in desperate times. You consult Craigslist.

Under GIGS, buried in calls for *18+ nude girl models for $$$$$*, you find none of the English tutoring jobs you are hoping for. Instead, three ads catch your fascination. The first reads:

DRIVERS WANTED MAKE $500 A NIGHT
(MIAMI/FT. LAUDERDALE)

Looking for reliable drivers to take our gorgeous ladies to appointments this is an adult entertainment reply for more info.

do NOT contact me with unsolicited services or offers

You envision yourself driving a white limo through the streets of downtown Miami. You envision escorts sprouting through the moonroof, pearls streaming from their wrists and necks as they blow kisses at the world. You blast "Material Girl." Blast Trick Daddy's "Nann."

There are three weeks before school starts again, and if you drove every night between now and then, you could come away with the money you need to buy the house—if the job is real, and if the pay is, and you've been around long enough to know it likely isn't. But these two words halt your daydream: *sex trafficking*.

The second ad reads:

DRUMMER NEEDED FOR BATTLE OF THE BANDS
(CUTLER BAY)

Seeking experienced drummer/percussionist to join indie reggae band w/ male/female vocalists to compete at Battle of the Bands / Bayfront Park on December 23rd. First prize: $100,000 recording deal with Sony Records.

Reply to Delano for audition details.

do NOT contact me with unsolicited services or offers

"Unbelievable," you say.

The third reads:

WATCH MY BOYFRIEND AND I
(DOWNTOWN/MARY BRICKELL AREA)

. . . compensation: Negotiable. We are looking for someone to watch us in bed. Preferably 6'2" or taller. Preferably 200+ pounds. PREFERABLY BLACK. I'm 28 and my boyfriend is 29. We're both attractive young professionals who love to experiment. Him: 6ft 170lbs, white. Her: 5'11" 145lbs curvy (NOT fat) blonde, white. May ask you to film. NO sex, no touching—just watch! Send pics and measurements, we'll host.

do NOT contact me with unsolicited services or offers

═══

They are attractive, you note, when you meet at the Bar in Coral Gables. Conventionally. Morgan is sitting alone on a barstool when you arrive. It's her height that first impresses you, even seated. As you move beyond greetings and into conversation, you note that she has the longest torso you've ever seen. Or maybe it's that second shot of Hornitas she fed you. You try sitting up straight. You picture a pole impaling you from crown to asshole. But despite being several inches taller than Morgan, you manage only to bob up to her eye level before sinking back down again.

"Tim should be here any minute," she tells you. "He often works late."

"Who's Tim?" you ask, and she playfully slaps your arm.

"I'm sure he'll love you. You seem like the type everyone loves."

"Not really." You compile an inventory of unprovoked adverse reactions you've inspired. "It's hit or miss. My students like me well enough. But my boss has it out for me." You tell her about Bob's email.

Morgan nods attentively as you speak. You give her the kind of honesty you can give strangers, people you're likely never to see again: I have bad credit. I haven't pissed straight since my first ejaculation. My father never loved me like he does my brother. "My girlfriend isn't crazy about me, either, these days. She thinks she can do better. She can. And I'm pretty sure she's racist. I'm not sure what to do about that." You tell Morgan about Jelly's wholehearted agreement that your fro has grown offensive.

"Don't you dare cut your hair," Morgan says. "Oh my god, I'll kill you." Her fingers thrust into your damp curls. You're grateful when she doesn't ask if it was raining when you arrived or if you'd jogged here. You showered several hours ago, but you'll likely be asleep before it air-dries. "The thing about institutions like racism and sexism," Morgan says, "is that you have to work around their rules. That's why my parents gave me a unisex name."

"Good point," you say, wondering, *Fuck am I supposed to do with that?*

"So I'd get called in for more job interviews."

You nod. "I get you."

You sip Maker's Mark, even though you don't care for whiskey when it's eighty-eight degrees out; when you requested the house tequila on the rocks, the bartender's beard twitched. That you are here at all is asinine. Jelly believes you're at one of your temping gigs, circling celebutantes with mojitos and bruschetta, and at any minute one of her girlfriends may walk in and spot you chatting up an elongated blonde.

Still, you take this opportunity to spew your anxieties, telling Morgan that your brother's Battle of the Bands competition is in a week, not that there's a chance in hell of his winning—there's more of a chance he'll change the locks when you're not around to stop him. And unless this couple plans to fuck nonstop for the next seven days, there's little chance that whatever they are offering could add up in time for you to take control of the house. This last part you don't say.

Nor do you share your concern that in Miami, great city of cons, you're as likely to wind up getting your organs harvested as you are to make a profit here. You consider that Morgan prefers Black guys because when one goes missing no one bothers to look for him. You keep your palm facedown over the mouth of your tumbler to ensure she slips nothing in. "Your boyfriend put you up to this? Or was this your idea?"

Her response is warm and composed. "We're a team," she says. The smile that creeps up one side of her face might be a wink, but you don't fool yourself into believing you can read her. She's barely touched her Malbec. Morgan's eyelids are the kind of heavy that makes you think you've seduced her when clearly you haven't. You wonder if this has gotten her everything she's wanted in life or if it's made it impossible for people to take her seriously.

"And you've done this before?"

"No, crazy." She laughs and taps your knee with her fingertips. "It's our ten-year anniversary, and we just want to shake things up a bit. You know how it is."

"Indubitably," you say, shaking your head. "Your first anniversary, paper. Your tenth, Black guy."

Morgan shrugs. "It's not that important to us. Tim didn't really think you looked all that Black in the picture you sent. He thought you might be Puerto Rican. Are you? He's been down here a lot longer than I have, so I guess he can pick up on that sort of stuff."

"I thought you said you were together ten years?"

"We did long-distance," she says.

A hand gently clasps your shoulder, and you turn to meet Tim, who looks as though he stepped out of a Banana Republic catalog. "I wanted to be an actor," he explains, a full PBR later. "That's how the two of us met. But the loans, the parents." You've all moved to a corner booth now. Morgan sits to your left, blocking the booth's opening, and Tim faces you, leaning forward on his elbows. "We had lead roles in—"

"*Baby with the Bathwater*," Morgan says.

"Sophomore year of college. That was a huge deal." Tim's hands sign along as he speaks, balling into fists, then flaring. He waves a palm over his face. "This isn't really me. This . . . corporate Boy Scout look."

"Tim had a bleached streak in his fringe when we met." Morgan bumps her shoulder against yours. "Tim had a fringe."

The three of you laugh.

"It looked a little skunky. But still hot."

"I never should have come to this city," Tim continues, his eyes darting from yours to Morgan's and back. "That's the truth of it." He starts to work his tie loose. "Too much beauty. The people. The cars. The weather. Well, not the weather. Hot as balls isn't really beautiful, but it beats thirty below."

"You guys are from where—Fargo?"

"Duluth. Milwaukee," Tim says, nodding at Morgan.

"Tim was ensnared by Miami. He hates it, but he'll never leave."

"At least if we were in L.A. we could audition on the side."

"So move," you say.

"We make too much money here," Morgan says. "Finance. We are trapped."

"Tough break," you say.

"I should never have done my MBA, you know?" Tim crumples his tie and tosses it onto the table. "We should never have bought our condo, M."

Morgan hangs her arm over your shoulder. "At least we're not in the suburbs. Right? At least we're not in Kendall or Doral or some god-awful suburb."

"That's true," Tim says, lifting his second tallboy, pointing it at you. "At least there's no picket fence, white or otherwise."

Morgan pats your chest. "We are anti–picket fence in this relationship. That's a hard rule."

"Sounds reasonable," you say.

"So tell us," Tim says. "Are you up for this? I know it's a weird ask."

"Not weird," Morgan says. "Don't say 'weird.'"

"Unique, then. Trelawny, we like you. What do you say? You down for a unique experience?"

And fool that you are, you say yes.

———

The first time, you simply watch. You drive your '87 Dodge Raider up Old Cutler Road, through Palmetto Bay, Pinecrest, then the Gables and Coconut Grove to Brickell, to a high-rise that overlooks the Miami River. When the valet sees your headlights approaching, he rushes out to greet you. But as your Raider rumbles near, he slows and takes you in with bewilderment.

"I'll need to show you where the kill switch is," you tell him as he approaches.

He passes his hand through his greasy hair and clenches his teeth. He has the expression of a man charged with cutting the red wire or the black. "You going to be long?" And knowing, before you answer, that you won't be, he says, "Just park it on the curb over there."

You sign in with security. You print your name legibly, and write *of Cutler Bay* beside it, like there's another Trelawny zipping around this city making poor life choices. The guard phones for approval before pressing a button that slides open a frosted-glass barrier to the elevators. Before you go, you ask, "You know the couple in forty-two-oh-three?"

"Tim and Morgan? Sure. Good peoples."

On the forty-second floor, marble tiles in the corridor reflect your half-solid silhouette. Ceiling-high mirrors separate the units' entryways, presenting startlingly vivid duplicates of you. You pause to view yourself before entering unit 4203: black slacks and tie with a tucked-in white button-down. You're less recognizable as a voyeur and might instead be mistaken for a waiter, just off a shift at Olive Garden. As long as you're not mistaken for a burglar, you've done well. Still, you wonder, as you did while rifling through your closet, what the appropriate dress is for watching others fuck.

You remember an eighteen-year-old Delano appearing unexpectedly on your doorstep one evening during your first year in high school. He nestled his girlfriend's hand in his, and the pair exuded springtime love. Your mother would have been excited to see him, but as she was already passed out on the living room couch, letting TV chatter wash over her, Delano said not to wake her. He explained that they'd been in the area, and that he hadn't seen his little brother in too long, so the three of you decided you'd watch a movie together in your bedroom. And while you faced the television from the floor, leaning back against your bed, they fucked gently behind you. His girlfriend breathed soft moans into your ear as he pumped into her, the mattress throbbing against your back. It was the smell that shocked you most, the smell of spread-open human. You wonder, even now, if they had wanted you to see, if that had been the whole idea, but you were too afraid to turn around before the movie ended.

And one summer in college, your friend Caitlyn flew you to Amsterdam, where you were both too sheepish to enter a sex show in the red-light district. "Seventy euros," she said, groaning. "Just to watch? It can't be worth it." You agreed, but you wondered if "worth it" was the point. As you strolled the cobblestone streets, you discussed sharing one of the women perched in the entryways to their brothelettes. What were you wearing then? Something dignified? The two of you speculated about what these women charged and whether they spoke enough English for you to negotiate. Would it cost double if you both took part? What if Caitlyn only watched? The whole thing seemed overly complicated, you agreed, as if you'd been expecting they'd wear price tags around their necks. Truthfully, how were you to negotiate anything when, walking past, you couldn't even meet these women's eyes?

Had the sun been low, or had you visited a bar first, it might have turned out differently. Afterward, you decided you'd learned something about yourself in Amsterdam, something you did not like. It had little to do with morality. It had everything to do with a lack of courage.

You enter 4203 without knocking, as arranged. The apartment is dark, but the wall of windows to the right displays a twinkling cityscape, foregrounded by the near-identical high-rises that hug the far side of the river. The adjacent condos cast an ambient glimmer around the room.

On the far side of the living room, you locate a door and enter. Here, you find Morgan and Tim, illuminated by a slightly different cut of Miami's skyline. They've already begun, basically enough. You figure they timed it to start when security called. Morgan sits at the edge of the bed, leaning back on her elbows. Her robe hangs open, exposing her breasts and stomach. Tim's head eclipses Morgan's pelvis. His left knee digs into the shag carpet; the other leg is extended in a ballerina stretch. The light from across the river soaks Tim's naked back and ass.

They are paying you to watch, but you avert your eyes. And although they'll want to know you are present, you shut the door behind you as quietly as you can. As the darkness thins, you inch toward a bar cart near doors that let out onto the balcony. A white envelope rests against a bottle of Patrón, perched on a fresh bucket of ice. Your name in marker extends across the envelope, which you lift, then quickly pocket. How strange that someone who has been broke his entire life can recognize the weight of cash. There is at least two hundred dollars here, the amount you'd negotiated.

Morgan's murmurs bring you back to her. She braces Tim's head with both hands, stifling him with her crotch. She's saying something, but it's unclear what. "You . . . You . . ." The rhythm suggests it's the same words over and again: *You one, two. You one, two, three, four. You one, two. You one, two, three, four.*

Tim's fingers work vigorously just below his chin.

Morgan comes. Or Morgan approximates the signs of orgasm. Her body tenderly spasms, and she catches Tim's hand, then collapses into silence.

Tim keels backward, panting, as though he's emerged from the depths of the Atlantic.

A few hundred seconds pass before either moves. You uncork the tequila and tilt back as much as you can without choking. Should Tim or Morgan turn to acknowledge your presence, you are entirely too lucid to respond.

Morgan stirs and crawls over the mattress to the bedside table. Tim lifts himself onto his knees. He faces the skyline, his profile to you. Morgan approaches from behind and slips something around Tim's neck. A tie, you think. Tim takes his semihard dick in his hand, and Morgan tightens the tie so the knot squeezes his flesh. He strokes himself furiously, and Morgan digs her knee between his shoulder blades, tugging.

She starts into her rhythm: *You one, two. You one, two, three, four.*

But you can distinguish her words now. They rise from a whisper, culminating in a shout:

"You little man," she says. "You little, worthless White man."

———

Your mom calls. She's calling through an internet connection that makes her sound a thousand miles away, which is fortunate, you suppose, since she says she's five thousand miles away, in Florence.

"Vacation?" you ask from your bed, staring up at the popcorn ceiling.

"A job interview," she says. "The embassy has an opening. It'd be an opportunity to finally practice my Italian."

"You're moving to Italy now?" It's been three and a half years since she left the United States for Jamaica. "I thought you wanted to be with Jamaicans? I thought you missed your people?"

"Sometimes you just aren't one of your people anymore. I don't know if that makes sense?"

"It does," you say. And sometimes, you think, you never were one of your people. You know better than to sour your mother's mood by mentioning him, but desperation rears its malformed head. "Dad wants me to buy the house from him."

"How you mean, 'buy'?" she asks. "He's supposed to give you and your brother the house." She adds, "When he's dead."

"Is that in writing somewhere?"

"We agreed," she says in that familiar tone that denotes, *Don't ask me another question on this matter*—the tone that has shut down many a conversation, left many a mystery between generations of Jamaicans.

"He says he'll sell to whoever if I don't buy it. Do you have any money you can lend me?"

Thousands of miles can't dim the teeth-kissing she unleashes. "Is he put you up to asking? What kind of fool would buy back the house she already bought and gave 'way?"

She pauses for your response, but a fool is a fool is a fool, as far as you can tell.

"And what about your brother? Him going buy it with you?"

"Delano's the problem. He hasn't been covering his half of the mortgage."

"Mortgage? Trelawny, we bought that house thirty years ago, with a fifteen-year loan. Do the math."

You'd try, but thirty-two years have taught you that things rarely add up.

"Anyway," she says, "you don't need that house unless him giving it free, and even then you should sell it off quick." Then she says something you'll consider for days after. "Tell me, who has that house ever brought happiness?"

———

When next you bump into your brother in the hall, he says the two words you've never heard him say to anyone: "I'm sorry."

Not when he dislocated your shoulder wrestling in your mom's yard when you were fifteen. Not when he borrowed your father's car without asking and totaled it. Not when his kids' mother tired of his fruitless fidelity to his musical aspirations (or so the story goes) and left him.

"You're sorry?"

"Sorry for what I have to do."

You would like to believe his aggression derives exclusively from whatever insanity is overtaking him, but its origins spring from a source that's long been festering and harder to cure: entitlement.

"What is it you think you have to do?"

"Not 'think,'" he says. "We are on a course. We're racing toward destiny, rude boy, and mine is the top." He stabs his finger at you, halting it an inch from your chest.

The hairs on your neck jolt up.

"You feel it?" he says. "It's bigger than us."

"That's your ego," you respond. "That's Sadie gassing your head up. You haven't gigged in how long now? What happens when you lose your competition?" You watch for his reaction, but his face is as blank as the sun. "You can't even cover your half of the rent. How do you figure you'll cover mine?"

"It's fate," he says. "Not only mine, but my sons'. I win and I can get them back. God help the man who stands in my way."

You feel the walls and ceiling inching near as you ask, "What about my fate?" Your bodies crowd the dim hall, yours holding a thirty-pound advantage.

There is such a thing as skinny-man strength, though, and Rastaman strength, and big-brother strength besides, the three of which advantage Delano. And there are other unlikely sources of power—desperation, for instance—from which you both may draw. But what of strength derived from bearing the brunt of underestimation? What of underdog strength, strength developed carrying thirty years of fuckery? "What if I'm the man who stands in your way?" you ask him.

"Then you will lose, Trelawny. And God help you when you do."

=====

When Morgan texts, *Can you come over now?* it's been three days since your visit to their freak show. It's early afternoon. A Thursday. You didn't think you would hear from them again, not after flitting from their bedroom a breath after Tim ejaculated on their rug. You weren't altogether sure they'd seen you that night, but Morgan writes, *Can you wear baggier clothes this time? Do you own a hoodie?*

You write, *This is a little short notice, folks. Busy week ahead,* and hit SEND before pulling the covers back over your face. You're technically off till January. But this, you declare, is a mental health day. There will be no scanning Craigslist for harebrained schemes, no lying to Jelly, who is out Christmas shopping with her mother. There will be no run-ins with your madman brother. And there will be no answering your father's phone calls. You can tell him tomorrow, or the next day, or whenever, definitively, that you will not purchase his house.

Your reply to Morgan feels like the end of it, so you exhale in relief. You're $11,398 short—you will not find the money now. Not before your father finds another buyer. Not before Jelly leaves you. There is safety in accepting defeat. Were you within reach of your target, there is no telling how you might destroy yourself to hit it.

But Morgan responds, *We'll bump you to $300 this time,* even though last time you discovered, on returning to your SUV, that they'd put $300 in your envelope, $100 more than you'd agreed on. You're certain this was no mistake. The ability to perform simple addition must be a requisite for the appellation *finance people*, whatever their jobs entail. You assume it's not a gratuity but guilt money, since they so easily out-negotiated you, since they so obviously exploited your need.

Make it $500 and I'll drop what I'm doing, you write back.

Morgan's text comes through immediately: *Fine. BUT DON'T FORGET THE HOODIE.*

You wear the baggiest jeans you own, a pair earmarked for yard work, and bring along your university sweatshirt, the only hooded sweatshirt you did not hawk or toss after returning to this hotbox city of sin back in 2009. You are not nostalgic for your college days, but you hope, even now, to one day romanticize your stint in the Midwest.

You imagine telling your children and their children that you escaped Miami, if just for a short while; that you once inhabited a land so cold your hair froze while trekking to campus, a land where white semisolids shat down from the sky, as if from flocks of leviathan pigeons. You assume that, should you survive long enough to become a grandfather or great-grandfather, you will outlive winter; you will outlive glaciers and polar bears and snow. And it occurs to you now that, should you survive to see your progeny reproduce, you will outlive and thus need to explain Miami to these descendants—who in your mind's eye split your features and Jelly's—as the city, by then, like much of Port Royal and Atlantis before it, will have returned to the sea.

It occurs to you that people like you—people who burn themselves up in pursuit of survival—rarely survive anyone or anything.

This time, when you pull up to Morgan's building, you ask the valet, "Should I just park it on the curb?" You point to a space behind a mint green Lamborghini.

"Why would I let you do that?" he asks, and he drives away in the Raider. You'll have to accompany him, or whoever is on duty when you return, down to the garage to start the car yourself. You've been here before; the valet will judge you, whether you tip him well or not.

Security lets you up to floor forty-two. Before you knock, you pull your sweatshirt on to expedite things. You hope this will be over quickly and that you'll beat Jelly home. When Morgan opens the door, she is in a bikini and sarong. "We're going up to the pool!" she announces.

"I didn't bring swimwear."

"That's all right," Morgan says. But she doesn't offer you a pair of Tim's trunks, and there are none to be borrowed from the pool deck's bar.

From the parapet you can see out to the yacht-studded bay, and for a moment you are struck by the aroma of promise Miami has dangled in front of you your entire life: you are a single lucky break from becoming one of the haves.

Tim is swimming laps as you two approach the pool. He waves briefly before continuing. Most of the pool's guests aren't concerned as much with exercise as with tanning and posing beside cocktails. "Don't you people work?" you wonder aloud. You can't all be teachers, off for winter break.

You start to pull off your sweatshirt, but Morgan grabs your arm and says, "What are you doing?"

"It must be ninety-five degrees out."

"For what we're paying you, I'm sure you can deal." Morgan moves in front of you and pulls down your sweatshirt's hem. She gazes at the university crest. For the first time, you feel as though she's your boss, evaluating. "I would have preferred something less . . . academic," she says. But she's playful as she pulls the hood over your head. "Put these on." It's a pair of Eazy-E-era shades. She leads you past the cabanas to two tightly woven wicker chaises in the deck's far corner.

Morgan produces a blunt and a lighter from god-knows-where, sparks up, pulls, and puffs weed smoke in your face.

"Lady," you say, "I told you I teach high school, right? Random drug tests mean anything to you?"

"Relax," Morgan says. She takes another drag and blows clouds at you. You doubt if she's even inhaled.

"What's the idea here, Morgan?"

"Look," she says, holding the blunt over your head, using her free hand to waft smoke into your hoodie. "Tim's had a rough week at work, so we need to do something special for him." She drops the blunt through a grate near the chaise, the smoke streaming up from the shallow catch beneath. "The idea is, you sit here and don't move till I get back." With that, Morgan removes her wrap and dives into the pool.

There was a time when December brought relief from the swelter, but even Miami's shallow winter has begun arriving later in the season. As more pool guests crowd your end of the patio, you sit broiling in your sweatshirt and watch people sniff the air, examining you with suspicion or curiosity or outrage.

You don't need to engage in whatever game Morgan is playing. Pull out your phone, check your email. The inbox contains a new message from Bob, the subject line and body identical: the query *????* and nothing more.

You delete it, open your web browser, and search *Why is my house sinking?* The results show that any number of factors could be causing the house to sink, but the most compelling possibility is this: *Surrounding trees may be stealing moisture from the soil near the house's foundation.* You think of the jungle that is your front yard. Of course Delano is responsible for this. A section at the bottom of one of the more useful web pages is titled *Professional Help.* It says: *Stabilizing a foundation with concrete or steel piers will cost $1,000–$3,000 per pier.*

"Christ."

You look up to see, staring down at you, a woman with wispy, silver-white hair and skin like thinly sliced soppressata. "And how are you today?" you ask.

Her knuckles bore into her hips—a superwoman pose. She has somehow materialized in your personal space, and somehow, judging from her countenance, she feels empowered to stay there. "Who are you here with?" she asks.

You stare back through your tinted lenses, thinking, *Say nothing, say nothing, say nothing,* but say, "Could you skip ahead to the intent behind your question?" This elicits no response, so you rephrase. "Say more."

"This is a private pool." Emotion rocks her like a wooden roller coaster, as if her enslaved ancestors died erecting the platform this pool deck was built on.

"You're telling me you own this pool?"

The white threads of her eyebrows rise.

"You're saying all these people are your personal guests?"

"This pool is for residents and *their* guests."

"Superb," you say. "Nice that two strangers can concur on such a divisive topic."

"You don't live here," she says. "I'm on the board of directors for the association. You'd have had to go through me."

"Congrats. You're two for two. I agree that I do not reside here."

"Then I'll ask again. Who are you here with? Who let you in?"

You point to the pool, but when you look over, Morgan and Tim are nowhere to be found. They're not at the bar. They're not by the cabanas. "They were here a second ago. Tim. Morgan." You snatch Morgan's sarong off the ground and hold it up, as if to say, *See?*

"Well, I don't know any Tim or any Morgan. And if they're not here now, you can't be."

This game you are familiar with, and there is no competitive way to play it, because the fact that it has begun means you have already lost. Morgan could round the corner and straighten things out, but that would only further prove that this rando can require you to justify your existence at any moment she chooses. "Is this your job?" you ask. "You seriously have nothing better to do?"

"I'm going to count to five."

"Then what? You'll nag me to death?" The woman teeters, clutching for pearls that aren't there, and, without thinking, or perhaps thinking with the sun-licked part of your brain, you say, "Eat a dick."

The woman staggers backward, her decorum ablating like microwaved Styrofoam. As she crumbles, you recognize that you have made an error for which there is no RESET button. She screams, "Jerome!" It's bloodcurdling. A wave of faces shifts your way.

Act natural, you think. Tuck your head, lift your phone, and commence scrolling. "*King Tides Arrive in Time for Noche Buena*," a *Miami New Times* article announces. *Break out the kayaks and get your cars to high ground . . .*

"Jerome!" she cries again. You're unsure if she is beckoning someone named Jerome, or if she thinks all Black guys are named Jerome and she's addressing you directly. Perhaps urban legend among a certain demographic has it that yelling *Jerome* five times will make a Black man vanish, the reverse of repeating *Candyman*. Soon enough, the answer reveals itself. The sea of spectators parts for an entity with the speed and size of a silverback gorilla.

You feel yourself plucked from the chaise by a force so powerful you can hardly tell what body part you've been lifted by—perhaps you've been swept into its gravitational pull. Your phone plummets to the ground. The screen detonates into a web of shards. The entity is a massive black suit with a moai head balanced on its shoulders. "What's going on?" he asks, but your accuser answers first.

"He accosted me," she says. "He threatened to expose his genitals."

"I said *a* dick. Not mine."

"Uh-uh," Jerome says. He drags you through the crowd of onlookers to the bank of elevators. "You don't talk to ladies that way. You would talk to your mama like that? Uh-uh." You trip, then skid behind him, yanked along by the massive fist crushing your triceps. Your accuser follows, whipping you with "Don't you ever try that" and "Somebody ought to have taught you" and "Unacceptable!"

In the hall, Tim and Morgan stand before the elevators, as if in wait. "What's going on?" Morgan asks. "Take your claws off my guest, you ogre."

"He was troubling a resident," Jerome says, but he releases you. "Ms. Mann."

"I very much doubt that," Tim says.

Ms. Mann steps forward and asks, "Do you know this young man?"

"He's a very important guest of ours," Tim says. "And a guest of our bank, in fact."

"For fuck's sake, don't you recognize him?" Morgan says.

Jerome leans back to inspect you as Ms. Mann lifts her palm to her mouth.

"Don't you people watch CNN?" Morgan asks. "Don't you read the *Times* or the *Post* or anything?"

Ms. Mann emits a chirp and says, "I couldn't have. With the glasses and the . . . I mistook him for . . ."

"How many celebrities want to get hassled everywhere they go?" Morgan turns to you. "Are you okay? Did he hurt you?"

Though the security guard has freed your arm, it feels as if a nurse is checking your blood pressure. You, like a child, say, "He broke my phone. It's probably been stolen by now."

"Oh, no," Jerome says, dashing from the hallway back toward the pool.

Ms. Mann says, to no one in particular, "I don't know what to say."

"This is because he's Black," Morgan says. "Admit it." She bears down on Mann, making the woman appear miniature. "This is textbook profiling."

Ms. Mann fingers her collarbone. "I just don't think that's

true." She turns to you. "You have to agree"—and when you don't, she adds—"that you look suspicious."

"He *looks* suspicious? He's Black. How else do you want him to look?" Morgan asks.

"It still works," Jerome calls breathily, returning with your phone. "I checked, and it's just the screen that's cracked." He hands you the phone. "Sorry about that, brother."

"That's not good enough," Tim says. "You assaulted my guest and damaged his property. *Sorry* doesn't cut it by a long shot. I'll be speaking with the building manager."

"Cut it out," you say.

Tim says, "We can't allow you to be treated—"

"This isn't his fault." You press the elevator call button. Ms. Mann fidgets in your periphery, but you don't give her another look. You step into the elevator, and when Tim and Morgan follow, you press the button for forty-two.

"We're so sorry," Morgan says. "I can't believe that crone."

"Let's just get on with it," you say quietly.

Inside their condo, Tim walks directly to the bedroom, but Morgan lingers near you and says, "I feel terrible. Really."

You study her face, a window to nothing you are capable of accessing. "That wasn't exactly what you engineered?"

"How could I have known? Look, I have an idea. I know what might help you feel better." She motions for you to follow her into the bedroom, but you clasp her forearm.

"Answer me this first. Do you know those two? Jerome? Mann?"

Morgan thinks for a second, then says, "I promise you I've never seen either of them in my life."

"Then how did they know you live here?"

Morgan raises her palm to your cheek and says, "Oh, honey."

Inside their bedroom, Tim is already naked on his knees. You remove your sweatshirt, ball it up, then throw it out onto the living room floor before heading for the bar cart.

"Hey, put that back on," Morgan says.

"Fuck off," you say. You scan the cart for your payment, and when you find none, you pour tequila halfway to the brim of a tumbler. You lift the ice bucket's lid. "No ice for your special guest?" When you turn around, that same smirk has crept up into Morgan's cheek. Tim focuses through the glass doors, his head slightly bowed. Any shame you might have felt in looking at this naked man has been replaced by something seething inside you. Tim is in magnificent shape, and you wonder if it's the swimming that has sculpted his body, or if tight swaths of muscle build simply from being an American psychopath.

Morgan produces the tie from the nightstand, but instead of pulling it over Tim's head, she holds it out to you. "Here. I want you to do it this time." The sunlight pouring in from the west catches in her irises, giving them a savage radiance.

"I'll have to respectfully decline," you say, but Morgan returns to the drawer and takes out a stack of cash. She drops five one-hundred-dollar bills on the bed, and this does little to shorten her stack. Ben Franklin makes eye contact, intimating, *This is awkward.*

"What is it you want?" Morgan asks. "Why are you even here?"

You empty half your glass and think. You want to be out of the grasp of these perverse puppeteers. You want not to be their plaything. Your list of wants expands beyond the moment, though. You want eleven thousand three hundred and ninety-eight dollars, plus the three grand to fix the foundation.

You want a home.

You want to win back your girlfriend's admiration.

You want to prove that your father bet on the wrong son.

But you don't say any of this. "A loan," you say. "A loan for fifteen thousand dollars. That's what I want."

Tim's head jerks by a few degrees.

Morgan smiles and holds the necktie out to you.

You take the tie and yank it over Tim's head, dig your knee into his spine, and begin tightening the knot.

━━━

On the drive home, you can't quite believe you've won. You desperately need a shower, but you've come away with five hundred dollars plus an appointment to meet Tim at his office tomorrow to pick up a check and the paperwork for the terms of repayment.

You want to dance. You turn on 99JAMZ and Biggie's "Juicy" is playing. This is a sign. You turn up the volume and rap along, shoulders bopping, hands chopping at the air. At McFarlane Road and Grand Avenue, the driver in the Aston Martin to your left raises their windows and pulls forward, but three young guys in a Honda Civic behind them find the station and join your sing-along, ad-libbing, "Ayyy—ayyy—ayyy," through the hook. You don't care that rush hour traffic will see you home in an hour and a half, and when you realize that your seat-dancing made you miss several of Jelly's calls, you don't worry that she'll wonder where you've been all afternoon.

"Bebe!" you yell into the cracked phone when she answers.

"He did it," she responds, so you turn the radio off.

"Did what?" you ask. "Who did?"

"Your brother. He put all our stuff on the front lawn." You're shocked to hear Jelly crying. "He changed the locks, Trelawny. What are we going to do?"

"I'll handle it. I'm on my way. Don't worry, Jell."

"Okay." For the first time in a long time, she sounds like she believes you. "I'll be at my parents', all right?"

"Everything will be good." For the first time in a long time, you believe yourself.

———

You do a drive-by. The setting sun's flare dulls the contours of Cutler Bay, but you can distinguish your possessions—through leaves and limp fronds—strewn across the yard, just as Jelly described them. Your bed straddles the yard's belly—frame, box spring, mattress, and all, arranged under the dangling ackee and coconut clusters like a jungle-themed Rooms to Go showroom. You wonder how Delano got it out of the house to begin with, and if he actually reassembled it.

You drive to your father's house, another fifteen minutes back the way you came.

Before knocking, you try peeking over his back gate to see if his ackee tree has recovered, if it's borne fruit since you tried to take it down. But the angles are all wrong.

He cracks the door after several rings of his bell and pushes his head through the narrow space he's allotted. The house is an enormous tortoiseshell around him. You're not allowed inside, not since the incident, not since your episode. You tell him your brother has lost his mind. "You need to do something."

Your father nods judiciously, scratching his chin in deliberation, but when you finish talking, he says, "I can't choose sides, you know."

"Since when?"

"You two will have to work things out."

"And what about the mortgage? The rent? You think I'm paying to live in the front yard?"

"Well," he says, "I talked to your brother, and him says he'll have the money to buy the place next month. So I'm giving him the chance."

"And me?" you ask. "What chance are you giving me?"

Your father says, "You can feel sorry for yourself, eey? The boy has responsibilities you don't. Think of your nephews."

"Of course I'm the bad guy. As usual." Your flight impulse kicks in, but you hold your ground before your father's craned tortoise neck. "Did he tell you how he plans to get the money? He thinks he's going to win some competition. He thinks he's going to hit the lotto."

"He might," your father says.

"He won't, though. You know he won't."

"Sometimes you have to believe in people," your father tells you.

You know this. You just wish you were one of the people that people believed in.

━━

The sun is tucked below the horizon by the time you try your key. Which does not work. You bang on the front door, switch to

kicking it when the bones in your fist start to ache. Music rever-
berates through the walls. A speaker projects your brother's voice
as he chats patwah in a rhythmic staccato over Sadie's melody.

The croaking lizards scatter over the stucco wall as you pace
the length of the front yard. Trashmore's funk fumes burn in
your lungs, and as you work yourself up, the stink laminates your
skin, slowly suffocating you. You kick the door harder, then start
at the windows.

The playing halts, eventually, and a husky dread pries open
the door. He leans out, his broad fingers engulfing the doorknob.
"Bredda," he says, "you pound 'pon me door like Babylon, but
you no look like Babylon."

"Your door?" you say. "Why are you in my house?"

"Oh," he says, and nods sympathetically. "You must be the
boy we helped move out. The singerman's brother."

You move to enter, and he presents his palm. "Can' come in,
bredda. You don' hear we magic making?"

"Let me talk to my brother. Delano!" you call out.

"You no hear? Me say the singer busy. Him can' stop for
every boy de wan' sneak preview."

At this, you rush the opening, grasping for a foothold, a gap
to stick fingers through and pry your way in, but the dread is tree-
trunk solid. He swats you back with the power of Marcus Garvey,
Emmanuel, and Haile Selassie himself.

"You can't keep me out. This is my house."

"Bredda," he says, "if this were a your house, you know say
you would be in it."

Your fingers fly toward the stiff knob as he closes the door.
You jab at it and cry out in anguish.

With your uninjured hand, you text Jelly: *I'm still working on this. What's the chance I can crash with you tonight?*

Jelly texts back: *There is no chance.*

You should have known. Just last month, at her family's Thanksgiving dinner—a dinner Jelly insisted you attend, though you were not technically invited—from across the long table, sandwiched between Tía Betty and Tía Linda, her mother lifted her finger to use you as a reference each and every time she uttered the word *black*.

"But no, Linda, that's like the kettle calling the pot black," she argued, and pointed at you. "Betty, if it were burned, the skin would be black," she said, and pointed at you. When she began recounting a story about her childhood dog, a black Lab, you turned to Jelly and said, "You're just going to sit there?"

Jelly made a face that you interpreted as *Please don't make a scene*, so you said, "You're not going to react at all?"

"Mom, stop it," Jelly said. "Please."

"Stop what?" her mother asked.

Jelly's father said to her mother, "That's enough."

"¿Por qué? He doesn't know he's Black?"

You rose from your seat and walked out to your Raider, slowly enough that Jelly might chase you down. She didn't. The next day, when her cousin dropped her off, Jelly said, "You just have to give them time," as though racism were a phenomenon best outwaited.

There are conversations you should have initiated by now, but when you're always exhausted, always one gig away from destitute, and always afraid this is the best life has to offer, it's too easy to let time slip by, to tell yourself, *Soon*.

The rehearsal resumes, and as you descend the steps of your childhood home, your next-door neighbor, the father, comes out and approaches. You accelerate, skipping a mildewed step. Another. If you can reach the street and your parking space, you can lock yourself in your Raider, then watch through the windshield. Perhaps neighborman's complaints can convince the band this is no place to hold rehearsals, but he cuts your trajectory short, focusing his attention entirely on you.

"Loud," he says.

"Loud," you agree. You step aside and motion toward the front door, inviting him to register his complaint directly, but he faces you instead. "Maybe you should call the police," you say.

"¿Policía?" He shakes his head. "No." He makes a gun with his hand and aims it at your forehead. "They shoot you."

"They do shoot us," you agree. "That they do." You see how this might backfire. You imagine the headline: *"Homeless Man Shot Dead in Bed in Bushes."*

"No. No police," your neighbor says. "How the rappers say it: *Snitches get stitches?*" He chuckles and lights a cigarette. Seeing him standing there minus his wife and kid, you realize he's younger than you thought. Not much older than you, if at all.

"Snitches do indeed get stitches," you say. "Solid observation. Still, they shouldn't disturb your family's sleep. Go and tell them." You wave at the door.

"Sleep?" he says, and laughs again. "It's seven o'clock, brother. I just came over to hear better. They sound kind of awesome."

He listens long enough to finish his cigarette, and as he returns to his house, what bothers you most is that he is right. Despite the odds, they do not sound bad at all.

=====

That night, under the ackee tree and the mango tree and the bed-covers, Jelly glides into your arms, her forehead pressing cool against your hot cheek, her hair wrapping around your shoulders like a shawl, fingers curled soft as a baby's at your collarbone. In your half-conscious state, you understand her return to signify loyalty, proof that whatever rough patch you are struggling through is passing. You will get through this together.

You wake in the night to find your arms empty, all but Jelly's scent having absconded from your too-hot bed.

In her ghostly absence, the animals of your youth revisit, everything you killed as a child. Millipedes nest in the crooks of your arms and neck. When you shine your phone on them, they evaporate, but when the battery dies two hours before sunrise, they grow heavy, multiplying.

A *crick-crack* rustles the underbrush, and you imagine the crabs that once washed over Cutler Bay's roads, returning to pick out your eyes and drag you into the sea. Something hammers your solar plexus, then launches itself over your head, into the surrounding grass.

Fruit is falling. You can hear it every so often snapping from overhead branches and hitting the dirt. Though whatever launched itself from your body did appear to have feet . . .

You refuse to collect your bedding and cram yourself into the back of the Raider as though you're homeless again. This is your home, and tomorrow, once you pick up the check from Tim, you will lay claim to it. You will show your father that you have the money, and he will come down on the side he has always chosen: his own.

You blink and the sun has come up. Your skin is mostly insect-free, barring the odd ant or gnat. The mosquitoes have tagged your body only from the neck down. These are good omens. Above, in the trees, sit dozens of pigeons, leering intelligently. Perhaps they, too, know a change is coming, that the home you share will soon be under new ownership, that soon they'll be in your domain; they sit in salute. But as you kick out of bed, they do not take flight. Instead, they scatter on paws, and you realize they are no flock of pigeons but scores and scores of rodents.

<hr/>

When you return to Brickell to visit Tim's bank to collect the check, they won't let you see him. Instead, a younger, shorter version of Tim leads you to an austere office, where he asks a series of intrusive questions: What is your mother's maiden name? Are you still at this address? Why are you very, very behind on your student loan payments? His expression suggests questions his mouth doesn't ask: *Why are leaves crumpled in your hair? Have you ever heard of an iron? When is the last time you showered?*

He shakes his head and makes a *tsk*ing sound. "I'm afraid we can't extend credit to you."

"Credit? Tim is supposed to be loaning me the money. That's why I'm here."

"You thought Tim was going to personally loan you fifteen thousand dollars? Like, out of his pocket?"

You nod. "We have an arrangement."

"Then why did you come to a financial institution?"

"He works here, right? Why don't you find him and ask?" You survey the bare office, suspecting that Tim is watching from somewhere, fondling himself, getting off on your degradation. You take out your cell phone, charged on the drive to the bank, and send a group text to Tim and Morgan: *I'm here with your minion. Tim, I hope you're enjoying this. But can we please, please, please get on with it?*

Morgan texts back on a separate thread: *We had a fight. Tim says the deal's off. Meet me in 2 hours at my place?*

In the fury that's suddenly blinding you, you send Morgan a response, then stagger out of the office. It's not until you exit onto the sidewalk that you see what you have written her: *daafuqqqqqq qqqqqqqqqqqqqqqqqqqqqqqqqqqqqqqqqqqqqqqqqqqqqqqqqq?*

─────

Morgan's condo is minutes from the bank by foot, so rather than arriving early and receiving the vagrant treatment, you saunter up Brickell Avenue toward Bayfront Park. As predicted, the road and sidewalk are flooded and malodorous, as the king tides have brought not just the sea but Miami's sewage up to street level. By the time you reach Bayfront, your sneakers are soaked through, likely ruined.

Banners line the park's gated perimeter, announcing upcoming concerts, including tonight's musical battle. You walk into the empty amphitheater and lower your weary body onto one of the concave benches facing the bandshell. As you stare down at the stage, it hits you: your brother is going to win the competition and buy the house out from under you. You can't possibly know this is true. Yet you know this is true.

You pull out your phone and type a reply to Bob's original message:

An outbreak of naps? You're likening our Black students to Ebola monkeys? Is this the type of email you want to go public? You hit SEND.

Bob's response comes in minutes: *IS THIS BLACKMAIL??*

You compose a new email and type in the subject line: *This is setting an example.* Hit SEND.

Bob responds: *Let's just be reasonable now. There's no need for rash, emotion-led actions here, Trelawny. Cooler heads prevail, after all. Let me appeal to your loyalty to Palmetto Preparatory and its larger community. I can't make decisions about advancing your salary without calling a meeting with the board, and they might take weeks to convene. But I'm willing to consider doing so in the new year, if you can give an assurance of discretion.*

Don't bother, you reply.

Trelawny??? he writes. *Don't be foolish.*

But you are foolish. And if you aren't going to get the money for the house, then you will bring ruin to anyone involved in stopping you. You mark his email as spam, then spend a half hour researching editors. You forward Bob's original email, changing the subject to *Palmetto Preparatory's war on natural hair.* It goes to *The New York Times, Miami Herald, Miami New Times, Caribbean Today, The Root,* Color of Change, and WorldStarHipHop.

You close out your email and Skype your mother. It takes several tries before she picks up, and when she does, she says, "Boy, you look wretched."

"Buongiorno to you, too."

"Buona sera. It's nighttime here," she says. "Is everything all right with you?"

"Sure." It's the lie you've been telling for so long, you hardly remember why you began telling it. "But actually, this isn't how I thought life would turn out."

"You sound depressed, honey. Is this about the house?" Before you can respond, she says, "You know, I called your father to ask him why he borrowed against you boys' inheritance, and you know what him told me? He said it's not just mortgage you been paying. It's fines. Them put a lien on the house, you know."

"That feels right."

"So now there's fines, plus late fees on fines, plus interest. Plus whatever it costs to fix the house in the first place. No wonder him wan' pawn it off on unoo."

"He admitted all this?"

"I have my ways, son. So you see, it's not a can of worms you want ownership over."

But you do. Because you are a fool, you still want it.

=====

An hour later, on Morgan's white couch, she says, "Tim wants a Black girl."

You tell her, "Good luck with the adoption."

"No," she says, as though you've misunderstood. "A woman. He wants you to find her."

"So I'm a pimp now?"

"He figures you'd know some. Don't you?"

"To do what with?" you ask.

Morgan shifts her eyes to the coffee table.

"More than watch?"

Morgan's eyelids retract, and for once she looks wide-awake.

You say, "You may not know this, being a gentrifier and residing in your tower. But you live five minutes from Biscayne Boulevard. Drive north for a mile and you'll run into all the sex workers your freaky hearts desire—every hue and gender imaginable. There." You hold out your hand. "Services rendered. Now where's my check?"

"Tim doesn't want that," Morgan says, her eyes meeting yours again. "He wants . . . he needs . . . humiliation. He needs . . ." She rests her palm on her forehead and closes her eyes. "I don't know what he needs anymore."

"What about what I need, Morgan? We had a deal."

She shakes her head. "He says you do this for him or the loan's not happening."

"Then you write the check."

"I told you. We're a team."

"Right. But you neglected to disclose that you're sociopaths."

Morgan doesn't react. After a minute of silence, she says, "Tim doesn't want a professional. That would defeat the purpose. Don't you have a cousin or something? A childhood friend, maybe?"

"We're not all for sale," you say. "Your money doesn't entitle you to everything."

"I doubt if that's true." Morgan opens her eyes again. "I suspect you've never seen real money." She goes into her bedroom and returns, not with cash, but with two ice-filled tumblers and a tequila bottle. "Let's drink," she says. "I bought this special for you."

"I should go."

"Because you have somewhere to be?"

"I have a house to save. It's sinking, goddammit."

"The whole city is sinking," Morgan says. "Just sit with me. If it's gone in an hour, what difference will anything you do make?" She fills her glass, then yours, her hands trembling.

"What is it *you* want, Morgan?" She doesn't answer. "You really want to spend your life chasing Tim's next nut?"

Morgan guzzles, then pats your thigh. "I want you to stay. Tim won't be back for almost a week. He flew out this morning on business. We can order in and make a night of it."

"He flew out this morning on business," you repeat. "Unbelievable." You get up to search the balcony, the closets, the en suite, including the shower. "He's not here, really?" you ask, back out in the living room. "This isn't another level in your game?"

"He left," she says, reaching up and twisting her fingers around yours, "so you might as well stay with me." This time, you are certain Morgan's sleepy eyes are seducing you. "Or will your racist girlfriend miss you?"

You can't say that she will, but you tell Morgan, "I can't stay here. If you're not honoring our agreement, I have to figure out something else."

Morgan says, "Maybe we can work out a side arrangement. Just between us."

And because you have nowhere else to go, or because no one has yearned for you in a long time, or perhaps because you're addicted to fucking up your life just a little bit more, you say, "Just until the concert begins."

———

You and Morgan finish the bottle, and when you do, another appears, as though teleported in. Day turns to night. You wait for her proposition, unsure what you're willing to give her. She asks for nothing more than your company at first, and so you wait.

You talk, and Morgan talks, and this time she reveals secrets: the pill addiction that was marginal and the eating disorder that was full-blown. The mommy issues and the daddy issues and the college boyfriend who was like Tim, only more vicious.

She hikes up her skirt to show where she cut herself in high school, on the inner thigh so no one would notice, and says it makes Miami hard for her to deal with, since she's expected to walk around half-naked here.

You feel sad about her sadness, and sad for the both of you because your wounds are not particularly original, however genuine. You tell her what it's like to not be the favorite, to be the opposite of the favorite, and she tells you, "Try being an only child." You tell her what it is like to be hungry, and she leans in and says, "That's fucked up, man. No one should be hungry," and you tell her she's right, that she has come to the correct conclusion.

You tell her why your father threw you out of his house. Not just the event, but the subtext. Because he said something during his retirement party about your being defective and the lesser son, so you took an ax from his shed and chopped to bits your patrilineal ties. "I molested his favorite tree."

Morgan responds with a clipped titter.

"I guess I'm nuts," you say, but she assures you, "We all are."

She goes to the kitchen to refresh your drinks, and as you hear her salting the rims on the kitchen counter, you look at your dying phone and see there's time enough. The tequila courses through you, making you feel as though you are simultaneously on Morgan's couch and diffused across the universe, on an infinite trajectory away from your troubles.

In this state of multiplicity you see clearly enough what will happen, though once the vision passes, you will forget—too quickly and completely to prevent it from occurring.

Morgan will return and you will empty your glass. You'll tell her you have to go and she will offer you something to keep you here, because she is lonely in the way only coupled people can be. Whatever she offers, it won't be enough.

You'll wade through Miami's bowels and its regurgitated refuse to the concert. You will pay the entry fee, and when Delano's band takes the stage, you will hop the front barricade, exploding past security, sending a guard careening to the ground. You won't know what you will do or say once you reach Delano, straddling the mic stand, Sadie and their drummer in place behind him. When he sees you approaching, he will step away from the mic and take a fighting stance, and that's when you will know: that he will go to war for the both of them, his children. You'll reach him and lift your fisted hand to offer him a bunks, say, "Good luck, bredren," because in that moment you will not want to take what was taken from you, and because you will finally understand that this has never been about defeating your brother, that beating him is not a route to getting what you need.

Security will snatch you, carry you offstage through the crowd, taking every opportunity to punch you in the ribs and face, before handing you off to the police. You'll hear Delano's opening riffs and his voice saying, "Big up me brother," before the patrol car door seals you in.

In jail, three things will strike you. The first is that it is undoubtedly the coldest place on earth. The second is the cruel irony of the corridors' placards supplying a 1-800 number for you to report rape, despite the COs having removed any possibility of your accessing a phone after your initial call is granted. As they've confiscated all writing implements, you'd have to glimpse, then memorize the number—if you needed it—in the event you ever did come in contact with a telephone again. This is still the second thing. The third is that jail hosts the cleanest public walls in Miami. Only hours after you've been processed and brought to a cell packed with bunk beds will you climb up to see the solitary line of graffiti scrawled on the too-close ceiling in fine blue ink: *Jail is bad for everyone.*

But before you are fully processed, before the cell with the bunk beds and the hall with the rape hotline, you will queue up to make your one phone call. The guards will pace the line, chanting, "Make it quick," yanking those who don't heed this warning away from the wall-mounted phones.

As your turn draws near, you'll make a decision: you will not call Jelly. Because whether or not she would come, you'll know, in that moment of choice, that the two of you could never work, that whatever love or obligation she feels toward you could never overrule her ties to her family.

Instead, you will dial your father's number and leave instructions for bailing you out. On his voice mail.

Then you'll wait.

Hours will pass.

Detainees will shift in and out.

You'll categorize them. This one was here when you arrived. That one they definitely brought in after. These three are DUIs. That one hurt somebody he loves. A couple of them will speak to themselves and shriek at the too-clean walls and shit in the seatless toilet in the middle of the cell, despite there being no tissue with which to wipe themselves. Others will do push-ups to warm their bodies and occupy the time. Most, like you, will hug their torsos and keep their eyes low.

The COs will begin an hourly game of head counts. They will chase you from your cell and line you up against the corridor wall, *six inches apart, head straight, eyes on the man in front of you, don't move, don't you fucking move.* Then they'll call roll, and it will horrify and relieve you to hear yourself counted. One of these times, before returning you to your cell, they will hand you a tray with a bologna-and-cheese sandwich.

Why'd I put myself here? you'll think over and again. *I don't belong here.*

There's a distinct sound in jail—you'll notice that, too— a hollow white noise in which you'll hear your name spoken over and over, as though from the far end of a tunnel, and so you'll swallow incessantly to clear your ears of pressure and look to the heavy door confining you, in fear of missing hearing your name called, in fear of being forgotten here forever.

By the time most of your cellmates have filtered out, you'll understand that you have been abandoned to the perpetual freeze. You'll rack your brain about public defenders and your right to a speedy trial, the things you learned in civics class and the things you learned from TV. Then an officer will holler your name, loud and unmistakable, and you'll be processed out, your belongings—phone, wallet, keys, belt, and shoelaces—handed back to you in a vacuum-sealed bundle.

When they release you into the sticky Miami dawn, what feels like a lifetime after you were booked, your father will be waiting in the parking lot.

He'll exit his truck—"What happened?"—concern and melancholy etched across his face.

You will hesitate before speaking, unsure how to state the onerous truth.

But for now, you are on Morgan's couch, listening to the salt grinding between granite and glass, a moment away from losing this premonition, this portal to your future, now my past. Tell him—across the expanse of time and distance, as I am telling you now—all that I can't say to him. Start with the resentment and the feelings of neglect and your resulting recklessness. Recount every injury, every scar you carved into each other. And when you're finished, and you are certain your father has heard, do what might divert you from the path to self-destruction: forgive yourselves.

ACKNOWLEDGMENTS

When you spend a quarter of your life working on a book, the number of people who offer meaningful contributions, directly or indirectly, is staggering. Words are insufficient to express my gratitude, and there just aren't enough pages.

To my wise and steadfast agent, Renée Zuckerbrot, who guided me and guarded me against my whims and impatience, and who might have read this book as many times as I have, I thank you. Thanks to Rob McQuilkin and Maria Massie, and to Rachel Clements, Dr. Petra Eggers, and Catherine Lapautre for finding homes for this project overseas.

To my editor Jackson Howard, thank you for your belief, your enthusiasm, and your vision—and for helping to make *IISY* that much better. Thanks to the rest of the team at, or working with, MCD and FSG, and especially to Sean McDonald, Caitlin Van Dusen, Gretchen Achilles, Brian Gittis, and Na Kim. Thanks to Michael Taeckens for your support and encouragement.

Thanks to my U.K. editor Kishani Widyaratna for your

careful notes and your dedication, and to the 4th Estate team, and especially to Sade Omeje and David Roth-Ey.

Thanks to Thomas Tebbe and Hannes Ulbrich at Piper Verlag, Francis Geffard at Albin Michel, and Joe Lee and Jared Bland at McClelland & Stewart, for your belief in the book.

My thanks to the programs and institutions whose funding, education, space, and community made the completion of this book possible: the National Endowment for the Arts, Aspen Words, the Bread Loaf Writers' Conference, Kimbilio Fiction, the Writers' Room of Boston, the Anderson Center, the Somerville Arts Council, the DOVE Fellowship Program, the Community of Scholars Program, Wellspring House, the MFA program at the University of Minnesota, the PhD in Creative Writing and Literature Program at the University of Southern California, and the Stegner Fellowship at Stanford University.

Thanks to my many teachers: to Debbie Gyenizse for reminding me that I had a gift and that I had better use it; to Diane Marshall, John Dufresne, Lynne Barret, Debra Dean, and Campbell McGrath, for giving me my footing; to Charlie Baxter for—among many other things—helping me become a more careful reader of the world around me; to Julie Schumacher for being a lifeline to your students; to Dana Johnson for being a powerhouse and an inspiration for how to be; to Aimee Bender for the most careful, brilliant feedback; to Danzy Senna for challenging me to make stories that move us forward; to Percival Everett for pushing me to write unflinchingly; and to Adam Johnson for prompting intense inquiry into my characters' motivations.

Thanks to Emily Nemens (you changed my life!), and thanks to the *Paris Review* team, especially Hasan Altaf, Nadja Spiegelman, and Jeanne McCulloch. And thanks to all the magazine editors who've shown support over the last decade, especially Kwame Dawes, Jennifer Maritza McCauley, Bill Pierce, Oscar Villalon, Brandon Taylor, Adeena Reitberger, Sarah Green, and Jennifer A. Howard. I'm better for having watched you all work.

My thanks to all the writers who looked out along the way: Mat Johnson, Danielle Evans, David Haynes, Tiphanie Yanique, Gary Dop, Dr. Ralph E. Rodriguez, Nana Kwame Adjei-Brenyah, Maurice Carlos Ruffin, Gabriella Garcia, Kerry Ann Moore, Kathleen Glasgow, Ani Gjika, Alysia Abbott, Shubha Sunder, Xochitl Gonzalez, Desmond Hall, Val Wang, Jenn De Leon, Jeff P. Jones, Stacy Mattingly, Christopher Romaguera, and Dolores Johnson. To my insanely talented 2018 Bread Loaf Waiter crew, my Kimbees, my Aspen Words EW fellows, and my Stegners, thanks for your community.

To the good people of Kingston who housed me, fed me, and fed my spirit, this book would not have happened without your generosity: Jennifer, Tubby (RIP), Andrew, and Christi Grahame; Liane Chung; Ruddy (RIP) and Joy McHugh; Neville (RIP) and Pauline Bryan; Tiffany Chérie Simmonds; Aunty Marie Evans; and Aunty Chubby. And massive thanks to Uncle Greg and Aunty Pat for putting me up and putting me in touch with so many good people.

To literary Boston, and especially to the staff at GrubStreet, past and present, what a world-class education you gave me. Thanks especially to Eson Kim, Sonya Larson, Chip Cheek, Chris Castellani, Eve Bridburg, Ian Chio, Alison Murphy, Lauren Rheaume, and Colwill Brown.

To my L.A. writing fam, Leesa Fenderson, Tom Renjilian, Laura Roque, Erin Lynch, Marcus Clayton, Melissa Chadburn,

Tisha Marie Reichle-Aguilera, Taneum Bambrick, and Ben Bush—we're doing the damn (literary) thing.

Thanks to my Miami crew—Ashley Barrington-Calunga, Kelvin and Eunice Rivers, Evelyn Suarez, and Priscilla Jade—who give not one damn if I'm talented, and care only that I'm here.

To my forever brothers-in-arms, Dariel Suarez and Fausto Barrionuevo—we knew our words would save us. Special big ups to Dariel, who first saw that I had a book on my hands with these characters, and Alina Collazo, who had a couch for me to sleep on in good times and bad.

For Carol Bellak-Escoffery (gone too soon), who read every story—I wish I'd been faster.

To the Escofferys and the Grahams, and all the diasporic Jamaicans, this book is for us.

Special shout-out to Aunty Lizzy, for letting me borrow her books as a pickney.

And most of all, for Mom, who taught me to dream. And for Dad, who preached pragmatism. And for my brother, Jason, who taught me how to live in the world.

And for Aja, my heart.